What People Are Saying About Laura V. Hilton and *Married to a Stranger*...

Married to a Stranger. How does that happen in modern times among a closely connected Amish community? Author Laura Hilton works out the circumstances believably, and left me wishing her characters the best possible future together.

—*Heidi Dru Kortman*
Devotional writer

Married to a Stranger hooked me right from the beginning and held me till the end. What are two strangers who suddenly find themselves married going to do? Laura Hilton does a wonderful job putting the reader inside the minds and hearts of her characters. I highly recommend this book.

—*Linda Hoover*
Author, *Mountain Prophecy* and *Lighter Than Air*

Married to a Stranger is an engaging story—deeply moving and heartwarming, artfully plotted to keep the reader turning the pages.

—*Marie E. Bast*
Publishers Weekly bestselling author, *The Amish Baker*

"You can't ride in all directions at the same time."—wisdom from Bishop Miah
Married to a Stranger by Laura V. Hilton is a mesmerizing and creatively penned story with dimensional characters with strong traits and flaws. It was with pleasure and honor to read this captivating story to catch up with characters and the events in the Mackinac County, Michigan, Amish community. A forced marriage, hidden wisdom from Bishop Miah, hidden secrets, an encounter with a stranger, and hospital visits, along with other intense scenes, brought this story to life, where I was right in the midst of each trauma and victory, whether a gentle kindness or a dangerous situation. Bethel

and Gideon had a lot to overcome, but with their resilient spirit, faith, fortitude, tenacity, friends, and family who cared, maybe their marriage had been lovingly orchestrated by God, even though it had been forced. *Married to a Stranger* is filled with picturesque scenes, compelling characters, love, faith, and Scriptural references that make this a shiny, winsome story. I look forward to reading each new release by Laura V. Hilton, knowing I'll be reading a golden nugget story with a strong faith message.

—*Marilyn Ridgway*
Book reviewer

An inconvenient marriage of convenience—can love eventually bloom? Laura Hilton's Amish stories touch the heart with realistic characters and captivating plots. I love this story!

—*Kathleen Friesen*
Author, *Hearts Unfolding*

Once again, Laura V. Hilton takes an impossible situation, adds sparks between the hero and heroine, characters to root for, and an Amish community that could either help, or share secrets that could destroy everything. *Married to a Stranger* is another page-turner where everything else takes a back seat.

—*Julie Arduini*
Author, *Match Made in Heaven*

I found the story insightful in how the truth can set us free, how trust can be restored and achieved with small steps and acts of kindness and faith. The characters in *Married to a Stranger* are very likeable and the read is sweet and engaging.

—*Linda Maran*
Author, *The Stranger*, White Rose Publishing

I was caught up in this story. The characters in *Married to a Stranger* became so real to me, I wanted to whisper advice.

—*Debi Parm*
Retired librarian

Laura V. Hilton has done it again. Her new novel, *Married to a Stranger*, is so captivating, you will not want to put it down. It's filled with spiritual inspiration, romance, and drama. Her characters come to life, as if they were your neighbors or friends across the field. You'll imagine yourself wanting to encourage, comfort, and give advice to this young couple trying so hard to make things work.

—*Jackie Pruett*
Retired librarian

I was engrossed in reading *Married to a Stranger* till the end. Powerful detailed words describing how some grieving humans can struggle with dealing with multiple emotions at the same time.

—*Tina Watson*
Amish Book Previews

As becoming the "norm," Laura V. Hilton catches your attention from the very first page of her new novel, *Married to a Stranger*, and holds your attention throughout with many unexpected twists and turns. You will find her characters come to life through her use of descriptive words and real-to-life experiences that they are confronted with. While reading this latest novel, you will find that you are experiencing tears of both sadness and joy, having feelings of mental anguish and a warm feeling of newfound love. Laura V. Hilton is very effective in incorporating unexpected twists and turns into her stories that are thought-provoking and trending with current topics of today.

Married to a Stranger is the third book in the Mackinac County Series, the first two being *Firestorm* and *The Amish Candymaker*. In *Married to a Stranger*, you will meet Gideon Kaiser and his family,

Bethel Eicher and her dad, and other members of Mackinac County. You will follow their lives for about six weeks through both sad and happy times.

—*Lucy Nix*
Reader review

When I realized we were visiting to learn more about Gideon's story, I stopped and grabbed my tissues. The little peek we had before [in *The Amish Candymaker*], I immediately recognized and started tearing up; however, if this is your first book by Laura Hilton, you will be fine as you will be all caught up quickly. I love that if you happen to miss one or are just now finding Laura's books, it will be fine...except you are now hunting for more and longing for another when you finish the last page. We visit with characters previously introduced and pick up in their lives like you do when having a family reunion. You may not have seen them yesterday, but within minutes, everyone is all caught up and making new memories.

—*Christine Bronner*
Book reviewer

LAURA V.
HILTON

Married
to a
Stranger

WHITAKER
HOUSE

Married to a Stranger

Laura V. Hilton
http://lighthouse-academy.blogspot.com

ISBN: 978-1-64123-249-4
eBook ISBN: 978-1-64123-228-9
Printed in the United States of America
© 2019 by Laura V. Hilton

Whitaker House
1030 Hunt Valley Circle
New Kensington, PA 15068
www.whitakerhouse.com

Library of Congress Cataloging-in-Publication Data
Names: Hilton, Laura V., 1963- author.
Title: Married to a stranger / Laura V. Hilton.
Description: New Kensington, PA : Whitaker House, [2019] |
Identifiers: LCCN 2019015594 (print) | LCCN 2019016524 (ebook) | ISBN
  9781641232289 (e-book) | ISBN 9781641232494 (alk. paper)
Subjects: LCSH: Amish—Fiction. | GSAFD: Christian fiction. | Love stories.
Classification: LCC PS3608.I4665 (ebook) | LCC PS3608.I4665 M37 2019 (print)
  | DDC 813/.6—dc23
LC record available at https://lccn.loc.gov/2019015594

1 2 3 4 5 6 7 8 9 10 11 **ᴜᴊ** 26 25 24 23 22 21 20 19

Acknowledgments

Thanks to Michael and Mallory for information about the Upper Peninsula of Michigan Amish, for cell-phone snapshots of buggies, for actually driving out to the area where the Amish live, and for bringing home some Mackinac Island fudge. Yum. I love you both. Also, thanks for housing us when we came up to visit/research in person.

Thanks to Jenna, Candee, Lynne, Linda, Heidi, Marie, Christy, Kathy, Julie, and Marilyn for your parts in critiques, advice, and/or brainstorming. Also to my street team for promoting and brainstorming. Candee, this story would not have become what it did without you.

Thanks to Jenna for taking on the bulk of the cooking while I was working toward a deadline.

Thanks to Whitaker House for taking a chance on me, and to Tamela Hancock Murray for representing me.

Dedication

To the God who loved me enough to die for me because
He loved me first.

Glossary of Amish Terms and Phrases

ach:	oh
aent/aenti:	aunt/auntie
"ain't so?":	a phrase commonly used at the end of a sentence to invite agreement
boppli:	baby/babies
bu:	boy
buwe:	boys
daed:	dad
"Danki":	"Thank you"
der Herr:	the Lord
dawdi-haus:	a home constructed for the grandparents to live in once they retire
dochter:	daughter
ehemann:	husband
Englisch:	non-Amish
Englischer:	a non-Amish person
frau:	wife
Gott:	God
grossdaadi:	grandfather
grossmammi:	grandmother
gut:	good
haus:	house

"Ich liebe dich":	"I love you"
jah:	yes
kapp:	prayer covering or cap
kinner:	children
koffee:	coffee
kum:	come
maidal:	young woman
mamm:	mom
mammi:	grandmother
maud:	an older unmarried woman (old maid/spinster)
morgen:	morning
nacht:	night
nein:	no
"off in den kopf":	"off in the head"; crazy
onkel:	uncle
Ordnung:	the rules by which an Amish community lives
ser gut:	very good
sohn:	son
welkum:	welcome
wunderbaar:	wonderful
youngies:	young unmarried individuals in the Amish community

1

Today's the day! Adrenaline and excitement surged through Gideon Kaiser as he parked his buggy next to the midwife's buggy. He couldn't wait to hold his first boppli—and just after Thanksgiving! An extra blessing to give thanks for.

He jumped down onto the ground, which was covered with an inch of snow. After quickly tethering his horse, he raced inside the three-story haus he shared with his parents, his sister, and his frau, Lizzie. He pounded up the half-flight of stairs from the landing to the main floor, then turned to run upstairs to the bedrooms.

Lizzie had awakened that morgen with mildly painful contractions. He'd wanted to stay home with her, but Lizzie had assured him that the first boppli often took hours to be born and he would be better off occupying himself elsewhere rather than hovering over her. So, he'd reluctantly gone to work at the grocery he owned with his daed. When a customer had reported seeing the midwife's buggy at his haus, though, Gideon had informed Daed that he was leaving. Hovering or not, he would be there when his boppli was born.

Mamm came out of the kitchen and hobbled toward him, clutching the four-footed cane with one hand, her prayer book in the other. Her mouth dropped open, as if she had something to say, but movement on the landing midway up the stairs caught Gideon's attention.

The midwife, Emma, stood there talking frantically on her cell phone. When she ended the call, she looked at Gideon…and something in her expression chilled his excitement. "I called for an ambulance."

He stared at her, his jaw dropping. His heart stopped. Restarted with a painful lurch. "What? Why? Nein. Lizzie wants our boppli born here." And he would do anything to make sure Lizzie got what she wanted.

Emma reached out a hand and held it up as if telling him to hush. "Don't worry. Everything will be fine. I just have some concerns about how long her labor is taking and I think she'd better get to the hospital. I'll go along, of course."

"The first boppli always takes a while." Gideon set his jaw and shook off his sense of alarm. "Lizzie told me that just this morgen."

"Jah, but…." Emma frowned. "This is just a precaution. Everything will be fine."

"Everything will be fine," Gideon repeated. "May I see her?"

"Briefly. I'm going to call a driver."

Gideon nodded before taking the rest of the stairs two at a time and dashing into the bedroom he shared with Lizzie. She sat on the edge of the bed, cradling her stomach. Pain had etched lines on her face. So had fear. Annoyance.

He dropped to his knees in front of her and peered up. "It'll be fine, sweetheart. It's just a precaution, she said."

Lizzie put a hand on his shoulder.

Something in her expression scared him. "What's wrong?" He turned his head and kissed her hand, then leaned forward to bury his face in her lap. Her belly tightened against his forehead. "How can I help—"

"Get. Off. Of. Me." Lizzie's hand tightened on his shoulder, her nails digging into the skin, before she pushed him away and concentrated on breathing.

He dismissed her gesture of rejection and tried to think of a way to help ease her pain. Somehow he'd make this better and take care of his frau as he vowed before Gott just over a year ago. Maybe a massage? He reached for her swollen belly.

Lizzie held up her arm. "Don't. Touch. Me."

Emma entered the room. "Let's get you downstairs. The ambulance is on its way." She nudged Gideon's leg with her foot, indicating he should move.

He shifted to the side and stood as Emma grasped Lizzie under one arm and pulled her to her feet.

Lizzie groaned, clutching her stomach again.

"Breathe through it," Emma encouraged her. She supported Lizzie as she panted.

If only Gideon could take the pain from his frau. Carry this burden.

A loud knock sounded on the door downstairs and then someone called up, "First responders!"

Lizzie would never manage the stairs in this much pain. Besides, the sooner they got her downstairs, the sooner they would get to the hospital and her pain would go away.

Gideon scooped up Lizzie in his arms. She moaned but wrapped one arm around his neck, the other arm still cradling her stomach. "Don't drop me."

"Don't worry, honey. I won't. Relax. Everything's going to be okay." He strode out of the room and carried her downstairs. It felt gut to be able to do something to help.

The first responders met them on the landing but backed out of the way as Gideon carried her past them and out the door.

He set her down beside the ambulance, her black socks sinking into the snow. He should've thought to grab her shoes. Her coat. What would she need at the hospital? A nacht-gown? An extra dress?

Lizzie screamed and grabbed the arm of one of the first responders.

Ach, it hurt to see her holding on to another man. He wanted to be her hero. He shook off his jealousy by reminding himself that she was in great pain and probably couldn't think or act rationally right now. Lizzie was getting help from professionals, so it was up to him to make sure everything else was taken care of. He forced himself to look away and glanced at the midwife. "I'll go get a suitcase ready for her."

"Don't forget something for the boppli to wear," Emma told him. "And a blanket. A boppli blanket."

Gideon nodded and went back inside.

Mamm still stood where he'd left her, limbs shaking, peering down the stairs as if she wanted to go along, too.

Gideon touched her arm. "It'll be okay. Emma said so. Go sit down. We're taking Lizzie to the hospital. Naomi will be home shortly to stay with you."

Mamm nodded. "I'll be praying. All this pain will be forgotten when Lizzie holds her boppli. Remind her of that. Ich liebe dich, Sohn."

Gideon leaned in and kissed her cheek. "I need to pack a suitcase for Lizzie and the boppli. And then I'm headed to the hospital with Emma." He ran upstairs.

When he returned, the ambulance had left, but a driver was waiting.

When they reached the hospital, Emma charged inside and hurried down a hall to the labor and delivery ward, Gideon on her heels. "I'm her midwife and you're her ehemann, so we'll be allowed in unless they do a C-section," she explained over her shoulder.

Panic seized his heart at the thought of a knife cutting into his frau. "Do you think they will?" Lizzie had wanted to deliver naturally, at home. "She'll be disappointed."

"I'm sure it'll be the last resort. Leave the suitcase out here." Emma pushed through the swinging doors. "But I think she has labor dystocia. It's basically an obstruction that occurs if the mamm's pelvis is too narrow or the boppli is too big."

Gideon dropped the suitcase next to the wall and felt his eyes start to glaze over. A fresh wave of panic shook him.

"And—"

"Stop!" A nurse in scrubs held up a hand.

"Midwife and husband," Emma told her

Gideon peered over the nurse's head. Lizzie lay on a bed, a blanket over her lower half, a strange-looking yellow thing on her upper body. Her face was flushed. A host of wires attached her to some sort of machine that had lights flashing all around.

The nurse sighed, then grabbed two facemasks and two sets of shoe covers. "You can stay for a little while. The baby's crowning, but we're waiting for the doctor, because—"

Lizzie screamed and bore down.

Hadn't they given her something for the pain?

The nurse rushed back over to Lizzie. "There, there, honey. Don't push now. You need to wait for the doctor."

How was she supposed to resist the urge to push if the boppli was ready? Gideon pressed his lips together to mask his ignorance about childbirth as he quickly yanked the mask over his face and then shoved his feet into the slippers. He hurried to his wife's side and smoothed his hand over her soft, black hair. They'd taken off her kapp. "Ich liebe dich, Lizzie. You can do this." He kissed her cheek.

She looked at him, her eyes brimming with tears. Silently asking, pleading, begging him to help.

He turned to the nurse. "Why haven't you given her anything for the pain?"

"I will as soon as the doctor approves it. The doctor and the anesthetist will be here in a moment. Don't push, honey."

Lizzie bore down again. Screaming. Again. Agony filled her eyes.

"The baby's coming." Emma stood at the foot of the bed, the blanket that covered Lizzie partially hiding her and completely obscuring what she was reaching for.

An alarm sounded, an awful squeal that hurt Gideon's ears. "Can't you turn that off?"

The nurse spun away from what she'd been doing, checked the screaming machine, and then reached beneath the blanket for a button. "We need a doctor in here, stat."

"Her name is Elizabeth," Lizzie ground out, then gave a big push.

The midwife gasped, but with the blanket covering Lizzie's lower half, Gideon couldn't see why.

Gideon smoothed Lizzie's hair. "It'll be okay, it'll be—"

"It's a boy." Emma held up the boppli.

The boppli screamed, his face bright red, as if he were angry at the world.

Gideon kissed Lizzie's cheek again. Smoothed a tear away. "It's a bu, sweetheart."

"Gideon, choose love. Not loss." Lizzie gave a quiet sigh and then her eyes rolled back in her head.

"Lizzie? Lizzie?" He rubbed her forehead and shook her shoulder slightly. "Liz?"

"Lizzie?" The midwife echoed him. "Nurse, something's wrong. She's gushing blood."

Gideon transferred his wide-eyed gaze to the foot of the bed. He stopped breathing as the door was shoved open. Someone took his child away.

Emma tried dragging him away from his unresponsive frau.

The door swung open again and a doctor rushed in, tugging on scrubs.

"We need to leave the room, Gideon." Emma's tone was urgent as she dragged him toward the door. "We need to stay out of the way."

Gideon collapsed against the wall beside the doorway to the room, his ears straining to hear what was going on. The doctor spoke tersely to the nurse. Another long wail from an alarm made

Gideon's skin crawl. He stared at the closed door. A voice on a loud-speaker called out some sort of code.

Gideon straightened. What was taking so long? He moved toward the door.

Emma grabbed his arm, jerking him to a stop. "Nein. Stay here."

Nurses rushed past with a cart and went into the room he'd just left.

And then, finally, the door opened and the sober-faced doctor exited, his scrubs saturated with blood. "I'm sorry. We did all we could, but we couldn't revive her."

"Nein!" A horrible scream ripped out of Gideon's throat. He slid down the wall, hands over his face, and wept.

2

Three months later

Her time had run out. She should've known she couldn't avoid the Amish man forever. In spite of the warm coat she wore, Bethel Eicher shivered in the February weather that chilled her as much as the fear of being stalked by him.

She crouched behind the round hay bale and peeked around the side.

"Where are you, my pretty?" His gravelly smoker's voice hissed through the barn. Not loudly, of course. That would draw attention.

He was handsome, but somehow, the hardness of his expression took away from his gut looks. She shuddered, thinking of his stinky breath. The dark anger in his eyes. The way every pretty, young woman who was unlucky enough to end up betrothed to him went missing…and was never seen again. Five, so far.

Though that might be a blessing for the women.

Even her younger sister, Ruth, had disappeared without warning. Without a trace. Bethel didn't know where to look for her and Daed had warned Bethel not to get involved.

Evil suffused the atmosphere, like the stench of rot.

And now his sights were set on her. Her!

Tears burned Bethel's eyes and clogged her throat.

Maybe if she screamed, someone would hear and kum to her rescue. Maybe to-nacht wouldn't be the nacht her life came to ruin. Maybe....

Nein. It wouldn't work. The two of them would be forced together and if she didn't go missing, she would have to marry him.

Was that what had happened to her sister? Had she left the Amish so she wouldn't be forced into a marriage with this creepy man?

But what if Bethel stayed quiet and managed to avoid being found? If they were caught alone together, the assumption would be that she had been violated. And if she was accused, what would she do? Could she turn it around, somehow, and point fingers at someone else? Such as the wunderbaar-nice auctioneer who had been in town several times last year? He'd liked her, she was sure. At least, he'd teased her, though he'd treated her more like a pesky little sister than a possible girlfriend. Still, love could grow from that. She definitely liked him...more than she wanted to. She and Daed had talked on more than one occasion about the possibility of her marrying Isaac Mast.

Something snapped nearby. Bethel retreated deeper into the shadows.

She didn't want to be wed to a man who was forced to marry her.

Nor did she want to be married to any member of the parade of older widowers who'd started coming around after Mamm died. True, at almost twenty-five years of age, she qualified as an old maud; but she didn't resent the time she'd spent as a caregiver for her precious mamm—a duty she had shared with her sister until Ruth's disappearance. Then had commenced the campaign started to marry Bethel off.

Of all the men who'd lined up to try for Bethel's hand in marriage, this man was the most determined. And he had a child with a leukemia diagnosis. It broke Bethel's heart, really, but she couldn't do it. Not even for the sake of the child.

"Bethel?"

She closed her eyes. He was close. Too close. She caught the whiff of his cigarette smoke.

"Where are you, my precious? Kum on out, now. The time for games is over—" A violent coughing spell interrupted him.

Nein. The games were just beginning.

She didn't want a widower. She would be happy to remain a single woman and spend the rest of her life taking care of Daed and working as a cashier at the local auctions. She loved her job.

Which was why her favorite auctioneer would be a perfect match.

Maybe Daed would work something out. Arrange to make her off-limits. But even their local bishop had introduced her to some aging widowers. The last one he'd brought around had been eighty if he was a day. Older than her own grossdaadi.

She shuddered.

"Hey, Rodney. I was looking for you." Daed's voice, lined with a tension Bethel alone would recognize, interrupted her musings. "I saw your buggy out front. Glad you stopped by, since I wanted to ask your opinion about my old plow. I think there's a problem with the teeth. I can't get them sharpened properly."

Bethel peeked again. Daed was leading Rodney out of the barn. *Danki, Lord.*

"Plow's in the back field."

Daed must've just taken it out there because it had been in the shed when Bethel went looking for him just before Rodney drove in and attempted to find her.

As soon as the men disappeared from view, Bethel emerged from her hiding place and ran for the haus. She locked herself in the upstairs bathroom, sank down on the closed commode seat, and buried her face in her hands. *Lord, help. Just…help. I don't want an ehemann. Well, I do, but not if he's going to be a widower who needs a caretaker. And I don't want to be forced to marry.*

She didn't know how long she'd prayed when her legs started to go numb and she forced herself to get up and move to her room. She paced until the painful tingling of her legs subsided, then knelt beside the bed and continued to pray.

Soon there came a quiet tap on the door. "He's gone, Bethel. You can kum out now. We need to talk."

Something about the tone of Daed's voice caused her stomach to knot. She pressed her hand against it as she stood and opened the door.

Daed's expression was grim, his eyes filled with pain. "You didn't tell me you were ruined."

"Ruined?" She blinked.

"You're marrying that man."

Bile rose in her throat. "Rodney?" *Lord, nein.* "He didn't ruin me." Not yet, anyway.

"Rodney was the one who told me. He offered to marry you in order to take your shame on himself. But, nein. You are going to marry the man who did it to you. Based on Rodney's description, I know just who it is and I've already contacted him." He set his jaw.

Already? Really?

"It's a lie." Bethel straightened. "Whoever he described has never touched me. Nobody has."

Daed's brow furrowed. "And that's why you're with child?"

"I am?" It was a question. Not a statement of fact. But, really, why would he accuse her of such a thing? And how would he know, even if it were true?

"You are." Daed nodded. "He gave me proof. He saw you leaving the midwife's haus."

Bethel's mind raced. "Jah, I was there, but I was taking her some dried cher—"

Daed slashed the air with his hand. "You will kneel and confess and marry either Rodney or the father. And I prefer that you marry the father."

Bethel's mouth gaped. She had nein words. None.

"His reputation will be destroyed if he doesn't marry you. And he's already agreed to."

"Already?" Was it Isaac Mast who'd been falsely accused of this sin and had agreed to rescue her? Isaac knew Rodney and didn't trust him. And she and Isaac had been alone together at auctions....

"Well, it took some talk, discussion, and threats. He hung up on me."

Threats? Not Isaac, then. But the unknown man must have a gut reason, because whoever it was hadn't touched her.

"Then he called back and agreed to my demands."

What? "Who is this man?" Shouldn't she know the name of the man Daed accused, at least? "This is beyond ludicrous, Daed. Whatever Rodney told you was a lie. Nothing more. I'll take a pregnancy test. Honestly—"

"You will do nein such thing. I won't be shamed that way." Daed pressed his lips together and strode off.

"Daed." Tears clogged Bethel's throat. "Listen to me."

Daed stopped and turned to face her. "You have two choices. Either you will marry Rodney to avoid the shunning, or you will marry the father on Thursday."

"This coming Thursday?"

Daed nodded, his eyes dark with some unidentifiable emotion. "Jah. That's what he said. Thursday."

Please, Lord.... It was the only part of the prayer she could get to form, as the only hope she had that Daed would listen to her was washed away.

If she was going to be forced to marry someone, it wouldn't be Rodney, especially after his lies. She sighed, her shoulders slumping.

It *had to* be Isaac, because if Daed had mentioned Rodney's name, Isaac would know she needed to be rescued. And that would mean he liked her enough to save her from this fate. Despair gave way to a bit of relief.

"Fine. Thursday, it is."

Thursday, one week later

The right thing was often the hard thing. That didn't make what he was about to do any easier.

Gideon straightened his suspenders, pulled his black vest over his shirt, and strode toward the door for his shoes, while Daed pushed the wheelchair holding Mamm, who cradled his three-month-old sohn in her arms, out the door.

Weddings were usually held at the bride's haus.

Weddings were generally happy occasions.

In this case, neither of those was true.

Gideon gritted his teeth as he shoved his feet into his shoes, then knelt to tie the laces. Straightening, he dropped his black hat on his head.

Forgive me, Lizzie. I had nein choice. Gideon swallowed and blinked against the burn. *Gott, help.*

There was nein choice. Either he marry the woman who'd accused him of sexually assaulting her—a woman he had nein recollection of ever meeting, not to mention the fact that he had never touched any woman besides his beloved frau—or his name would be dragged through the mud for a sin he hadn't committed, a sin for which he'd be forced to kneel and confess.

Since he needed a frau—for more reasons than one—and since a frau was being forced upon him, he might as well take advantage of the situation.

That didn't mean he had to love her.

He didn't even have to like her.

Right now, he didn't know her. Why had she singled him out?

Even her name meant nothing to him. She wasn't from this area. Wasn't from any area remotely close to the places he'd lived.

He grunted under his breath. Glared in the direction of the barn, which was newly cleaned and ready for the false festivities.

Daed said it was fair. Gideon's name in exchange for her services as a mamm for his sohn and helpful companion for his mamm. His name for a cook, laundress, and haus-keeper. His name for her silence about an event that had never happened. His name for her boppli that wasn't his.

Why him?

He should've talked to the bishop about it. Should've told him about the false accusations and asked his advice, instead of listening to Daed and allowing this…this farce to continue, unchecked, in hopes of keeping it out of the gossip mill.

It had worked. As far as he knew, nobody was aware that his bride and her family were blackmailing him.

And judging by the laughter and the sense of expectancy pouring forth from his haus and barn and from the pasture filled with the transportation vehicles of the wedding guests who'd traveled from near and far, everyone was happy, believing Gideon had found a new love.

They didn't know, didn't care, that this was a nacht-mare.

One he wouldn't wake up from. Ever.

3

When Bethel arrived that morgen, one of the strangers serving as her side-sitters looked at her. "I'm so excited to meet you. Have you ever been to this area before?"

Bethel tried to manage a smile. "Nein, but I've met Isaac at several auctions."

The girl gave her a puzzled look and then giggled. "Isaac Mast? He and Agnes have such a love story, and now they're on their honeymoon at Niagara Falls. Isn't that romantic? I went there with the other youngies in December...."

As the girl chatted on, Bethel struggled to keep her small breakfast down where it belonged. Isaac wasn't her groom, after all. She was truly marrying a stranger.

Over an hour later, Bethel's stomach still churned. She couldn't bear to look at the man she was marrying, other than to notice that he had a beard. A kind of reddish-gold beard that probably matched his hair color. A beard that meant he'd been married before. A widower. And the beard, plus its shade, only drove home the realization that he definitely wasn't Isaac coming to her rescue.

She swallowed the bile in her throat and wordlessly obeyed the murmured instructions to kneel while the minister prayed over them.

Usually, it was ministers. Plural. But for whatever reason, only this unknown bishop did the honors today. None of his words registered with her in a way that she would remember. Her knees hurt from kneeling for what seemed to be an abnormally long time and she couldn't get past the beard.

What had she agreed to?

Fear grabbed her by the throat. The kind of fear that left her paralyzed. Not a physical fear, like when Rodney stalked her in the shadows. It was the kind of fear that told her, nein matter what she might try to do, her life was about to fall apart.

Irritation and annoyance almost radiated from the man in waves. His resentment was almost tangible.

The only thing that could make this worse would be if he needed her to be a caregiver.

She would curl up in a fetal position and just die if she needed… nein.

She sighed heavily.

Nein, an abusive man would be worse.

But it wouldn't do any gut to ask der Herr for this stranger—what was his name, anyway?—to be nice to her, because it seemed apparent Gott hadn't heard one word of her endless prayers over the last few days. Either that, or He callously chose to disregard her requests.

They rose with a word from the bishop and went into the other room, where they sat through a long wedding sermon—another thing she couldn't seem to comprehend.

Then, finally—finally!—it was over.

Over except for the meal, complete with well-wishes from more strangers. Because as far as she knew, nobody from her district was aware of the nuptials. She hadn't invited anyone. It hadn't been published in the church. It was all hush-hush.

The Amish equivalent of a shotgun wedding.

At least in her district. Around here, the news had gotten out. The barn was packed. They'd even rounded up a bunch of maidals to be her attendants, since she hadn't brought any friends.

And she didn't know a single one of her attendants. In fact, the only woman she knew even remotely in this community was Agnes, who'd evidently won the heart of Isaac Mast for gut, having married him the week prior. And now they were honeymooning at Niagara Falls.

A honeymoon was something Bethel would never have.

Love was something she'd never have.

If only she had an appetite for the plate of wedding food before her. She cast a sideways glance at her groom, sitting silently beside her. Caught the beautiful reddish-gold color of his beard. Again.

Tears blurred her vision and she returned her attention to her plate.

This day couldn't be over with quick enough.

Except for the nacht. *Ach, dear Lord. The nacht.*

She put her fork down and stared, unseeing, at the colorful clusters of food on the cream-colored plate.

⌒

Finally, it was over. And Gideon hadn't exchanged more than a word or two with his new frau, other than the appropriate murmurs during the wedding ceremony when a response was expected. He hadn't even looked at her fully. Probably wouldn't have been able to identify her in a room full of people.

Sad commentary on a wedding. On a marriage. On...him.

Why, why, why had they targeted him? They had to know it was all a lie. Well, maybe someone had sexually assaulted the woman he'd married, but it certainly wasn't him.

Strangely, her body language didn't match the smug, gloating demeanor he would have expected from someone who'd lied and gotten away with it. Nein, she seemed sad. Resigned.

Almost fearful.

As if she were as much a victim in this drama as he. As if she wasn't the one he should be angry with. As if....

He shook his head. He didn't know who deserved his anger, but the emotion was there, simmering in his gut. He had nein control over that.

Well, he could choose not to let it show. To treat this stranger with civility and even kindness.

He needed to try.

Dinner over, Gideon was greeting a few cousins from another district when he noticed a man he didn't recognize hugging his bride. Her daed, perhaps? He excused himself from the well-wishers and made to approach the man—though what he would say, he didn't know. But the man disappeared in the crowd before Gideon could reach him.

And, ach! The expression on his new frau's face! She looked like someone who'd just lost her last friend.

She probably had.

That hurt. Gideon continued to make his way back to her, not wanting her to be alone. She needed a protector. And it was time for the two of them to retreat to the main haus anyway. His parents and sister had already done so because the cold weather had been affecting Mamm. And even though Elam was bundled up, Gideon's parents had taken him back to the haus with them.

Someone opened the barn door, blasting Gideon with a gust of bitterly cold air. He steeled himself and sent his new frau a smile. A forced smile, but a smile nonetheless.

He'd wasted the effort. She didn't look at him. Instead, she studied the ground at her feet.

Well, he'd tried.

Not really.

⌒

He sucked in a breath as they walked briskly to the main haus. Neither of them wore a coat.

"I…um…." He cleared his throat. "I didn't catch your name." Though he could have—should have—read her name on the wedding certificate they'd both signed an hour before.

"Bethel Eicher." Her voice was barely above a whisper.

"Kaiser," he corrected her.

She looked quickly up at him just long enough for him to catch a glimpse of her face. Beautiful girl. Gorgeous hazel eyes, in spite of the fear he read in them. Blonde hair and…wait. His heart lurched. He'd seen her before. At an auction. She was…Beth?

Nein, she couldn't be the girl he'd seen as a teenager, long years ago. The one to whom he'd given his heart as soon as he'd spotted her. The one who'd made him a believer in love at first sight. He'd told everyone around him he was going to marry that girl someday. And he'd intended to hold out for her. Until Lizzie.

Something inside him flared to life. It *was* Beth. There was nein way, but it had to be.

His view of her was, once again, the top of her kapp.

He tried to school his reaction. "That's my last name. Kaiser. Yours now."

She nodded. "What's your first name?"

That question seemed to prove she was just an innocent pawn in this game they were both unwittingly playing. A game that had suddenly changed its dimensions.

"Gideon."

She nodded again.

"Bethel, you should know, before we go inside…my mamm was recently diagnosed with multiple sclerosis. Her condition isn't very serious right now, though she has some not-so-gut days. She might need occasional assistance dressing, she'll need watching so she doesn't fall, and if she leaves the haus to go to the barn or to shop, Daed wants her in her wheelchair. I also have a sohn, only a few months old, named Elam. My daed's name is Ben, my unmarried sister is Naomi—she owns a bakery—and we all live here together.

Daed and I run the Amish salvage-grocery and the temporary post office."

He'd figured she knew all these details going into this. But by the way she'd withdrawn into herself, it was apparent she didn't.

Should he tell her anything else? Like his favorite dessert? The way he preferred his koffee? Or any of the zillion other things Lizzie had known long before they'd said their wedding vows?

"I'm a caregiver, then." She made a sound that might've been a sob. "How long have you been a widower? Not long, since your sohn—"

"She died in childbirth." He tried to keep the overwhelming grief out of his words, but he wasn't sure he'd succeeded, since she paused and glanced up at him again.

"I'm sorry," she whispered.

He stomped up the stairs to the haus, both to knock the snow off of them and to warn his parents they were coming inside.

"I don't know what you were told, but I'm not pregnant," she said bluntly.

He jerked his head to the side and stared at her.

Her face flared red.

He could feel his own face burning, too.

He pressed his lips together briefly, to keep his demand for an explanation unsaid. Then he nodded as unexpected sense of immense relief filled him.

Answers would kum.

In time.

⌣

As Gideon held the door, Bethel entered the rambling farmhaus, where she was greeted by two unsmiling adults and a sleeping boppli.

Ben. Elam. Had he mentioned his mamm's name?

Naomi? Nein, that was his sister. Probably the side-sitter who'd stood the closest to her. The one whose flaming reddish-gold hair matched Gideon's. She was pretty. Probably a year or two younger than Bethel.

Ach, Lord. I can't do this.

She supposed it was better than being married to Rodney. It had to be. She shuddered at the thought of Rodney kissing her. Of the rights he would have received if she said, "I do."

The very rights this man now had.

Ach, dear Lord.

She glanced again at the man now stooped beside her as he untied his boots and pulled them off upon entering the kitchen. She quickly did the same.

Gideon straightened, then put his hand on her lower back, urging her further into the next room. Unexpected sparks shot up her spine and down her arms and legs, leaving her fingers and toes tingling.

She peeked at his lips. What would it be like to be kissed by this man? Would it make her feel loved? In spite of her fear of the unknown, she experienced an odd sense of excitement.

She would find out soon enough. It was her wedding nacht, after all. And Daed had already warned her that this man would expect to exercise certain liberties. Though Daed had also rather rudely accused her of giving those same liberties away. Resulting in a pregnancy that was more real in his mind than in her body.

"Mamm, Daed, this is Bethel. Bethel, meet Ben and Reba. And my...your...our sohn, Elam."

He pressed his lips together and strode from the room.

Reba stared at Bethel, her mouth pursed, her eyebrows drawn together. Then her gaze dipped to Bethel's midsection.

Ach. She'd heard the same false story and had already judged Bethel and found her lacking. Bethel cringed. Her face heated again. She needed to set Gideon's parents straight about that rumor.

Ben gave Bethel an odd look, then glanced in the direction Gideon had gone, his eyebrows rising. Then he stood. "Welkum, Bethel. Your daed carried your things upstairs to Gideon's room just before he left. We hope you can make yourself at home. Admittedly, this has been quite a shock to us."

Jah. To her, too.

"But I daresay, we'll adjust." Ben frowned.

Bethel's stomach churned.

So much for her welkum in this haus.

4

It was probably the only wedding nacht in history during which the groom had hidden in the basement and raged, huddled upon and beneath a pile of blankets for warmth—warmth that never seemed to reach his core—before he cried himself into a fitful sleep.

As shameful as that was, it was easier than, and preferable to, going upstairs to the bedroom he'd shared with Lizzie and crawling into bed next to a stranger.

Even if that stranger was the one he'd never dared to imagine she might be.

"Bethel." Gideon tried out her name first thing the next morgen. It felt foreign on his tongue. And it hurt to speak. He stubbornly firmed his shoulders and said it again. "Bethel."

To-nacht, he would sleep in his bedroom. Not the dark, cold basement.

But that would mean that, in addition to the normal chores and post-wedding cleanup, he would have the job of transforming his room.

Exactly how, he didn't know just yet.

But he couldn't share with Bethel the same room he'd slept in with his beloved Lizzie. And there were nein spare rooms in the main haus. Mamm and Daed had the downstairs bedroom. Naomi and Elam each had a room upstairs and the additional room had been Lizzie's sewing space. He couldn't touch Lizzie's sewing supplies. He'd never even been allowed in there to see her creations in progress. The third floor was unfinished attic space. Full of black flies in the summer. Definitely not a place to put Bethel.

He certainly couldn't share the bed with Bethel. Which meant one of them—probably him—would sleep on the hard floor.

Gideon sighed deeply and once again wished he'd taken this false accusation to the bishop instead of acting on Daed's advice. "Keep it quiet. You're a new minister. This news will ruin you, ruin our business. Ruin us. Might even ruin your sister's business. You can't do this to us. Besides, you know you need a frau...."

It had seemed like wise advice at the time. Still did, when he focused on Daed's concerns. But if Bethel wasn't pregnant, why had someone accused him of fathering a child with her? Sometime, when he could think clearly, when his temper wouldn't get the better of him, he'd try to get to the bottom of it.

Now didn't seem like a gut time. He was still angry. Not at her, if she was as innocent as he believed, but at someone. And he might say or do something he would regret, like demanding an annulment, which was just not done. And it would ruin his reputation—and his family's, as well. Not to mention destroying hers.

He couldn't do that to her. To them.

"Bethel," he said again. Apparently, saying a name three times in a row meant you would never forget it.

He couldn't risk forgetting it.

Not if he had any hopes of pulling this off.

Then again, the name she'd given—Bethel—was so close to what he'd always believed her name to be—Beth—that nobody would be the wiser and suspect the truth—that he didn't know his own frau—if he accidentally used the latter. They'd believe it was a nickname.

At least, with this situation being handled directly between Gideon and both their fathers, with nein preacher or bishop involvement, none of the potentially damaging dirty laundry was hung out to dry. Daed had been the one to approach Bishop Miah, telling him only that Gideon was marrying for convenience's sake and asking him to officiate the ceremony.

Bishop Miah hadn't spoken to Gideon about it. Yet. But judging by the concern in the older man's eyes yesterday at the wedding, that conversation would be forthcoming. Along with some much-needed marital counseling.

Gideon went over to the laundry tubs and turned the faucet on enough to splash some cold water on his face. He didn't have a toothbrush down here, but he'd take care of that upstairs. Hopefully, the cold water would disguise what he'd spent most of the nacht doing.

He puffed out a breath and trudged upstairs. Still in his wedding clothes. Changing out of them would take priority, too.

At the top of the stairs, he opened the door to the kitchen and a smorgasbord of delicious smells and sights hit him broadside in the senses. His stomach rumbled. Loudly.

Mamm, Daed, and Naomi were seated at the table, already eating, while Bethel bustled about the kitchen, cleaning up and washing dishes. She must've done the cooking. And judging by the aromas and appearance of the food, and the expressions of contentedness on his family's faces, she was a far better cook than Lizzie. Lizzie had always relied on Naomi to do all the cooking while she did the sewing. Lizzie hated cooking. And it showed.

Hopefully, that mental acknowledgment wasn't dishonoring her memory. It was just a fact, ain't so?

And while Naomi could work wonders when it came to breads, muffins, and other baked goods, her main dishes and sides always tasted bland.

Daed looked at Gideon and opened his mouth, but Gideon put his finger to his lips and crept past, out of the room. He wanted—needed—to be presentable before he greeted his family.

And her.

Bethel.

The one he'd given his heart to years ago, now beside him at long last.

But still, the interloper.

⟋

The condemning stares from Gideon's family members seemed to bore into Bethel's back the entire time she prepared their breakfast and then washed the dishes. She'd intended to sit down and eat with them, maybe initiate a heartfelt conversation about why she'd played along with the false accusations. They needed to know the truth. But given their judgmental glares, her appetite and the entire "speech" she'd mentally prepared both abandoned her. As did her nerve.

But it had to be done.

She had just finished washing the meal-preparation dishes and was turning toward the table when Gideon came into the room. He looked as bad as she felt, with his eyes red and bleary. Where had he slept while she cried herself to sleep alone upstairs? She'd spent a semi-sleepless nacht surrounded by another woman's things. All yesterday, she'd dreaded the nacht and it had ended up being miserable—albeit for a different reason from what she'd anticipated.

His attempt at a smile wasn't entirely successful as he took his place at the table. "It smells amazing in here, Bethel."

Daed had always praised her cooking. And she'd gone all out this morgen, trying to impress these people. Her efforts had only tied her stomach into knots. It was a mark in Gideon's favor that he'd been the first—and only—one to compliment her cooking. And he hadn't even tasted the meal.

"Danki," she murmured, reaching for the plate she'd kept warm for him on the back of the stove. She set it in front of him, then poured him a mug of koffee before sitting down in the only empty chair.

"Aren't you going to eat?" He reached for the pitcher of cream.

"I'm not hungry."

"You obviously aren't still suffering from morgen sickness," Reba said snidely with a pinched-lip look. "You need to eat to keep up your strength. You're eating for two now."

Her ehemann, Gideon, and Naomi jerked their heads to stare at Reba.

Gideon frowned. "Mamm...."

Bethel pulled in a deep breath. "Actually, I'm not."

Three forks clattered to the table.

Gideon took a sip of his koffee, but the quiver in his hand betrayed his nerves.

"Then...." Ben glanced from Bethel to Gideon and back again. "Why...?"

"Why? I don't know. I mean...." She needed to do something with her hands, so she wrung the fabric of her apron as if it were a filthy dishrag. "There's this man. A widower. Who, I'm told, is a very gut catch. He's wealthy. But he creeps me out. One by one, he tried to court a series of maidals, all of whom disappeared. Including my own sister. Then he set his attention on me and one day, he stalked me when I was alone in the barn. Daed caught him. And he—this man—told my daed he'd caught me in a compromising position with another man and that he knew I was with child because he'd seen me leaving the midwife's haus." She got up, poured herself a glass of water, and returned to her seat. "It's true that I had recently been to visit the midwife at home, but it was only to take her some dried cherries. She loves cherries."

Ben's brow furrowed. "You're saying this man—your accuser—lied."

Bethel took a drink of her water and choked. Wow, it had a strong sulfur taste. She set the glass aside. "Jah, but my daed believed him over me. I think that man, Rodney, made up a description of the man he claimed to have seen with me. I don't even know what he said, but Daed thought he knew who it was and told me I had two options: marry Rodney or marry Gideon. I didn't know Gideon, but marrying a man I didn't know seemed the lesser of two evils."

At least the truth was out. And she'd be able to breathe freely without feeling she was caught in a lie. Sort of. She wouldn't mention she'd believed her ehemann would be Isaac Mast until just before the wedding started. She also wouldn't tell them how she'd prayed her ehemann wouldn't be a widower. Or that she wouldn't need to serve as a caregiver. What gut would that do? He was and she would.

"So, who *did* violate you?" Naomi asked. "And why didn't you tell your daed the truth about who it was?"

"It was nobody. I'm a vir—untouched. And the only ones coming around asking to court me were—" Her gaze skittered over those seated at the table with her. She couldn't tell them her would-be suitors were old, sick, widowed, or had family members who needed care. That would never do. "Uh, weren't appealing."

She would've rejected Gideon, too, if he had kum calling.

She should've packed her bags and run away instead of going through with the wedding. Which was probably what her sister had done, kum to think of it. That would explain why Daed refused to speak of her. Bethel puffed out a breath. Where was Ruth now? If she managed to locate her, could she go to live with Ruth, even though she was married to Gideon? She had to try.

"Why would Rodney ask to marry you then?" Reba asked. Suspicion still filled her eyes.

"I'm not sure. Daed said Rodney was willing to take my shame." Bethel ran her finger around the rim of the water glass. She couldn't mention his sick son without offending this family even further. And she couldn't mention that look in his eye when he stared at her because it was inappropriate for mixed company such as this. "I didn't mean for…well, I don't know what I expected. But Gideon had the right to say nein." He certainly shouldered some of the responsibility for their getting married. Considering he'd spent their wedding nacht away from her, he obviously hadn't wanted to get married, either. Why hadn't he fought to get out of it?

"Nein, I didn't." Gideon's voice was hard.

His harsh comment and the sting of rejection pierced her heart. Had he truly felt forced into the marriage as much as she? They could never have a happy, loving union after such a sorry beginning. Just as she'd feared while huddled in the barn, hiding from Rodney, she now bore the brunt of a man's resentment.

Gideon drained his mug of koffee and pushed his empty plate away. He'd somehow managed to finish his food. Bethel's insides still churned too much to stomach even one bite. "Breakfast was ser gut, Bethel. Danki for preparing it." He glanced at the clock. "Guess we best be getting to the store, Daed."

Ben made a little noise that might've been a masked chuckle. "They aren't going to be expecting to see you there, Sohn."

Gideon's face flamed red. "Right. I forgot."

"I'm not going into work today either." Naomi pushed away from the table and glanced at Bethel. "I'm a baker and I usually start my days super early." She sighed. "I guess I'll help with wedding cleanup and"—she looked at Gideon—"if you want my help packing up Lizzie's things, then we can get Bethel's unpacked."

Gideon made a choking noise. "Don't touch Lizzie's things. Just don't." He jumped to his feet. "In fact, move Bethel *out* of my bedroom."

Ach. That hurt. Bethel took another sip of the foul-tasting water just to ease her suddenly dry mouth as Gideon jammed his feet into a pair of boots and then stalked from the haus, slamming the door behind him.

From the other room, Elam screamed.

It took Bethel a moment to respond. She wasn't accustomed to caring for a boppli.

She hadn't expected to have to continue seeing the belongings of Gideon's much-loved first frau on a regular basis. They would serve as constant reminders that Bethel wasn't wanted.

Worse, now it seemed she was being banished. But to where?

Gideon stormed out to the barn. Apparently, his lack of adequate sleep was negatively affecting his ability to be nice. Well, not totally, because he'd thought to compliment Bethel on her cooking, even if he hadn't quite managed to soften his voice and not snap like an angry monster. If breakfast was anything to judge by, he and his family would be eating like kings.

The church wagon was still parked off to the side of the barn, waiting for the copies of *The Ausbund* hymnals to be collected and loaded into the bottom before the benches were piled on top. It'd be gut to get this reminder out of sight.

But first, the chores. At least, those that Daed hadn't done before breakfast.

Odd that Daed hadn't called Gideon to kum help. Though maybe he hadn't wanted to disturb the newlyweds.

Gideon snorted.

If that was the case, then his emergence from the cold basement would have communicated clearly to Daed that there had been nothing to disturb.

And there never would be, because this was a marriage of convenience. Nothing more.

"Gideon."

The quiet voice drew Gideon's attention and he turned.

Bishop Miah stood in the barn doorway. "I'm sorry. I was remiss in not talking to you directly instead of taking Ben's word that you'd met a pregnant widow, had fallen in love, and needed to marry right away."

So that was what Daed had told the bishop. Lies. A bunch of lies. And he'd lied to Gideon as well, in telling him he'd described it as a "marriage of convenience." Or maybe he hadn't…because it was. Although who it was convenient for remained a mystery. It wasn't Bethel and it certainly wasn't Gideon.

Lies. Their marriage was based entirely on lies.

Bethel sounded sincere that morgen over breakfast as she shared her story. He could see the hurt and bewilderment lingering in her eyes, as if she still didn't fully realize how she'd gotten here, or why her father had chosen to believe an old widower over his own dochter. Perhaps he was eager to see her wed. Gideon did wonder why Bethel hadn't married before. Admittedly, she was easy on the eyes, with flawless skin and beautiful, honey-blonde hair streaked with highlights, as if the sun had reached down and kissed it.

"I was suffering from the flu and didn't want to go out, but I figured you knew what you were doing," Bishop Miah continued. "Probably you were busy, which is why you didn't kum by yourself. And when I prayed about it, all I heard was, *'My ways are not your ways, nor are My thoughts your thoughts.'* Which meant, to me, that maybe Gott intended for you and Bethel to marry."

Pray.

Gideon dipped his head. He'd neglected to pray. He'd been so stunned—so distraught—by the false accusations, praying hadn't even crossed his mind. Daed had been pressuring him to marry because, with Naomi working at the bakery and he and Daed working at the salvage store-grocery, Mamm was left alone with Elam. And that was not gut. For her or for the boppli.

"She's not a widow. She's not pregnant," Bishop Miah said bluntly as he advanced into the room and started gathering the hymnals from where they lay. "And you don't love her."

"Did Daed tell you?"

"Nein. I have eyes. Not to mention, my senses still work. I felt the anger, the mistrust, the fear, the…I don't know. I didn't see the glow of new motherhood or the sadness a widow usually carries. Nor did I sense any love between you. I should've stopped the wedding right then and there. Refused to go through with it. But again, Gott seemed to tell me you needed to marry her. Why, I don't know. But…." He stopped, balancing a small stack of seven or eight hymnals on his left forearm as adeptly as a waitress with a tray laden with plates.

Daed came into the barn just then. "Bishop Miah. I didn't realize you were here until I looked outside and saw your horse and buggy."

"I'm here." The bishop sighed. "You lied to me about the situation behind the wedding."

Daed paled. "Not intentionally. And not totally. I believed her to be pregnant and I knew you'd never approve the wedding if you had the whole story. And with Gideon being a new preacher...." He shook his head. "I found out just this morgen, over breakfast, that she really isn't pregnant and her father didn't believe her."

"Or...maybe he did. And maybe there were other, more sinister, reasons behind his accusation." The bishop picked up another hymnal and added it to the pile he held.

Gideon stilled as a sudden chill, not related to the frigid temperature of the barn, filled the room. His gaze went to his father, whose eyes widened.

"What!" Gideon took a step nearer to the bishop, his heart pounding. "What do you mean by that?"

"I don't know. I just...I don't know. I want to hear the whole story sometime. Later." The bishop handed the stack of hymnals to Daed. "I need to go. Now."

5

Bethel's first time changing Elam's diaper didn't go as badly as she'd feared. Lying on the changing table in his bedroom, the boppli waved his feet in the air and blew bubbles at her, completely winning her heart. She scooped up the clean and dry boppli and kissed his sweet little cheek. "You are a little lamb."

She carried Elam downstairs to the kitchen, where Naomi handed her a warm bottle of formula and pointed her to a rocking chair in the living room.

Reba clumsily pushed to her feet and took shaking, shuffling steps in that direction, then sat in the chair beside the rocker. "You go ahead and feed him. I'll make sure you do it right."

Bethel nodded, resisting the urge to say she knew how to feed a boppli. How on earth had this older, ailing woman managed to care for Elam on her own? And on top of the cleaning, laundry, and cooking? True, Naomi probably did the majority of that work when she was home, but what about the long hours she surely spent at her bakery?

"You'll want to have a burp rag on your shoulder. He tends to spit up after he eats. I think it's due to the formula because none of my boppli ever did that. But it can't be helped. Don't really think Lizzie would've fed him the natural way anyhow. She said as much when I talked to her about it, telling me she planned to get a shot to dry up. I didn't even know such a thing was possible." Reba shook her head as she handed Bethel a flannel boppli blanket.

Bethel's face burned at the too-personal talk. She somewhat awkwardly draped the blanket over her shoulder. Elam had already begun to guzzle the contents of the bottle, gulping as if his last meal had been days ago. She'd never seen a boppli eat like that and pulled the bottle away from him. He screamed while she studied the nipple.

She leaned closer to Reba and held the bottle out for the older woman to examine. "I think the formula is coming out too fast. Don't you think the holes look a little bigger than they should for a boppli his size?"

Reba waved her hand dismissively. "We bought the kind with the biggest holes. Takes less time to feed him. Who can sit around half the day holding a boppli? Though Naomi showed me how to prop the bottle up so he could feed himself, since I can't lift him on my weaker days."

Bethel frowned. She didn't know a lot about caring for boppli, but neither the larger-than-proper holes nor the propping up of a bottle for self-feeding seemed like a gut idea. Even so, she didn't want to just kum in and take over. This was Reba's home. Naomi's home. And this boppli was the sohn of Gideon's first frau. His perfect frau.

Nothing about this was hers.

By now, Elam had turned red with rage. Bethel brushed her finger over his soft cheek. He needed cuddling and the best care she could give him. The boppli's crying eased and he stared up at her.

"I think he's swallowing too much air with the way he's gulping," Bethel said carefully, not wanting to sound overbearing. "That's probably why he spits up so much. I'll look for bottle nipples with smaller holes next time I'm at the grocery store."

She just wasn't sure when that would be, with Naomi working in town and both Ben and Gideon owning the salvage-grocery. She'd probably need to ask either Ben or Gideon to buy the nipples.

Reba offered a slight smile as she pushed herself to her feet. "You do seem to know what you're doing." She took the bottle from Bethel and hobbled into the kitchen. "Naomi, put one of the old nibbles on this bottle, if we still have any. Bethel is right—this one is too big. We won't torture the poor boppli any longer now that Bethel's here and has time to sit around feeding Elam." She looked back at Bethel. "If you want, we can sit and visit. But if you'd rather be left alone, I'll go do something else."

"Visiting would be nice." Bethel snuggled the warm boppli closer to her chest. At least someone in this haus was on her side. Maybe she could start winning over the others.

Reba's smile grew as she settled back into the chair. "I'll have Naomi join us, too. She can get us some koffee, unless you prefer tea?"

Elam started rooting. Bethel gave him her finger to suck, but he started screaming and turned red.

"Koffee is fine." She raised her voice to be heard over the angry wails. She rocked, jostled, patted, hummed. Maybe the boppli didn't want her here.

Naomi hurried in with the bottle, now fitted with a different nipple, then returned to the kitchen and came back moments later with a tray holding three cups of koffee. She pulled up another chair.

They chatted quietly while Elam ate. By the time Bethel rested the boppli upright against her shoulder and gently rubbed his back to burp him, she felt that she'd made two new friends. She liked her new in-laws. And judging by their frequent smiles, they liked her, too. Or were starting to.

Except for those angry stares at breakfast....

"Naomi will need to start making bread soon," Reba said. "Would you mind doing some laundry? We're behind on it, with Naomi working and me unable to climb stairs to the basement, where the wringer washer is. I can watch Elam if you put him on a blanket on the floor." Reba nodded to a colorful folded quilt on a nearby sofa.

Bethel nodded. "I don't mind. I can do laundry. But first, I should make sure all my things are out of Gideon's room."

She would put them beside the back door. He was probably banishing her to the barn loft anyway. Where else would you put an unwelkum frau?

Both Reba and Naomi stared silently at their laps.

Bethel shook her head, ashamed of giving in to a pity party. True, she hadn't known Gideon's circumstances, but she'd chosen him over Rodney. And if she were given the choice again, even knowing what she knew now, she still would choose Gideon. He made an effort to be nice, he wasn't creepy, and he was grieving. She could afford to do what she could for this family. At least until she could find her sister and leave.

Besides, he couldn't put her in the barn loft. She had to be close in case Elam needed attention or Reba needed help. Putting her suitcase inside by the back door would be overkill. He was likelier to banish her to the attic.

At least the attic would be warmer than the barn.

Gideon prayed for guidance and wisdom while he finished clearing the barn of any remaining wedding supplies. The boxes of copies of *The Ausbund* and all the pews had been loaded onto the wagon, which was ready to be parked out of the way until the following church Sunday. Or the next wedding, whichever one came first. Any discussions Gideon had previously had with Bishop Miah about published couples planning to marry before spring planting had been erased from his memory when he'd heard the accusations from Bethel's father.

Gideon was trying to get through each day moment by moment. One thing at a time. Just like he had done since Lizzie's death.

Chores done, barn cleaned, he trod through the snow to the haus, then stomped up the stairs to knock as much snow accumulation as possible off his treads. He opened the door to find Elam in a swing in the kitchen while Naomi kneaded dough nearby. Mamm sat knitting in the living room. Whatever it was that she was working on, the rows wouldn't be as tight as those on her former projects. Daed was right—Gideon did need a frau to help out. And Bethel seemed nice and also competent, even if she had been pushed on him.

Elam kicked his feet and sucked on the leg of a stuffed toy frog. Gideon knelt to ruffle the boy's dark hair and then kissed his rosy cheeks—both features of Lizzie's. Elam had her brown eyes, too.

Lizzie should be here for this domestic scene. Instead, Gideon was stuck with Bethel. Not stuck. Married to. He glanced around. Straightened. "Where's Bethel?"

Mamm glanced up from her knitting. "That sweet girl is downstairs doing a load or two of laundry. I told her to hang everything on the line down there. Nein point in putting anything outside, with those heavy gray clouds ready to empty at any time."

Gideon nodded and started for the cellar door. He'd take his shoes off when he came back upstairs. It was cold down there.

"She packed her things," Naomi said, a hint of irritation in her voice. "They're in the hallway outside your room, waiting for you to tell her where to put them."

Gideon turned to face his sister. "Can she share your room?"

Naomi narrowed her green eyes and pursed her lips. "Nein."

"Kum on, Naomi. There's nein other place to put her, except maybe on a cot in Elam's room. That wouldn't be ideal."

"And so—what? You'll stash her in the attic with all the other unneeded junk nobody wants to get rid of? Or in the cold cellar?" Naomi put her flour-covered hands on her hips. "I like her, Gideon, and I hate to see her treated like this."

Gideon held up his arms in surrender. "Hey, now. What did I do to get on your bad side?" He was the victim here. Well, one of the victims, anyway.

"You know who she is, ain't so? I think she's that girl you talked about for years...until you fell in love with Lizzie."

Naomi had recognized her, too?

"And now—now she's your frau!"

He stared. "You think I don't know?"

Naomi slumped, the fire going out of her. "Court her."

It seemed a little late for that, but he could see the wisdom in Naomi's advice. How else would he learn to at least appreciate Bethel? To get to the point where he wanted—where they both wanted—a marriage in more than name only?

But the thought pained him. How could he even think of such a thing?

He swallowed. "She's in the basement?"

Naomi nodded and returned to her kneading.

Gideon descended the cellar steps and peered around the corner once he reached the bottom. Bethel had sorted the laundry, making piles that matched like kinds together, and now she hung a row of men's trousers—his and Daed's—from one of the several clotheslines that spanned the basement.

"Bethel." He tried to speak with a soft voice. To sound kinder. More welcoming. Less resentful.

A tiny gasp escaped her lips as she fumbled with a clothespin. She spun around to face him, her eyes wide.

"I didn't mean to scare you." He approached her slowly with one hand outstretched, as if she were a dog that might want to sniff it. He grunted at the foolishness of the gesture and returned his arm to his side. Shoved his hand in his pocket.

It was freezing cold down here. And she wasn't wearing a coat.

"Do you...uh, would you like to take a walk with me later? We should talk." Though he didn't know what they would talk about, exactly. Where she would prefer to sleep, maybe?

She shrugged. "If you want to."

He really didn't want to. Would it be better to force communication or let it kum naturally? He didn't know. Would communication ever kum naturally? Probably not. They'd get into the habit of ignoring each other. He blew out a breath. "We need to talk."

"You indicated as much."

He felt like an idiot. "Jah, but...well, we do." He tried for a smile. "I don't know anything about you."

She stared blankly at him. The damp pants she held started dripping on the floor.

"Okay." He cleared his throat. "Well, I...uh, I'm going to pack up Lizzie's things. It's been three—almost four—months." He swallowed hard and his eyes burned. He blinked and then gazed, unseeing, at his feet. "I'll probably rearrange the room, too. But you...and I...um, will share the room." He gulped. "Not the...the, uh, bed."

At least that would make his sister happy. Maybe his parents, too.

He raised his head in time to see Bethel's eyes widen. "Are you sure?" She clutched the wet garment closer to herself, probably soaking her dress.

Nein. Nein, he wasn't sure. Because even if his heart recognized her from a long-ago meeting, he didn't know her. They'd never even talked. Assuming she was even the same girl he'd loved at first sight all those years ago.

She must've read his answer in his expression because she made a noise that was kind of a half-sob, half-cough. "I'll be fine on the couch."

"Maybe so, but that wouldn't be right. We're married now." The words were meant mostly as a reminder for him.

"How about a cot in Elam's room?"

He felt more than a touch of alarm at her suggestion—the same idea he'd dismissed earlier because it wouldn't be ideal.

But her bringing up the idea made it seem as if der Herr was behind it. And a cot would work, on a temporary basis. At least until he bought a twin bed for the room. He'd need one eventually for Elam anyway.

He sighed, not bothering to conceal his relief. "Jah, we could do that."

He definitely needed to spend more time in prayer. After the odd discussion he'd had earlier with Bishop Miah and now this one with Bethel, Gideon needed godly wisdom on how to proceed.

He pulled in a breath. "We still need to get to know each other. We're kind of doing it backward because most marriages occur following courtship. So...a walk later?"

She hung the trousers on the line. "We could go for a walk." Her sudden smile lit the dim space and also transformed her pretty features into something beyond beautiful.

Gideon was enchanted. He needed to figure out a way to make her smile more often.

⌒

Bethel's smile faltered and her face burned. Why was Gideon staring at her?

Instead of reaching for the last pair of pants, she flicked at her cheeks, thinking perhaps she'd somehow smudged them on a soiled garment.

Gideon blinked, as if whatever spell he'd been under had been broken, and he turned away. "To-nacht. After dinner. I'll ask Naomi to do the dishes."

"Ach, I'd hate for you to bother her. It's my job now."

"It's her job, too. And she'll be in favor of doing anything that will enable me to court my frau." He glanced over his shoulder. Met her gaze. "She and Mamm both told me they like you. And Naomi made her displeasure over our having separate bedrooms very plain. But I'm not quite ready for sharing. And, I daresay, you aren't, either."

Bethel swallowed. Lowered her gaze. She might never be ready. But it would be expected. If this community was anything like her old one, people would be expecting her to have a boppli within a year of getting married. And if word got out that she and Gideon didn't even share a bedroom, a bed, they'd be subject to marital counseling.

Of course, they might need counseling anyway once word got out about the circumstances surrounding their forced marriage.

Booted feet entered her scope of vision. A finger brushed her jaw and lingered at her chin. She looked up. Gideon's green eyes gazed into hers and she caught a hint of cinnamon on his breath. "I won't force you. It'll happen when we're both ready."

Her face burned hotter.

His finger slid away, curving up her jaw and over her cheek. "You really are very pretty. Gorgeous when you smile."

Her heart pounded. She moistened her suddenly dry lips.

His gaze dropped. Lingered.

Her lips tingled in response. A flicker of something ignited deep inside her.

Then he abruptly pivoted on his heel and strode away.

She pressed her cold, damp hands against her hot face. It wouldn't take much for Gideon Kaiser to win her affections.

Not much at all.

6

Gideon's hands sweat as he held Bethel's coat while she slid her arms into the sleeves. His fingers trembled. How many times had he done this simple kindness for Lizzie? Not on their first date though. Not even the first several times after they'd started courting. They'd known each other for years, having grown up in the same community, and had courted for three years before marrying. Slow and steady.

Much better than being rushed without warning, as he'd been with Bethel.

His fingertips grazed her neck as he pulled away. Shockwaves worked up his hands and into his arms.

He pressed his lips together. He refused to acknowledge any smidgen of attraction to this woman, even though far more than a smidgen was there. It was too soon. He hadn't finished mourning Lizzie. Or their shared dreams that died with her.

And now he was expected to court his new woman. His...frau.

He didn't turn to glance at his parents and sister, all watching them. How had Bethel won them over already? Or was it that unbelievable? After all, he'd fallen in love with her—or imagined he had—the moment he'd seen her as a sixteen-year-old. She did seem sweet.

And she was very pretty. Not to mention, she was a wonderful cook and made the boppli happy.

Gideon tugged his own coat on, donned his black hat, and opened the door to a world of wind and swirling snow. The blizzard almost erased any visible sign of the dark shadow of the barn.

Maybe a walk in this weather was a bad idea. They might wander off and not be found until the next day. Or even later.

He could play it safe. Take her to the barn, find some hay bales to sit on, and do their courting while chaperoned by a couple of cows, three horses, a pig, two dogs, and innumerable cats.

The flickering light of the lantern would probably make for a more romantic atmosphere than the moon and stars, now hidden by snow-laden clouds.

Lightning flashed. Thunder boomed.

On second thought—make that third thought—maybe staying indoors and courting over a game of checkers would be better than a walk, even one across the yard, in this weather. Warmer, too. And much better chaperoned. Not that they needed any chaperones. They were married, after all.

Bethel stepped outside, sucked in a sharp breath, and started down the porch stairs.

Okay. The barn it was. Gideon shut the door behind him and followed her into the icy, thundering snowstorm.

A far cry from the weather they'd had a year ago that had them battling forest fires.

He reached for Bethel's mitten-covered hand with his gloved one. "To the barn," he shouted over the wind.

She nodded, then surprised him by not pulling her hand away. In fact, she clung to him all the way to the barn. It was slippery underfoot, though, so maybe she just wanted to safeguard against falling. Once they'd reached the shelter of the barn, she released his hand and hugged herself. Because she was cold? Or was it a defense mechanism? Lizzie used to hold throw pillows on her lap when entertaining or visiting people she didn't know well, as if those items would protect her. As if they could somehow mask her insecurities, her self-consciousness.

He lit the lantern, then pulled over a rectangular hay bale and motioned for her to sit down. She did, at one end. As if she expected him to sit next to her.

Which he would've done if she had been Lizzie.

She wasn't. And being that close would violate the laws of personal space. For him as well as for her.

It wouldn't be a gut place to start. It was too soon for his broken heart, still on the mend. And he might be tempted to act on his growing attraction for her before they accomplished the important task of establishing a foundation of friendship, a common understanding.

He dragged another bale of hay over and sat across from her.

She stared at her lap.

"I, uh, spent the morgen—and most of the afternoon—praying. Trying to get past myself to actually listen." He cleared his throat. "This marriage didn't take Gott by surprise. Just us. With that in mind, I'm telling you now: if love is a decision, then I am determined to love you as Christ loved the church."

She glanced up at him, her eyes shimmering with moisture.

"We make our plans, but Gott directs our paths. When we follow where He leads, things fall into place. And…." It was his turn to stare at his lap while he searched for the right words. "I think we need to start this marriage off with prayer. For us. As a couple. A prayer that we'll be open to His leading." He peeked up at her.

She nodded, her eyes now glistening with a look that might've been one of admiration.

He forced a smile that was rather wobbly and steepled his still-gloved hands, propping his elbows on his knees. After a moment, he stood and walked over to a nearby shelf where he thought he remembered stashing a New Testament/Psalms Bible that someone had given him. The cover was bright orange, as if to remind him, or anyone around, that the Word was meant to be boldly shared rather than hidden. And yet Gideon—or maybe Daed—had buried the book. Ashamed of its not-so-plain appearance.

Gideon rifled around in the clutter and finally found it. He pulled his hands free from the warm gloves and thumbed through the pages.

"First Peter, chapter three...I won't start with the 'submit to your husband' part because you were trained to submit to authority and, I think, if I treat you right, it will kum. Besides, Bishop Miah preached on that very thing during the ceremony yesterday." He flashed her a slight smile. "But verse seven says, *'Likewise, ye husbands, dwell with them according to knowledge, giving honour unto the wife, as unto the weaker vessel, and as being heirs together of the grace of life; that your prayers be not hindered.'"*

Bethel shifted, moving closer to the center of her hay bale, as Gideon lowered himself once more onto the bale across from her.

Gideon shuffled backward through the Bible's pages. "That wasn't the passage I had in mind. Ah, here it is. Ephesians five, beginning with verse twenty-five:

> *'Husbands, love your wives, even as Christ also loved the church, and gave himself for it; that he might sanctify and cleanse it with the washing of water by the word, that he might present it to himself a glorious church, not having spot, or wrinkle, or any such thing; but that it should be holy and without blemish. So ought men to love their wives as their own bodies. He that loveth his wife loveth himself....Nevertheless let every one of you in particular so love his wife even as himself; and the wife see that she reverence her husband.'"*

He closed the orange Bible and set it beside him. Then he reached across the expanse between them, holding out his hands.

After a moment's hesitation, Bethel pulled off her knitted mittens and slid her warm hands into his open palms. A tingle worked through him, sending a spark or two toward his heart, as if it wanted to melt the ice of grief that had formed there.

He squeezed her fingers and bowed his head. "Let's pray." Silence fell between them and as she bowed her head, he clasped her hands between both of his. "Lord Gott, please help me to be that husband, to love Bethel as You intended. Amen."

Her lips trembled as he pulled away and withdrew into his own space. A tear wandered down her cheek. Followed by a second one. She wiped them away and met his gaze and…jah. Unmistakable admiration filled her eyes.

He wasn't worthy. Because Gott knew, as well as Gideon did, that he would fall short of her admiration.

Still, if this moment had kum at a different time, or with a different woman, it might've ended with a kiss.

Gideon shook his head to shoo that thought away. That didn't work so well. "So, Bethel." He pulled his gloves back on to keep himself from pulling her into his arms—it was cold in there, after all—and looked into her hazel eyes. He leaned toward her. "Tell me about yourself."

$\backsim$

Bethel swallowed, keeping her gaze firmly fixed on Gideon's green eyes. Not his lips, which spoke words that were a balm to the hurt deep inside her. Not his reddish-gold beard, which shouted the fact that he'd belonged to another. "What do you want to know?"

"Everything." He chuckled and a blush tinged his cheeks. "Who are you? Where are you from? What did you do? Any brothers or sisters?" He shrugged. "We'll start there."

This was awkward. Bethel shifted, bits of hay stabbing her legs through the thin material of her dress. It would've been nice to have a blanket spread over this hay bale. Or to have worn a longer coat. "I'm Bethel. Bethel Magdalene Eicher."

"Bethel Magdalene Eicher Kaiser." He winked.

Her heart thudded. "Kaiser. My birthday is December twenty-fourth."

"And your parents didn't name you Carol?" he teased.

"That was my mamm's name. My daed is Elijah and I have one younger sister, Ruth. She left the Amish…I think. Rodney tried to court her and she…she vanished a year ago."

"Hmm." His eyes turned serious as he surveyed her, as if he wondered why she hadn't done the same.

Gut question. And one for which she didn't have an answer. She moistened her lips. "My daed worked as a clerk for an auction haus and I worked for him as cashier. I also took care of my mamm until she died."

Gideon grimaced. "I'm sorry for your loss. But cashier…?" His eyes skimmed over her, as if he were mentally evaluating her suitability for some unknown position. "And nein suitors emerged from among the auction-goers?" His eyes glittered with an unreadable emotion.

"No one I was interested in, except—" Isaac. The auctioneer. Well, one of the auctioneers. The most popular, most in-demand one. She looked away.

Gideon raised his eyebrows. "Except…?"

If only she'd controlled her tongue. "Except nobody."

"You're the one who said 'except'. Plus, there was a certain look in your eyes." He gave a slight frown.

She shrugged. "It's nobody," she said firmly. "Nobody." She was married now and so was that "nobody," so it didn't matter anymore. She focused on tugging her mittens back on, keeping her gaze lowered to hide the tears that stung her eyes.

"Nobody." Gideon nodded slowly, his eyebrows rising once more. "Okay. If I were to bring home a special gift from the salvage-grocery for you, what would you choose?"

⌒

Gideon studied Bethel, waiting for an answer. For the longest time, she said nothing, but only stared at him. As if waiting for him to tell her he was kidding.

Gifts were an important part of courtship. Generally, these gifts were items for the home: a dish, a towel, a clock.... But when one's home was already set up, then other things were acceptable. Such as candy.

"Rich milk chocolate with a caramel center." She closed her eyes, an almost dreamy expression on her face, as if she could almost taste the...what? Candy bar? Fudge?

He would check to see what he had at the store. If nothing in their inventory matched her description, he'd have a talk with Agnes when she returned from her honeymoon. She could whip up something special.

He stood and returned the orange New Testament to the shelf, but he didn't bury it this time, even though the flamboyant color still made him shudder. It screamed, "Look at me!" The opposite of the attitude that the Amish strived to live by. On the other hand, the Word of der Herr *did* need to be looked at. Read. Studied. Prayed over. A lot. And even more so by someone needing godly wisdom for dealing with his new frau.

Bethel had stood, too, so Gideon tugged the hay bales back to their original locations, then opened the barn door. The wind gusted inside, its force causing Bethel to sway. Gideon clutched at his hat and held out his other arm. "Hang on tight."

Her mittened hand curled around the crook of his elbow. And she clung tightly.

Was it wrong to admit, even to himself, that he liked the sensation?

As awkward as it had been, this hour of courtship had gone well. How often should he initiate these sessions? Once every two weeks, as most courting couples started out? Or should he schedule them more frequently, since he and Bethel were already married?

He feared that the latter might somehow betray Lizzie's memory. But her last words to him had been, "Choose love. Not loss." Almost as if she'd known what would happen and wanted to give him permission to pack up her things. It'd still been a hard process—putting her belongings into boxes, carrying them up to the attic, and then spending over an hour praying, crying, and trying to say gut-bye. Not quite succeeding.

He glanced down at the woman walking beside him, holding his arm. Her slight smile faltered.

Choose love. Not loss.

He swallowed the burn in his throat.

"May I take you out Monday for a second attempt at a walk?" He barked a laugh. "Or maybe a sleigh ride?"

"Sure." She turned to him and looked deep into his eyes. "You asked what I'd like if you were going to bring me something. I know you can't do anything about it, but I really want some white chocolate raspberry ice cream."

7

Bethel giggled at the look of pure shock on Gideon's face. He probably hadn't met many people who would get a hankering for ice cream in the middle of a February blizzard. Daed would've taken one incredulous glance at her and declared it too cold for the dessert.

Gideon finally shook off his wide-eyed, gaping-mouthed stare and nodded. "Your wish is my command. However, I might not be able to do white chocolate raspberry." He opened the door to the haus. "Naomi? Get us a pan. We're going to have snow ice cream."

"Bring in enough for all of us," she hollered back.

"Sure." Gideon held the door open a bit wider for Bethel. "You go on in and set out some bowls and spoons." He winked. "I'll be right in."

Naomi handed Gideon a kettle. He took it and headed back into the blizzard.

Bethel stood in the open doorway, watching until the blowing snow obliterated him from view. He wanted to court her—again—on Monday. Despite its awkward start, today's first foray into courtship had been eye-opening. Intriguing. And a relief, because it sure seemed that Daed couldn't have picked a better man for her to be forced into marrying. Gideon was strong. Courteous. Faithful in prayer. Determined. Loyal. Just. A man of Gott.

What would it be like if he kissed her? She swallowed. If he did as she'd feared he would do on their wedding nacht—if he'd taken her hand and led her to the…. A mixture of curiosity, disappointment, and anticipation mingled inside her as she considered the possibility of his lips even brushing her cheek.

To-nacht, she could have melted into a puddle at his feet. It was so sweet, the way he courted her.

She sighed, tears blurring her eyes, and shut the door. She pulled off her coat, mittens, and bonnet, and hung them by the door. Then she tugged off her shoes and turned, her black socks slipping slightly on the wood floor.

Naomi had taken out sugar, evaporated milk, salt, and vanilla and was measuring them into a mixing bowl. She looked up and smiled at Bethel. "I don't know what made him think of it, but it's been a tradition since we were little to make snow ice cream at least once every winter. I figured the tradition died with Lizzie."

At least it wasn't Lizzie's tradition. Bethel frowned as shame pricked her heart. "I mentioned being in the mood for white chocolate raspberry ice cream."

"I think we have some canned raspberries and white chocolate chips in the pantry," Naomi told her. "I might be wrong about the chips though. I know we have milk chocolate chips, if those would do instead."

A fresh round of tears burned Bethel's eyes. This family was so accommodating, reaching out to welkum her with open arms, as if she truly were Gideon's beloved.

She managed a mute nod, her throat suddenly raw from her unshed tears, and scurried to the pantry to see what she could find.

She turned on the battery-operated lantern-shaped flashlight in the dark room just as she heard the back door open. Peeking her head out, she saw Gideon blow into the kitchen with a flurry of flakes and a frigid gust of wind.

He handed the kettleful of snow to Naomi and removed his hat.

"It's really sweet of you to make snow ice cream for Bethel because she asked for it," Naomi said.

Gideon grunted.

That hurt. But maybe it was too much—and too soon—to hope for a gracious response. Really, what else had she expected? She'd known this wasn't going to be easy. Marriage was hard even when the ehemann and frau married for love, ain't so? If this was going to be a real marriage, they would have to work at it every day.

Bethel wanted it to work. She wanted to love her ehemann. For him to love her. Forever.

Not to be two strangers coexisting in the same haus for the rest of their lives.

She blew out a breath, firmed her shoulders, and grabbed a bag of white chocolate chips and a can of raspberries. Forcing a smile, she reentered the kitchen.

Gideon hung his coat next to hers on the hook and turned.

His eyes met hers.

And for a moment—the briefest of moments—they were the only two people in the room.

⌒

Gideon watched as Naomi stirred together the evaporated milk, sugar, salt, and vanilla, then dumped them on top of the snow in the kettle he'd brought in. It was a bittersweet moment…because Lizzie had been the one to introduce him to snow ice cream. She'd mentioned the treat in a school essay titled, "What I did this weekend," and he'd been curious enough to ask her about it. His own family's tradition had started soon thereafter, when he'd asked Mamm if she'd heard of snow ice cream and wondered whether they could they try it. He'd never told his family that the idea had kum from Lizzie, though, only attributing it to "someone at school." Only Naomi knew, as she'd had to write that same report and had listened to the other students read theirs. She'd been considerate enough not to tease Gideon for copying Lizzie.

And now he'd suggested making Lizzie's dessert for Bethel.

Bethel set a bag of white chocolate chips and a can of raspberries on the counter.

"Danki, Bethel." His sister reached for a measuring cup. "Gideon, go set up the checkerboard. You and Bethel can play a game or two while I finish up."

Snow ice cream didn't take that long to make. And the white chocolate chips and raspberries would make this wintry concoction all Bethel's. Lizzie had always added rainbow sprinkles to hers. Whoever heard of the combination of white chocolate chips and raspberries?

But Naomi didn't even blink. And Bethel appeared happy. Content.

Suddenly, Gideon didn't want her sleeping in Elam's room. He wanted her curled up beside him, her head on his shoulder, her—

He shook his head, turned his back on the intriguing woman in his kitchen and went to find the checkerboard. Though how he would be able to concentrate enough to strategize and make well-calculated moves was beyond him.

Lizzie hadn't been very gut at the game. She approached it the same way she did the rest of life, breezing through it with lots of giggles and little thought. She'd done well if she had even one king at the end of the game. While they were courting, it sometimes seemed to him that she'd deliberately set it up so as to get blocked in a corner. Later, after they married, she seemed to look for those corners to be blocked into. Though he supposed moving his frau into a home with his parents and sister meant the only privacy they'd get would be in corners.

Or the bedroom.

The same bedroom he now considered inviting Bethel into. Again.

A ball formed in his stomach and thickened into a heavy mass that sank to the bottom and expanded, filling him, blocking out everything but the pain. How could he even consider…?

Since moving the furniture around in his room hadn't erased the memory of Lizzie, he would have to start fresh. When he was ready—and Bethel was, too—to take that step, he'd need to have plans in place. An area that didn't scream memories of Lizzie. A sanctuary of their own.

For now, he would continue their evening of courtship with a game of checkers. He reached for the box. Then he hesitated without grabbing it. Nein. Nein, he wouldn't. He and Bethel would have to start fresh with courting activities he'd never done with Lizzie. Such as…. He surveyed the closet.

What about…? Nein.

Or…? Nein, again. All the games they owned, he'd played with Lizzie.

He'd check the store to see if they had anything new.

And the next time Gabe Lapp came in to do some shopping, Gideon would ask him privately for recommendations on remodeling a bedroom. So that, when the time came, he'd be ready.

"Gideon."

Gideon jerked at the sound of his daed's voice behind him. How long had he been standing in front of the game closet, staring blindly at it?

He grabbed a puzzle someone had given him as a Christmas present. It was still wrapped in plastic and, thus, untouched by Lizzie. He closed the door. "You know, Daed, I'm not up to a game of checkers to-nacht. A puzzle sounds fun. Would you open the box and get it ready? I need to find a cot to set up for Bethel in Elam's room."

"I was going to tell you the ice cream is ready, but you and Bethel…." Daed gave a slow shake of his head.

Nein matter. Gideon could guess.

"I'm not ready, Daed. I'm not. And neither is she."

This was Bethel's first time having snow ice cream. It was gut, but it melted faster than traditional ice cream. She happily helped the Kaiser family to sort edge pieces of the puzzle after they'd introduced her to another new tradition: assembling puzzles without the help of the box lid. She didn't have the beginnings of a clue about how the end result was supposed to look.

In some ways, the approach seemed unfair, since Gideon and Ben had seen the box cover in advance. But neither Reba nor Naomi seemed to mind having a disadvantage. And Reba multitasked, holding Elam against her shoulder and rubbing his back to get out any final burps before it was time to put him to bed.

Even though Bethel was still a stranger in their midst, it was nice being part of a happy, laughing, engaging family. Granted, Gideon didn't laugh much and his smiles were few and fleeting, but the general atmosphere was so different from Bethel's home. Daed had sunken into a bottomless pit of despair when Mamm died and hadn't laughed since. And in the days since Ruth had vanished, he'd mostly sat in silence, staring glumly into space. Either that or staring at Bethel as if he expected her to up and disappear, too.

And she had. By his own doing.

She swallowed the lump in her throat.

Did he even wonder what would become of her? Did he care? Or had Daed vetted Gideon ahead of time to discern his character before falsely accusing him of having fathered Bethel's nonexistent child? And, if he had, did he find his discoveries as intriguing as Bethel was finding her own to be?

"Whoo!"

Her attention jarred from her thoughts, Bethel looked up in time to see Naomi waving two connected edge pieces in the air.

"I got the first match!" Naomi crowed, grinning. She leaned closer to Gideon and shoved the two pieces under his nose. "I beat you."

He rolled his eyes at her. "My thoughts were on other things." With his spoon, he scooped up the last of his mostly melted snow ice cream and brought it to his mouth—with a tiny half-smile aimed at Bethel.

Naomi leaned closer to Bethel. "He always gets the first match when we do puzzles. But I guess I won't rub it in too much if his thoughts were on his bride."

A heavy silence fell and Bethel's face burned. She didn't dare look at Gideon. If this was awkward for her—

Gideon pushed his chair back. "I'm turning in. Didn't sleep so well last nacht."

Neither had she.

"You'll be able to find your way to Elam's room okay?"

Still not looking at him, she nodded.

Reba shifted. "Elam's asleep, Gideon. If you'll take him from me and carry him upstairs, you can show Bethel her new room." There was a note of disapproval in her voice.

Or maybe it was all Bethel's imagination. Because surely Gideon's parents didn't expect him to share a bedroom with her. Not yet. Gideon was still grieving. And Bethel had been thrust out of her familiar world into one filled with strangers. Love wasn't a factor, for either of them. And even if the number one rule of the Amish had been to be fruitful and multiply—which it wasn't— nobody would be so callous as to expect two mutually unknown newlyweds to make gut on it right away. Nobody.

Or maybe the tone was one of irritation with Bethel for still being there. Maybe the friendship Bethel thought she was forming with Reba and Naomi was just a ruse and they had decided to play along until this nacht-mare ended.

The same bad dream Bethel was living through.

She set down her puzzle piece, stood up, and forced a smile at her new family.

She had to have a little hope. This, too, would end. Eventually. Maybe.

"Gut nacht."

"Gut nacht," said Reba, Naomi, and Ben, almost in unison.

Gideon carefully lifted his sohn out of his mamm's arms and led the way upstairs. He laid the boppli on his back in the crib, checked the diaper, and turned to her where she stood in the doorway.

"I got it ready for you." He gestured to the cot, which was literally that—a piece of rigid canvas stretched tautly over a series of metal rods about six inches above the floor. Spread atop it was a green floral-patterned sleeping bag that was partly unzipped. Half opened, for ease of crawling in. A tiny tomato-red foam camping pillow waited not-so-invitingly at the head.

Wow. He'd gone to such great lengths to make her comfortable! Guess who wasn't going to get a gut nacht's sleep? Then again, he had mentioned the idea of their sharing a room but not a bed and she'd voiced the dumb alternative of a cot. Was it too late to accept his original suggestion?

Tears of regret burned her eyes as she remembered the comfort of the pillow-top mattress in the next room over, the softness of the full-sized pillow surrounding her like a cloud.

Not hers.

She attempted a grin. "I am *so* blessed."

8

Gideon didn't miss the sarcasm in his bride's quiet comment. Punctuating it with an eye roll had been completely unnecessary, even if the expression had been extremely subtle. He wouldn't have caught it if he hadn't been looking.

He'd looked, because Bethel was lovely. A vision, really. And she had a demeanor to match—one that was gentle. Kind. Loving. Hardworking. How had she managed to go unclaimed for so long?

Could it be that Gott had set her aside specifically for him to love, honor, and cherish, until death did they part? A replacement for Lizzie?

His heart hurt. How could he even consider such a question?

She stood in the bedroom doorway a moment longer, then turned and grabbed her suitcase from the hallway as if preparing to move in.

Here.

Elam's room.

Ach, wait. She was. By his own doing.

And not even two hours after he promised to try to be "that ehemann." The one who loved her as he loved himself. The one who had prompted a look of genuine admiration. Admiration that was now gone, replaced by hurt and rejection. And a touch of loneliness.

He could almost picture Gott writing a big, fat, ugly zero in bold red on his scorecard in heaven. Like the one he'd gotten on a school spelling test when he leaned over ever-so-slightly and peeked at Lizzie's test so he would "remember" how to spell a word. And the teacher caught him. An automatic zero. Public shaming by being sent to the dunce stool in the corner and then having to write "I will not cheat" fifty times on the chalkboard. Followed by a trip behind the woodshed with Daed. He'd never forgotten how to spell that word. *Recipient.* One he didn't really use in daily life, now indelibly etched in his mind.

Bethel was a recipient of his broken promises.

Ouch.

She shifted. "If you don't mind, I think I'll get ready for bed."

As if that uncomfortable cot qualified as a bed.

He chuckled as his eyes drifted southward, taking in her lovely curves all the way down to her skirt, still damp from their blizzard "stroll." She probably couldn't wait to change into something warm and dry.

"I don't mind at all. In fact, I'll do the same."

Only at the sight of her flame-red cheeks did he realize what he'd said. What he'd implied. And how she must have understood it.

Not what he'd intended to say. Or imply.

He cleared his throat, then stepped forward and picked up her suitcase. "You're sleeping next door. In...in my room. I'll take the cot."

She shook her head. "Nein. It's okay. I'll be fine here. Close to Elam. And you need your sleep. I'm sure the cot won't be very comfortable for you."

He shrugged. "I'm used to it. Lizzie and I went camping as often as we could." When would he learn to control his tongue? The pain of regret cut his heart like shards of glass.

"She liked camping?" Bethel's voice was barely above a whisper.

"Loved it. It was her favorite pastime. After sewing." Although, truthfully, it'd been a privacy thing and not necessarily a true love of camping.

He carried the lantern and her suitcase into the hallway. Into his bedroom. He set the lantern on the dresser and put the suitcase on the bed. "Do you like camping?"

Bethel had followed him as far as the doorway. She hesitated. Shrugged. "I've actually never tried it."

Gideon smiled as he pictured taking her into the woods and introducing her to his favorite spot. Not to mention, getting away from the crowded house and having a little privacy.

As Bethel stepped further into the room, her gaze drifted to the comfortable bed, her face showing obvious relief. Gut thing he'd decided to sleep on the cot. But he wanted to prolong this conversation and find out more about her. "You didn't camp out with the youngies from your area?"

"Nein. For most of my teenage years, my mamm couldn't be left alone at all. She couldn't walk. Some days, she couldn't even get out of bed. I didn't do much of anything with the youngies." She shrugged, as if it didn't matter, but there was a hint of regret in her eyes. "My sister, Ruth, would go along with the youngies, because we agreed that one of us should be courted and get married and she seemed the more logical choice. Besides, Mamm did better with me there."

That explained why Bethel had never married.

"I can see why. You possess a calming demeanor. And you're patient with Mamm." She would be the perfect caregiver, with her experience. Almost as if Gott had brought him more than just a replacement frau but one who would truly make their family better.

"Your mamm is a lot better physically than mine was." Her voice cracked. Had she watched her mamm fade daily until the end, as he would have to do with his? He wasn't ready for that either.

Gideon swallowed. "She has gut days and bad days. These past several days have been better ones." He studied her a moment, then reached out and playfully tugged one of her kapp strings. It was a gesture he'd often done with Lizzie just before taking her in his arms. A reflex he hadn't thought about before acting on. But he couldn't take it back. "When the weather improves some, I'll take you camping, if you'd like."

Bethel didn't answer, but a look of what might've been pain crossed her face.

He opened his mouth to ask what was wrong, but then bit back the words. It was none of his business. Still holding the kapp string, he allowed his fingers to trail over the soft skin of her neck, where the kapp string dangled, and down to the collar of her dress. Something else he'd done with Lizzie. It'd be so easy to pretend.... Watching his fingers, he'd missed any reaction she might've given, other than the slightest of gasps and a tiny shiver. He pulled away.

His breath hitched. He shouldn't have acted on his attraction. Things were escalating too fast and neither of them was ready. He gulped. Cleared his throat.

"I'll grab a few things and get out of your way."

◡‿◠

For one moment of insanity, Bethel wanted to ask him to stay. Her neck still tingled from his gentle touch and she loved the way he'd suddenly decided to put her comfort over his own. And the earlier prayer in the barn—the warmth of his hands holding hers—and the making of ice cream had helped to raise her hopes. Plus, there were his green eyes and his reddish-gold hair to consider...

But neither of them was ready to move their relationship forward in that way. Honestly, the very idea terrified her because of the high risk to her heart. Although, if they could eventually reach that point, being loved might be worth the risk.

Her heart was in enough jeopardy as it was. Especially if Gideon kept his promise to love her as he loved himself. It gave new meaning to the commandment to love one's neighbor as oneself. What would the world be like if everyone went out of their way to meet others' needs? To make sure they were happy and comfortable? She should strive to do the same for him. For his family.

Perhaps Gott had called all people to be a caregiver and the position wasn't a punishment but an honor. Well, it had been an honor to care of Mamm. Bethel just hadn't ever wanted to take care of other people. But she would. Because Gott expected it. And it wasn't as if the experience would be altogether unpleasant. Elam was a joy to take care of, for now, being tiny and adorable. Reba might require a bit more patience on harder days, but so far, she'd overturned Bethel's first impression by treating her with kindness bordering on affection.

Gideon grabbed a pair of navy-blue plaid flannel pajama pants, a navy-blue T-shirt, and what looked to be a change of clothes for the next day. Then he headed for the hall. In the doorway, he stopped and turned. "We'll have to talk sometime about future sleeping arrangements."

Ach. She might end up on the uncomfortable-looking cot after all. Only fair, since he was taking a turn.

"But until I can make other arrangements, this room is yours. I'll take care of Elam if he cries. Gut nacht, Bethel. Sleep well."

"Gut nacht, Gideon."

As he left the room, she pressed her hands to her chest as if to hold her heart in place. If she stayed around him much longer, he might just capture it.

⌒

Gideon woke with a start the next morgen. He blinked, trying to distance himself from the dreams that had kept him tossing and turning all nacht. Nobody would fault him for dreaming of his frau, but it was the wrong woman who'd filled his thoughts. Not the dark-haired, dark-eyed beauty he'd gradually fallen in love with and eventually wed, but the honey-blonde, hazel-eyed enchantress he'd married two days ago. Her impish smile when she mentioned white chocolate raspberry ice cream, which had actually been quite delicious. The admiration in her eyes at the end of their awkward first courtship session. The mystery of her. One he wanted to delve into and solve.

Thoughts he shouldn't already be thinking about the stranger sharing his life.

How could he remain true to Lizzie while courting Bethel?

Choose love. Not loss.

Ugh! What had Lizzie meant by her final words? Had she been giving him permission to embrace the possibility of loving—truly loving—another woman?

Or had she meant for him to love Elam and not blame him for her death?

That thought had not crossed his mind until just now.

Nein, he couldn't fathom not loving Elam. The boppli wasn't to blame. Lizzie's time had simply kum.

Gideon swallowed. Hard.

Elam gurgled, drawing his attention in the dim light of the early dawn. The bu had somehow rolled over onto his tummy and now peeked through the slats of his crib, gazing at Gideon.

Gideon sat up and then slowly stood, stretching his sore back muscles. He and Lizzie used to go camping every other weekend, but stopped soon after learning she was in the family way. Once the boppli had gotten big enough to push almost constantly on her bladder, she hadn't wanted to camp. And since she passed…well, it'd been a gut eight months or more since he'd slept on the cot. It barely beat the floor in terms of comfort.

At least it was warmer than the basement.

Elam made a cooing sound and Gideon stepped toward him. He scooped up his sohn, kissed his chubby cheeks, and then laid him on his back to change his diaper. Wet, but not overly so. Someone must have kum and changed him during the nacht.

He blew noisily into Elam's belly, zipped his sleeper shut again, and held the giggling boppli to his chest as he made his way downstairs. In his pajamas.

He paused halfway down the stairs when he remembered the presence of the alluring, curvy, altogether lovely stranger in his haus. He started to turn, ready to return to his room to dress for the day, but...nein. He'd make this quick. He would hand off Elam off to whoever was up or would leave him on a blanket on the floor while he ran upstairs and changed clothes. Hopefully, before Bethel noticed him.

Gideon paused again at the sound of voices coming from the kitchen. He heard Daed say something. Mamm answered moments later. He didn't hear Bethel. He slipped into the room and stopped just inside the door at the sight of Bethel bent over the woodstove, sliding a pan inside. She straightened, closed the doors to the stove, and turned, her gaze skimming over him and then darting back.

Daed shrugged his coat on. "I'll be in the barn. Send Gideon out when you see him so we can get started on chores while you prepare breakfast."

Bethel nodded, her gaze locked with Gideon's.

Gideon swallowed, his face heating. "I'll be right out, Daed."

If Daed had heard him, he didn't acknowledge it. Or maybe Gideon's sense of hearing—along with all his other senses—was compromised at the sight of Bethel coming toward him with arms outstretched and a smile on her face.

For one heart-stopping second, he almost thought she was about to embrace him. But then she took Elam from him, her fingers brushing his T-shirt-covered chest and kissed his sohn the same Gideon had, including a noisy blow on his stomach. Well, almost the same way. Elam's sleeper made the sound more muted.

Elam giggled.

Gideon's chest burned where she'd accidentally touched him. And the burn of jealousy coursed through him. Was it a sin to envy his boppli sohn because of the affection she gave him?

He reached out and grasped Bethel's arm. Her gaze rose from Elam to him. Gideon's eyes lowered to her lips, then rose to meet her eyes before lowering again. He leaned forward, and...and....

Her eyes widened. She drew a ragged breath.

And then his brain caught up with him. He jerked himself back, spun around, and ran upstairs. What was he doing, trying to kiss her? He hadn't even brushed his teeth yet! Not to mention, he should've courted her at least twice…or thrice…or maybe even four times.

Shoot, was it a sin to want to kiss his bride?

It was those dreams. It had to be those dreams.

He'd known Lizzie a lot longer before he even began to think about kissing her.

Maybe a cold shower would shock the thought of kissing Bethel out of his system.

9

Bethel's arm tingled from Gideon's light touch. Her lips unexpectedly ached at missing out on a kiss, even if the only kisses she knew had been in her dreams...dreams triggered by his gentle caressing of her neck just before she'd gone to bed. She stood there, staring after Gideon. Fighting the urge to run after him, grasp the dark blue material of his soft T-shirt and lean into him, inhaling the pine-scented body wash he used, tasting the hint of cinnamon on his breath....

She shook her head and moved around Reba's wheelchair to address the woman to her face. "Do you want to hold Elam? Or should I give him some floor time?"

Reba paused in her task of refilling the family's collection of salt and pepper shakers. "Floor time. His blanket is in the other room." She sounded abrupt. Cranky.

Bethel nodded and headed for the living room. As she passed the steps, she glanced upstairs. It was tempting. So tempting. But Naomi was likely in her room and could kum out at any time. Not to mention, it would be overly forward to chase Gideon like that.

She gathered the fuzzy blanket, carried it back into the kitchen, and, somewhat awkwardly, spread it out on the floor between her and Reba, close to the stove, which was still struggling to remove the chill from the room. She laid Elam on the blanket, then glanced outside. The blizzard was over, having left behind several inches of beautiful snow. It'd be fun to walk in it later. But right now, she needed to fix breakfast. She opened the refrigerator and surveyed at the contents, looking for inspiration.

Something hot because of the cold and snow. Maybe oatmeal with bananas, hash browns, bacon, toast, and scrambled eggs? She checked the pantry. There were a few bananas left. Very little bread. They'd really gone at the warm loaves slathered with butter Naomi had made yesterday.

"Do you think Naomi would be willing to make bread again today?" Bethel grabbed the bananas and the remaining loaf of bread and carried them into the kitchen.

"She left for work around four this morning. She'll be home after lunch. I figured we would have toasted cheese sandwiches and tomato soup for lunch." Reba grimaced as she struggled to twist the lid off a shaker.

Ach. Bethel put the loaf back in the cold pantry. She would make biscuits and sausage gravy instead. She wasn't sure the haus was warm enough for bread to rise rapidly—and her dough tended to fall. Often. She wasn't ready to reveal her not-so-gut breadmaking skills. Of course, Mamm had always blamed Daed, pointing to the fact that he stomped around and slammed doors and bread didn't like that. It was true that Bethel had better luck with breadmaking when Daed wasn't home. But this home had two men—and a professional baker.

She didn't like to think of herself as a coward, but with those odds against her, she was afraid to try breadmaking so early on. She wanted to impress Gideon and his family. And her efforts would have to start with Reba and her prickly demeanor this morgen.

Pride, all pride. But what else did she have?

Certainly not love. Not acceptance. Not yet.

In a fairy tale, a hero would swoop in and save the day. But her life was in the cinders. It wasn't in the fire that was blazing and the sparks Gideon's touch ignited but went nowhere. Not for her. Just ash and cinders and lonely days filled with endless work in the shadow of the much-loved Lizzie.

Not that she would complain. It wouldn't do any gut. It was her cross to bear.

She felt numb. Cold, inside and out.

Alone.

So alone.

~

Showered and suitably dressed, Gideon reentered the kitchen and was greeted by an amazing aroma. Bethel stood at the stove, a wooden spatula in her hand. Gideon sniffed again. Sausage?

He wandered closer to see. Jah, sausage. It was crumbled. On the burner beside it, oatmeal bubbled in a kettle, while a gravy-colored cream simmered in another pot.

"Smells great, Bethel." Before he could think better of it, he leaned over, intending to brush a kiss against her neck, just below her ear.

She jerked away before he could make contact, turning to stare at him, her eyes wide and filled with pain. Or fear. Or shame at his boldness in making a public move on her.

His face heated. Burned, actually. He grinned, though the expression probably made him look sick. Added a wink because it seemed like the thing to do. And turned away, catching Mamm frowning at him from her wheelchair, where she sat and fed Elam his bottle. Was her look intended for him or for Bethel? Or was she simply having a bad day? Probably the latter. On gut days, she refused the wheelchair.

He needed to apologize to Bethel for his bad behavior, but he'd do it in private. Mamm didn't need to overhear. He grabbed his outerwear, plopping his hat on his head and shoving his arms into the sleeves of his coat as he hurried out to the barn. In spite of the raw wind, it was a relief to leave the tension in the kitchen.

He and Bethel probably wouldn't be going for a walk to-nacht either. The barn was cold, but at least they would have protection from the wind during a private conversation. Or they could stay inside the warm haus and keep working on the puzzle in the living room. With nein privacy.

Probably not a bad thing, with Gideon's hormones raging out of control.

He shouldn't have dreamed of her last nacht. If he hadn't, then he wouldn't be suffering like he was right now.

As if he had any control over his dreams.

He pulled his coat tighter around him and entered the barn, where he could hear Daed singing a hymn. Daed must be in the cow byre. He always serenaded the cows when he milked them. Gideon, on the other hand, practiced his Sunday-morgen messages on them, shouting down fire and brimstone if they didn't repent and get baptized.

Their cows knew the Word, for sure. At least they heard daily songs or sermons.

Daed looked up as Gideon came into the cow shed. "Almost done. You took longer than I thought you would. You really should go ahead and kiss the girl. You *are* married to her, ain't so?"

Jah, well…. He couldn't exactly discuss the problem with Daed. How could he relate? And Daed's advice would be to consummate the marriage already.

Maybe that would be gut advice…and maybe not. Gideon wasn't sure. He was only certain of two things: Lizzie had been gone just four months and he was attracted to Bethel. Big-time attracted. But while he might have imagined himself in love with Bethel in the past and was determined to love Bethel now, he was still in love with Lizzie. And with that in mind, it just seemed wiser to wait.

"Hallo," yelled a male voice from the front of the barn.

Gideon glanced at Daed and headed for the concrete steps leading out of the cow byre. "I'll see who's here, then collect the eggs."

He stepped outside in time to see the front door of the haus open and his bride—*his* Bethel—run, coatless, toward the man standing beside a buggy. She flung herself into his arms and held on tight.

Jealousy reared its ugly head. Gideon forced himself to approach calmly, quietly, peacefully.

"How's my little sis?" the man asked and Gideon suddenly realized the voice was familiar. "He's treating you okay?"

"Sis"? Bethel hadn't said anything about a brother.

"I thought—I hoped—it'd be you. I didn't know you married Agnes." Her voice was muffled. "Congratulations."

She didn't sound like she completely meant it.

Pain pummeled Gideon. Pain and another heaping dose of jealousy. Agnes…and Isaac Mast. The auctioneer. Bethel had mentioned that she'd been a cashier at auctions. She had obviously spent enough time with Isaac that *he* felt free to hug her and call her sister.

Isaac released her and stepped back. He turned slightly and his eyes narrowed as his gaze fell on Gideon. Probably mirroring Gideon's own scowl. But Gideon felt his was justified. Isaac was *not* Bethel's brother, even if he called her "little sis" or thought of her as just that. He was the "nobody" Bethel had referred to yesterday when they were talking in the barn. Gideon was sure of it.

Gideon struggled to find his emotional footing. And his voice. Or maybe it was better that he couldn't find his voice. But he hastened—strode, really—to stand beside Bethel and reach for her hand. Possessively. He entwined his fingers with hers.

She gave him a sharp look but didn't pull away. Sparks shot up his arm at the contact. She looked at his hand. And took the tiniest of steps closer to him. The skirt of her dress, blown by the wind, whipped around his leg.

"I worked an auction on our honeymoon, at an Amish community near Buffalo, New York," Isaac told Gideon. "Found something I thought you might soon need: a very nice high chair. I know your sohn isn't quite big enough for it yet, but he will be in a few months."

Gideon managed a nod and a small smile. "Danki," he mumbled almost unintelligibly.

"How is Agnes?" Bethel stretched on her toes and peered into the buggy. "Where is she?"

"She's at the candy shop. She had some orders kum in while we were gone." Isaac moved to the back of the buggy and lifted down a high chair with a blue-cushioned seat and back. "She wasn't sure she should...ach. Never mind." His face reddened and he glanced at Bethel briefly, then looked away.

So Agnes knew of Bethel's crush on Isaac? Or was he thinking of the time when Gideon had proposed to Agnes for the sake of convenience because Daed had convinced him he needed a frau, pronto?

The same reason Daed had given to support his marrying Bethel when the accusations about Gideon had arisen. What does love have to do with it? You need a frau. She needs an ehemann. She's alone. Available.

Gideon cringed.

And...wait. How had Isaac known about Gideon's marriage to Bethel? Probably a dumb question. Through the Amish grapevine, nein doubt.

"The high chair looks great, almost brand-new," Gideon remarked. "Danki."

Isaac nodded. "Brought a few other things I figured someone in the community might need. They're stored in Gabe Lapp's barn. If you are interested."

"I'll take a look." Gideon hesitated. Swallowed. "Is there a...a bed?" His face heated.

Isaac nodded. "A couple of beds actually. Stop by and see." He winked at Bethel and then turned away. "Don't be a stranger. Bring Bethel to the candy shop, Gideon. I'm sure Agnes will gift you and your bride with a slab of fudge. Besides, Bethel will need another friend here." He climbed into the buggy and glanced at Gideon once more. Tilting his head toward Bethel, he added, "Take care of her."

Gideon nodded. "The best. Don't worry." It was a vow. A promise. And he meant it. He squeezed her hand to emphasize it.

With another wink, Isaac clicked his tongue and drove off.

Gideon released Bethel's hand, turned, and grasped her cold cheeks in both his palms. "You need to get inside. You'll freeze out here." But instead of letting her go, he leaned nearer, his gaze dipping to her lips. Then he looked up again.

She sucked in a breath, her eyes wide.

"Nobody, huh?" His hands slid away, one going around to the back of her neck, the other gently grasping her chin and tilting her face upward.

She shivered as she leaned slightly into him. "Nobody," she whispered. Her hazel eyes gazed into his green ones as if maybe she meant it.

He started to lower his head.

"Gideon?" Daed's call interrupted him.

With a sigh, he stepped back. "I'll carry the high chair inside when I kum in for breakfast. And we'll resume this conversation later."

⌒

"It's nobody," Bethel whispered to Gideon's retreating back as he returned to the barn. Then she shivered as a gust of cold air blew her dress upward from underneath. The high chair shook in the wind, but didn't topple. Thoughtful of Isaac to bring it, though it probably wouldn't be long before he and Agnes were in need of one, too. They could regift it to Isaac and Agnes when Elam nein longer needed it. It wasn't as if Bethel would have a boppli of her own anytime soon.

Isaac…. Gideon knew. Knew and let Isaac know, in nein uncertain terms, that she was taken. Unnecessary, really, with Isaac's calling her "little sis," plus the fact that he was married now, too.

Somewhere, a timer started dinging. Ach, the breakfast food! She ran to the haus, raced up the porch stairs and burst into the kitchen to find Reba struggling to her feet, still holding Elam.

"I'm sorry—somebody brought a high chair by," Bethel explained breathlessly. "Gideon's going to bring it in." She rushed to the stove, turned off the buzzer, and checked her white sauce and oatmeal. They were both done and not scalded, thankfully. Next, she pulled the oven door open. Biscuits were done. She grabbed the two pot holders from the countertop and used them to lift out the tray.

"A high chair? Who needs a high chair?"

Bethel turned to look at Reba, then glanced at Elam. "For when he's ready."

Reba settled herself back into her wheelchair with a low grunt and adjusted Elam in her arms.

Bethel set the tray of biscuits on the counter to cool. Then she rested both hands on the edge of the counter and leaned forward, letting the heat rising from the biscuits warm her cold face. Hopefully, the heightened color her cheeks had must have assumed would be attributed to her toiling in the kitchen and not to Gideon's almost, not-quite, but obviously intended kiss.

Nein wonder Lizzie had enjoyed camping. There was nein privacy in this haus at all. Not even for stolen moments.

And Gideon had intended to kiss her!

Admittedly, the gesture was born of jealousy rather than love or passion. But the truth remained that he had almost kissed her.

And she wanted him to.

Well, she did...and she didn't. The very idea still terrified her. But he was her ehemann. Would his reddish-gold beard feel soft or prickly? Would she experience the same tingles from his kiss as she did with every other point of contact with him?

Wait.... He had studied her lips earlier today, before Isaac showed up.

Maybe he truly wanted....

Exciting. And terrifying.

She slowly straightened, preparing to ring the dinner bell to summon Gideon and his daed for breakfast.

The door opened before she was halfway across the room. Gideon set a basket holding several eggs on the counter, then ducked outside once more to carry in the high chair, which he set down by the door. "Isn't it nice, Mamm? Isaac Mast brought it by. He also suggested I bring Bethel by the candy shop to meet Agnes. I see that you're in the wheelchair this morgen, but if you're feeling okay later on, would you mind if I took Bethel out and showed her around the community? We would probably be gone an hour. Two, at most."

He was going to court her again today? Not wait until Monday? Bethel smiled as her hope grew.

"That sounds like fun," Reba replied, her voice cheerier than it had been all morgen.

Was she excited at the prospect of having some time away from her new dochter-in-law? Ach, a terrible thought.

"I'm feeling all right. Elam and I will be just fine for a couple of hours," Reba assured him. "Be sure to show her your store and Naomi's bakery."

Gideon turned to Bethel. "We'll go after breakfast is cleaned up then."

Bethel nodded as Ben strode through the door carrying two covered milk pails.

"Breakfast is ready." Bethel peeked inside the egg basket. Three brown eggs. Just three.

"They aren't laying well right now," Ben explained. "It's too cold. We're doing gut to get any eggs all."

He and Gideon removed their coats and hats and hung them on hooks beside the door. Their boots were parked in a plastic tray underneath. Then Ben checked the fire in the stove while Gideon made his way to the sink.

Bethel went to transfer the biscuits to a serving bowl. As she did, a pair of icy-cold hands landed on her shoulders, the thumbs rubbing the skin of her neck. A chill worked through her and she shivered, jerking away. "Ach, you're cold!"

Gideon chuckled and then lingered beside her for a brief moment, as if he wanted to do something more. Like nuzzle her neck, as he'd started to do earlier.

Before Isaac arrived.

Surely, he wouldn't. Not here. Not now.

She wanted.... Nein, she didn't. Ach, she didn't know. She dared to raise her eyes to his.

His gaze was...heated. Intense. Focused.

It warmed her from the top of her head to the tip of her toes and did strange things to her stomach. Not a reaction she'd ever gotten from Isaac's presence.

Then Gideon frowned, looking everywhere except at her. He stepped away and went to the sink to wash up.

Leaving her feeling strangely bereft.

10

Gideon needed another cold shower. The first one hadn't done its job and neither had the frigid temperatures outside.

Did he need to apologize to Bethel for his beyond-bold, inappropriate actions? Jah, he was attracted to her, but that didn't equal love. He'd loved Lizzie. Still did. And Bethel apparently still harbored feelings for "nobody," also known as Isaac Mast.

Gideon could blame Isaac at least partially for his own foolishness in the driveway. For his almost kissing her. Danki, Gott, that Daed interrupted us. For his determination to stake his claim publicly—well, at least in front of "nobody." And on the heels of dreaming about her, then watching her run into Isaac's arms....

Ugh!

Jealousy was not a gut emotion for anyone to fall prey to, least of all a preacher. He needed to spend time confessing and repenting to Gott for his inappropriate thoughts, feelings, and emotions, and start by getting right with Him before he apologized to her. Maybe he could spend some time in prayer while he finished the chores as he waited for Bethel to do the breakfast dishes.

"Gideon?" Mamm's voice interrupted his musings. "Your daed is waiting his turn to wash up."

Right. And he was just standing there, staring into space, and thinking about Bethel. Again. Still. He'd have to be very careful to think of Lizzie right before bed that nacht so he wouldn't dream about Bethel.

He grabbed a hand towel and stepped aside to give Daed room at the sink.

A buggy ride around the community.

His stomach knotted.

Would that count as courtship or should he consider it a chore?

Bethel hurried to complete the kitchen chores after breakfast, more excited than she probably should be about a buggy ride with Gideon. And a trip to Agnes's candy shop would be on the agenda! Isaac had practically promised her a slab of fudge. Her mouth watered at the thought.

The dishes were done and the table and countertops wiped off when Gideon came inside with another gust of frigid air. He took off his outerwear, added another log to the fire, and warmed his hands a bit before closing the stove and picking up Elam from his blanket on the floor. "I'll feed Elam and change his diaper before we go."

"Danki, Sohn," Reba replied. "Get me a pad of paper and a pen and I'll make a list of things for you to bring back from the store. Has your daed left yet?"

Wasn't Bethel supposed to be responsible for feeding Elam and making lists? Should she step in and insist on doing those things herself? She didn't want Gideon's mamm taking burdens upon herself and then feeling resentful of Bethel for not stepping in. But she also didn't want to give the impression that she thought of Reba as being completely helpless. She wrung her hands, not knowing what to do.

"Nein, he had to repair a rung of the ladder first. I told him I would take care of it, but he said he could do it in a minute or so." Gideon prepared a bottle of formula, then set it near the stove to warm while he carried the rocker from the living room into the kitchen. He found a flannel blanket and draped it over one shoulder before gently picking up Elam.

Bethel tested the bottle and brought it to him as he got settled in the chair.

"Danki." He smiled as he took the bottle from her.

A strange fluttering sensation filled her midsection as she went to make up the bed Ben and Reba shared. She couldn't wait to be alone with Gideon in the buggy. What would happen during the ride? Would he try to find a secluded back road to park along so he could kiss her? More tingles tickled her stomach, cut short by a flash of fear. He was experienced. She was not.

She would focus on the promise of fudge.

Bed made, she returned to the kitchen. Since Reba seemed to be without paper and a writing utensil, she found a magnetic notepad on the side of the refrigerator and handed it to Reba. Then she separated the fresh milk, put it into jars, and refrigerated it. "Would you like me to try making some cheese?"

The door opened and Ben poked his head in. "I'm off to the store. I'll check in at lunch, unless it gets busy over there."

"Bye." Reba turned to Bethel. "There's a pen on the hutch. I don't know anything about making cheese. Have you made it before?"

Bethel found the pen and placed it on the table. "Nein, but my mamm did and I have her recipe."

"I guess you can try." Reba sounded a bit doubtful. "Not today though. I'd like you to make butter after you get back from town."

More assignments. She supposed it was too soon to set her own agenda. She forced a smile. "Sure. I can do that."

Gideon set the bottle on the table, lifted Elam to his shoulder, and patted the boppli's back. Elam emitted a hefty burp.

Gideon rose. "I'm going to change his diaper and then we can go." He carried his sohn upstairs.

Bethel checked the fire again and added another log, not wanting Reba to have to bother with it while they were away. She would have enough to do, taking care of herself and Elam. Bethel shut the dampers a little so the fire wouldn't burn so fast.

Gideon bounded into the room and gave Elam a noisy kiss before he laid him on the blanket on the floor. "Be gut for your mammi. Bethel, I'm going to hitch Prancer while you get ready to go. We have a heater in the buggy, so don't worry about heating a brick. Mamm, we'll be back soon. Be careful." He shoved his feet into his boots, grabbed his hat and coat, and dashed out the door.

"He's not anxious." Reba laughed. "Seriously, I haven't seen him this excited since he met his Beth—ach, since he married Lizzie. Or maybe the day Elam was born. Before...well, that's not a gut example. It didn't end well." She sighed. "Here's my shopping list. Feel free to add to it." She handed the paper to Bethel. "Gideon will put it on the store tab."

As much as she hated being compared to the perfect first frau, Bethel was glad Gideon looked forward to this trip to town with her. She stuffed the list in her purse, bundled up, and headed outside, where Gideon had just finished hitching Prancer to the buggy.

Gideon reached for her mitten-covered hand to help her up into the buggy. The vehicle dipped under his weight as he settled in beside her. She tucked her purse behind her feet.

Should she scoot closer to Gideon? Or keep a Bible's width between them? She wasn't sure whether this was to be a courtship outing or a duty-motivated, routine buggy tour so that she could learn her way around. If only she'd had some experience with courtship. She didn't know how to act, how to respond, how to think...

Gideon reached under the seat, pulled out an old quilt, and tucked it around Bethel. His hands danced tantalizingly close to her body, his touch heating her even through the thick fabric.

"Warm enough?"

She managed a mute nod, not sure of her ability to form coherent words right then.

Gideon clicked his tongue and Prancer started toward the road. A sudden gust of wind shook the buggy and Bethel grabbed the edge of the seat.

"Generally speaking, this is the way to town." Gideon tugged the reins to turn the buggy right at the end of the driveway. "Some Amish live out in the opposite direction, but the wildfire we had a year ago mostly destroyed everything on the west side of the pond. Bishop Miah lives about a mile away. Gabe and Bridget live in the opposite direction from town. They have the furniture Isaac mentioned when he stopped by this morgen. Isaac and Agnes are currently living in the back of her candy shop until Gabe can get started on the haus Isaac wants to build. I'm sure you saw Main Street on the way into town Thursday morgen."

She hadn't exactly paid attention during that trip. At the time, she'd been struggling not to cry, to let Daed know she would rather marry a stranger than cave in and marry Rodney. Although she'd hoped the stranger would be Isaac.

And Daed hadn't believed Gideon was a stranger.

Comfort zone? If she even had such a thing, she was way outside it. How should she act around this man she was married to but didn't know?

Scoot nearer to him. Near enough that he brushes against you with every jostle of the buggy.

She could almost hear her sister's voice directing her next move.

Bethel obediently shifted nearer...nearer...until her left side was almost touching his right arm. Close enough, ain't so?

She imagined Ruth scoffing at her attempt.

Do the things he likes to do.

Another piece of imagined advice. What did Gideon like to do? Go camping, he'd said. Not the right season for that.

This courting thing was harder than she'd thought.

Talk to him. Are you off in den kopf? Apparently so.

Bethel sighed.

Gideon glanced at her. "Are you comfortable?"

Physically, quite so. Mentally, not so much. Or emotionally.

Not exactly something she could say.

She looked askance at him. "So what do you like to do besides camp?"

There. She'd made an effort at conversation.

She pictured her sister rolling her eyes. But at least her imagined voice remained quiet.

Gideon frowned. "Well, now, I don't know. Fish, I guess. Read. I used to love volleyball when I was a youngie. But then I grew up and married. Life became about working, eating, and sleeping. I never go fishing anymore. Haven't since I married."

It was the wrong season for fishing, too.

How could she do the things he liked to do if he didn't do anything he liked?

The voice in her head stayed annoyingly quiet.

She decided to try again. "Where are we going?" Then she cringed at her own idiocy. He'd told her he was taking her on a tour. If only she could cancel that question and say something that sounded more intelligent. Like asking about his friends in the community, or inquiring after the identities of the other girls at the wedding, so she wouldn't embarrass herself when they were reintroduced.

Gideon gripped the reins with his left hand and moved his right hand to rest on her knee. In spite of the layers of material separating them, the weight of his hand seemed to sear her skin. "Don't try so hard, okay? It'll kum."

"It"? What was he referring to, exactly? And how long would it take? She stared at his hand, still stationed on her knee. If only he had the ability to put people at ease and have fun as naturally as Isaac did.

Guilt filled her. She shouldn't compare her ehemann to another man. Not even if he compared her to his perfect first frau.

Her stomach hurt.

"I'm taking you to town. We'll visit Naomi at her bakery, meet Agnes at the candy shop, and stop by the salvage-grocery store.

Then we'll drive out to Gabe Lapp's and take a look at the rest of the furniture Isaac brought to see if there's something we can use."

Like an actual bed for her to use in Elam's room? Something other than the cot Gideon had slept on last nacht?

"I also need to talk to Gabe about remodeling my bedroom so it won't be filled with memories of...her." His voice was low, raw, and oozing with pain. Shattered.

Memories of her. Bethel didn't know what to say. What to do. How to react. Except to offer comfort the only way she knew. The way she would've comforted Mamm. Or a small cousin.

She scooted even closer. Untangling one arm from beneath the blanket, she slipped it through his and pressed herself against his side. His hand shifted on her knee but stayed put.

After about five minutes of silence, his right elbow bumped gently against her side as he reached around to grasp the reins with both hands, pulling to direct Prancer to make a turn. Bethel leaned harder against him.

He didn't push her away. Instead, he straightened the buggy's course and then wrapped his right arm around her shoulders.

"Tell me how you met Isaac Mast. Have you known each other a long time?"

There was pain in those questions, too. A note of brokenness.

"Did you…. Did he court you?"

❧

He shouldn't have asked. Gideon hated the raw jealousy in his voice, in his question. And truthfully, he didn't want to know the answer. Not if it was jah.

Her chest rose and fell with her breathing, which he didn't see as much as feel, with her plastered against his side the way she was. Warming him. In more ways than one.

"Nein. I told you, I was never courted. Never dated. Isaac and I met at an auction in Mio a few years ago. I think I told you I worked as cashier. Daed was the clerk. And Isaac always stayed at our haus when he was in the area, which was about once a month. I'll admit to having had a massive crush on him, but he never treated me as anything more than a sister. And I had a front-row seat to watch him date some of the girls from the Mio area. Casually. Always casually. Agnes was the first woman who ever caught his attention in *that* way. The way Lizzie caught yours."

The last sentence was whispered.

He wanted to say, *Nein, Lizzie never caught my attention the way you did—and still do.* Which would be true. Brutally so. And also horrible to admit. He loved Lizzie and found her beautiful, especially after he'd gotten to know her. But when it came to physical appeal, she couldn't compete with Bethel.

Lizzie had dark eyes and hair that was almost black. Her features would be considered plain by most and she wore glasses. She was also short. Petite, she called it. The top of her head barely reached Gideon's chest. But her love of physical activity belied her size. She loved volleyball and despite her short stature, she was actually gut at it. And she enjoyed camping. He'd asked her out on a dare and soon discovered he liked talking to her.

She always talked about wanting to go mountain climbing. But there were nein mountains where they lived and Gideon was too cheap to hire a driver to take them camping far enough away to access scalable mountains. He regretted that. He should've taken her, despite his many misgivings.

Bethel didn't seem quite as adventuresome. He couldn't see her asking to go mountain climbing and he was more than fine with that. And her appearance was sunshine next to Lizzie's shadow. Honey-blonde hair, hazel eyes, and a height that brought her head level with his shoulders.

He didn't know yet if he enjoyed talking with her. They hadn't gotten past the forced-to-marry awkwardness. Besides, she was quiet. Not talkative like Lizzie. That fact probably contributed to the awkwardness. Not that he knew what to say either.

But Lizzie had never made his heart pound the way Bethel did. He hadn't felt the sparks with Lizzie. He didn't…well, the undiluted passion wasn't there. The temptation.

He couldn't build a relationship with those feelings alone. They had to find some common footing. Love needed to be present. Not mere lust.

The silence had elapsed long enough. He shifted, conscious—way too conscious—of her curves pressed against him. Warming. Comforting. Bonding, in some sort of way.

"Do you want to go mountain climbing?" The question popped out without conscious thought.

Her body jerked with apparent surprise and then she laughed. Not just a giggle, but a full-out laugh. The sound warmed him even more and he wanted to make her laugh again.

"Where did that kum from?"

He shrugged and searched her face.

"Nein, not really." Her eyes sparkled. "But I'll watch you climb if you want to go."

He'd rather stay safely on level ground. "What about Niagara Falls? Do you want to go there?" That was where the youngies went right after Thanksgiving every year. Lizzie had wanted to sign up as chaperones—her and Gideon—but Gideon refused. Too close to the time when the boppli would be born. If he could do it over, he would say, "Jah. Let's go." But she'd died before the youngies left. He would've let her do anything she wanted, if only he'd known.

Niagara Falls was also where Isaac had taken Agnes on their honeymoon.

What if Bethel wanted to go there because of that reason alone?

He couldn't live in the land of "what ifs." He couldn't.

Bethel sobered. "Maybe. But honestly, I'd be just as happy seeing the Tahquamenon Falls. Niagara Falls would be too commercialized, I think."

"Tahquamenon Falls is doable. When the weather is warm enough, we could camp in an unheated tent and not risk freezing to death. I haven't been there either. It sounds fun." They could do something together that he and Lizzie hadn't done. "We'll plan on it. For our honeymoon."

She didn't answer. Not verbally, at least. It could have been just his imagination, but she seemed to press even closer against his side.

They'd reached town. And just in time, too. Because his brain was fixated on the unsolicited advice Daed had whispered.

Go ahead and kiss the girl.

11

Bethel studied the old buildings as the buggy neared them. The right side of the street had a raised sidewalk accessed by two or three steps. They passed a shop bearing a wooden sign that read "Sweet Treats" in pink letters; the window next door featured the hand-painted words "Sugar and Spice." Sugar and spice and everything nice. Cute. Probably Naomi's bakery.

"Do you want to tour the bakery first or go to Sweet Treats?" Gideon asked. "I'm sure Agnes would gladly give you a tour, too."

She was more interested in visiting Sweet Treats because of the promise of fudge. It wouldn't be wise to express her preference, though, because Gideon might interpret it as an effort to see her not-quite-former crush again. A crush she needed to get over sooner rather than later, considering they were both married. And the crush was one-sided anyway. Always had been.

She tried to muster a measure of excitement over seeing a bakery that produced breads, pies, cakes, and other goods that she herself had baked by the ton. But Gideon's sister owned this bakery so, naturally, Gideon was proud of it. Naomi had been friendly toward Bethel yesterday. It was the least Bethel could do to keep an ally in her new home.

"We can see the bakery first," she finally replied. "What made Naomi decide to open one?"

Gideon grimaced. "Her fiancé evacuated during the wildfire last year and while he was gone, he was somehow 'discovered' by a talent scout for the White Caps in Grand Rapids. So he now plays minor league baseball. Naomi was crushed. The wedding's off and, like Agnes, she had nein other prospects. At least, none she wanted to consider."

Bethel could understand that part. But having a fiancé "stolen" by baseball, of all things? Her only experience with the sport was watching the local buwe play in the schoolyard, but only until they turned fourteen or so. "How did an Amish man manage to get discovered by a talent scout for a baseball team?"

Gideon shrugged. "I couldn't venture a guess. All I know is what I heard through the grapevine."

Jah. That grapevine spread news faster than any article in *The Budget*.

News of her marriage to Gideon probably hadn't been printed yet, since they were never "published" and only had a shotgun wedding. Bethel pressed her hand on her stomach as the contents from breakfast took a ride through a blender. She swallowed. Hard.

"I'm thinking we'll save the candy shop for last. As soon as we leave the bakery, I'll show you the store. We'll maybe get a piece of candy and some koffee at the candy shop afterward and take a moment to...talk." Gideon's smile was tentative. "They might have some of the milk chocolate candy filled with caramel you mentioned last nacht. If they do, we can take home a pound or two." He shyly glanced at her out of the corner of his eye. Red tinged his cheeks as he parked in front of the bakery.

He'd remembered? Sweet. Gideon seemed just as insecure as she felt and the realization calmed her a little. Of course, maybe the promise of chocolate contributed to the peace she felt. A peace that was threatened mightily by the stares of several curious onlookers driving by or shopping in nearby stores, gawking at the stranger in town.

Gideon climbed out of the buggy, tethered his horse, and then came around to assist her, even though she was more than halfway out. His hands settled around her waist, adjusted their grip, and tightened. Then he lifted her down as if she weighed nein more than Elam.

Tingles raced through her. She shivered.

"You're cold." His hands moved from her waist to the neckline of her coat and he pulled it tightly closed.

"Nein," she whispered. "Not cold." It was cold outside. Very. But that wasn't the cause of her shivers.

His lips parted. His eyes rose from his hands, still grasping her coat, to her face. His green gaze latched on to her eyes and darkened.

Her breathing quickened. Her heart pounded.

A muscle worked in his jaw. His gaze lowered to her lips.

She wished for some of her sister's flavored lip gloss. Instead, she used the tip of her tongue to moisten her lips.

His eyes rose again to hers, heating, as his hands very, very slowly slid along the unsecured opening of her coat from the neckline down to her abdomen. They grazed her body through the thick fabric and she burned with awareness.

Her muscles tightened and she shivered again. She'd never felt this way with Isaac. She wanted Gideon to do it again. Maybe there was hope for them, after all.

A horn honked. Someone made a catcall. "Get a room!" a deep voice yelled from a passing car.

Her face burned. But a room would be nice.

Gideon's cheeks reddened. He looked away. "I'm sorry." He swallowed hard, released her, and stepped back. Prancer sidestepped. Gideon moved enough to rest his hand on Prancer's head as he murmured calming words to the horse, his gaze still focused on Bethel.

She didn't hear, couldn't comprehend, what he said to Prancer.

He hadn't specified what he was sorry for. She didn't ask. Maybe his public—too public—display of affection. Or...whatever it was called when you were forced to marry someone but still loved another. Even if it looked like he'd wanted to kiss her or enjoyed touching her, she knew the truth.

Ach, that hurt.

She forced a smile to hide her breaking heart from the staring bystanders and headed toward the steps leading up to Naomi's bakery.

He followed her.

She may have added a little extra swing to her hips. A deliberate ploy to capture his attention because she needed to hope that he could kum to love her too. Eventually.

Because she was there. And Lizzie was nein more.

⁓

Gideon tamped down a groan. He should've taken Daed's advice on the way here and gotten what ailed him out of his system instead of letting it consume him. He wouldn't dare to ask Daed how he knew what Gideon suffered from. But they did share the same haus and Daed had eyes. It was probably too obvious.

That was an uncomfortable thought.

Gideon forced his attention away from Bethel's swaying skirt and concentrated on his feet.

She opened the bakery door and a blast of heat hit him, as did the sounds of many voices. He looked up. There was a line of customers winding around the room. Naomi wasn't in sight, but her part-time helper, Paris Kaufman, stood behind the counter, bagging someone's purchases.

The place smelled amazing. Like yeast, vanilla, cinnamon, and...ach, he couldn't begin to identify all the aromas. His stomach rumbled. He missed Naomi's baking up a storm in their own kitchen. Now, his family usually got the day-old stuff she brought home. Though she *had* baked bread yesterday.

Paris looked up. "Hi, Gideon. Bethel." She raised her voice to be heard above the crowd as Bethel paused just inside the door. "Naomi is in the back, if you want to see her." She handed the customer his bag, then hurried to open a half-door separating the shop from the space behind the counter for them to enter. She gave Bethel a quick hug. "How are you? You've been in my continual thoughts and prayers. I can't imagine being in your shoes."

Gideon frowned. What was she referring to? What rumor was going around town? The one about his marrying a pregnant widow? The one about their marrying for convenience's sake? Or had Paris somehow found out that they'd been forced to marry?

Gideon's throat threatened to stifle his breath. He pulled off his gloves and shoved them into his pocket. Naomi. She would've blabbed. He wanted to hurry Bethel into the kitchen to get her away from the stares and the gossip.

Coming to town had been a bad decision.

"And marrying a preacher, too—you must have the weight of the world on your shoulders," murmured someone else. Gideon didn't have to look in order to identify her. It was Debby Fisher, the biggest gossip in town. "And currently the only one in the district...."

Somehow he made his feet move. With a forced smile, he put his hand on Bethel's coat-covered back.

Bethel stiffened. "Preacher?"

He urged her toward the kitchen. "This way."

Naomi glanced up as they entered. A dusting of flour covered her forehead, her nose, and the front of her apron. Bread cooled on the counter nearby and she was mixing what appeared to be a sugar glaze for doughnuts or.... He looked closer at the loaves on the counter. "Raisin bread?"

Jah, there might've been more than a touch of longing in his voice. How long had it been since he'd had a warm slice of raisin bread?

Naomi nodded. "I got an order. The customer's probably here waiting."

"You need to consider hiring more help than just Paris."

He was trying to be helpful, but Naomi grunted and glared at him. "If you've kum here to offer me unsolicited advice—"

"Sorry." Gideon held up his hands in surrender. "I wanted to give Bethel a tour. I guess this is a bad time."

"You know your way around."

"Right. Can I order some raisin bread for us?"

"Sorry. Only paying customers may place orders. Not annoying big brothers who don't pay."

Gideon's face burned. He glanced at Bethel, but she kept her gaze on the ground.

"We'll get out of your way," he muttered to his sister. Then he turned back to Bethel. "This is the bakery. Obviously, it's doing well today."

"Saturdays are always busy," Naomi added. "And don't show her the office. It's a mess. I need to hire a bookkeeper, too." She gave him a pointed look.

Gideon nodded, trying to ignore his sister's raised eyebrows. He had been handling her books ever since she opened for business, but he hadn't looked at them at all since Lizzie died. Almost four months. He needed to get his act together. Taxes would be due in two months.

Just another thing he didn't want to face.

When had life become such a chore?

"You have a really nice place, Naomi. It smells amazing in here," Bethel said with a sweet smile as she exchanged some sort of nonverbal communication with his sister. "Gideon, let's get out of her way. I'm eager to see your store." She tugged on his arm.

Naomi snorted.

His store was a big mess, too. Two businesses he was failing. His sister's attitude was more effective than a cold shower…and on a day when he'd wanted to impress Bethel a little. Gideon rubbed his beard. "Maybe we'll stop by the candy shop first, since it's next door.

And the store is on the way out to Gabe Lapp's place." It'd also make this less like a date. Just a tour for a newcomer.

Not a date. Not a date. Not a…shoot. Who was he trying to kid?

Besides, he wanted it to be a date. It *was* a date. With his frau. Someone he would've wanted to court but, in reality, probably would've never been brave enough to approach. He likely still would've asked out his beloved Lizzie, but he would've been looking over his shoulder at the beautiful, unattainable Bethel. And Lizzie never would've known she was the replacement.

Of course, Lizzie had known, anyway, because he'd told her about his teenage crush.…

He shoved away the memory.

In some weird twist of fate, Bethel was the replacement for the replacement. Gott truly had a sense of humor.

Gideon bit his lip. *Lord Gott, danki for the gift of Bethel.* Even though he still didn't love…. Well, maybe he did. A little.

His fingertips tingled after taking a brief trip down the back of her coat.

He reached for Bethel's hand—when had she removed her mittens?—and grasped it in his. Sparks shot up his arm.

Was it possible to find love twice in one lifetime?

⌒

Bethel followed Gideon through the warm, crowded bakery and outside into the bitter cold. Gideon kept hold of her hand as they walked next door to Sweet Treats. More tingles from his touch teased her senses as he explained how he was called to be a preacher by the drawing of lots before Lizzie died. Bethel listened—or tried to—as bystanders called out greetings to "Preacher Gideon."

She was a preacher's frau living a lie?

He tugged open the door to the candy shop, causing the sleigh bells suspended from it to ring. Bethel heard banging coming from behind a closed door.

It smelled so gut inside. Like pure chocolate. And despite the banging noise, it was much more peaceful than the bakery. Bethel smiled.

An older Amish man, who looked vaguely familiar, sat alone at a table, nursing a cup of koffee. He looked up with a smile directed at both of them. "I've been waiting for you."

Interesting.

"Bishop Miah." Gideon made a sound that might've been a groan.

This was the man who'd married them two days ago? She gave him a closer look.

Gideon took a step nearer. "Did my daed tell you—?"

"He said you'd be coming this way."

Gideon furrowed his brow. "I'm trying to court my frau."

Trying to court? If this was trying, she had nein chance of emerging unscathed from a true courtship. She was close to falling head-over-heels already. But why the frown?

"I won't take much of your time." Bishop Miah's gaze shifted to Bethel. His expression softened. "How are you doing?"

"Fine." A lie, but how was she supposed to tell this stranger the truth? She was lost, confused, overwhelmed, hurt, and experiencing a whole host of other emotions that ended with an unexpected attraction to her ehemann. And she was in pain. Ach, the pain. It ripped through her without warning. And the cause varied from Daed's disbelief in her to the fact that this wonderful man she married was a recent widower who had loved another first. More. Still.

A fresh round of tears stung her eyes. She attempted to hide them by dipping her head and looking away, but somehow, the boppli-blue eyes of this man of Gott caught her gaze and held her captive. They peered deep into her soul, probing, accessing, analyzing.

"Forgive him. Your daed."

What? Forgiveness was important in their culture—to all Christians, really. But Daed hadn't asked for forgiveness. He didn't care. He believed a lie instead of the truth. He'd pushed her out.

Yet he had hugged her on her wedding day, with tears in his eyes. And whispered, "Ich liebe dich, Bethel. Stay safe."

She hadn't responded. If he really loved her and wanted her safe, why had he forced her out of her familiar, safe, comfortable world?

"Write him. Tell him you forgive him." There was a touch of urgency in Bishop Miah's voice. Tears shimmered in his eyes. "He needs to know, Bethel. I have a dochter—"

His voice shattered into a sob. He broke eye contact with Bethel and wrapped his trembling hands more tightly around the koffee mug.

"And Gideon, you have to grieve what you have lost before you embrace what you have now." The bishop's words were directed toward the dark liquid sloshing around in his cup.

Jah, please get over the grieving soon. Bethel wanted the "embracing" part.

The bishop's lips quivered. His voice shook. "What you have now could be much more than you can imagine."

That comment caused her hope to bloom and flourish. She might even be able to forgive Daed if she ended up in a happy, loving marriage.

The swinging doors separating the front from the back part of the store opened and Agnes bustled through, carrying a tray of candies. She stopped cold as her gaze skittered from Gideon to Bishop Miah and then to Bethel. "Ach! I didn't hear the bells."

"You need new bells, Agnes." Bishop Miah stood, grasping the table for support. "Either that or your hearing is going. Because they rang."

"I was making lots of noise back there," Agnes conceded, setting the tray down on the front counter. "You should've called me."

"I just needed koffee." Bishop Miah kept one hand on the table and lifted his cup to his mouth with the other.

Agnes came around the counter and approached Bethel. She wrapped her in a quick hug. "Welkum, Bethel. Have you had a chance to browse the selection of fudge? I hope Isaac told you that you'd be taking some home as a gift."

Bethel schooled her expression, hoping not to betray her former crush in her reaction to hearing his name. Maybe she, too, needed to grieve what she'd lost in order to embrace what she had now.

Agnes pulled back and glanced at the bishop. "Are you okay, Bishop Miah? You look a little gray."

Bishop Miah's mug fell from his fingers, koffee splattering. The mug shattered as he grasped his chest and crumpled into Agnes's outstretched hands.

12

Gideon jerked a chair out of the way and then lowered Bishop Miah in a sitting position, with his back leaning against the glass display case. The bishop's skin was pale and clammy. Gideon's heart pounded as he knelt in front of him. "Agnes, find him an aspirin. Bethel, run to the bakery and use the phone to call nine-one-one."

Now would be the ideal time to have a cell phone.

Agnes whirled around and ran into the back of the store, muttering under her breath. Probably praying.

Bethel just stood there. Staring.

"Go!" Gideon barked.

After another moment's hesitation, Bethel spun and dashed out the door.

"I broke the mug." Bishop Miah's voice was weak. He still clutched at his chest.

"The mug is the least of our concerns right now." Gideon willed Agnes to hurry. He was scared and didn't know what to do, other than administer aspirin. He tried to think.

Nothing came.

Lord, help.

The bishop rubbed his chest with his open hand. A tiny moan escaped his lips.

Agnes returned at a run and dropped beside Gideon, a bottle of aspirin in her hand. Tears streamed down her cheeks. "I can't get it open. Childproof lid."

Gideon snatched the bottle from her and gave it a quick turn while applying pressure to the lid with his thumb. He shook out a couple of the tiny pills and popped them into the bishop's mouth. "Chew." He tossed the bottle to the side.

Agnes picked up the bottle and peered at the label. "These aren't chewable." She sounded frantic.

Gideon shook his head. "Doesn't matter. Chew." *Lord Gott, let him be all right. I can't do it all alone.*

Though Bishop Miah had done it alone for the better part of a year.

The bishop dutifully chewed, grimacing all the while, then swallowed. "When someone you love dies...." He adjusted his hand on his chest and gasped. He tugged at his shirt, tearing at the material.

"You aren't dying." Gideon hoped. *Lord, please.*

Agnes caught her breath on a sob. "Nein...." The aspirin bottle rattled as she raised both arms and wiped her eyes with the backs of her hands. "Ich liebe dich. You're my substitute daed."

"Ich liebe dich, Agnes." Bishop Miah's eyes darkened with pain. "You, too, Gid."

Gideon had nothing to say to that. He merely nodded—a gesture that the bishop probably didn't see, with his eyes shut tight.

"Does your heart go...with the one you love?" Bishop Miah wheezed.

"Nein, but it feels like it does." Gideon swallowed. "It leaves a hole where that person used to live. I don't need a bishop-sized hole." Not when he already had a Lizzie-sized hole.

The door opened, sleigh bells ringing noisily, as Isaac came in. Agnes wailed and ran across the room to him.

Isaac wrapped his arms around her. "What's going on?"

Gideon opened his mouth to answer, but then shut it again as Naomi barged in, followed by at least a half dozen other Amish women. He didn't see Bethel among them. "Bishop Miah collapsed?" asked Naomi.

"You can't ride in all directions at the same time," the bishop said quietly. His gaze was fixed on Gideon.

Only the bishop would conduct a counseling session while suffering a heart attack. Unfortunately, his statements weren't doing much to clear Gideon's muddled mind. Especially that last comment. Unless....

Unless he was referring to Gideon's very public flirting with Bethel when he was still mourning Lizzie's death.

Gideon's stomach hurt. He'd failed so many: the bishop and his expectations for Gideon's behavior. Lizzie and her memory. His new wife and her feelings after receiving such mixed signals from Gideon.

"Quiet everyone." Isaac pulled out his smartphone and pressed something on the screen. Then he held the phone and disappeared into the kitchen with Agnes, one of his arms still wrapped around her shoulders.

"Bethel's talking to the nine-one-one operator on my office phone." Naomi came closer and surveyed Gideon's beloved mentor. "Bishop Miah, you're looking gray."

She was right. The bishop's color had faded even more since his fall.

The corners of the bishop's mouth lifted and fell in a movement that was barely perceptible. "I've felt better. I'm already missing the fried pies Katherine is going to make me give up from here on out." The words, though broken and separated by long pauses, were still laced with his signature sense of humor.

Only Bishop Miah.

"Ambulance is en route." Isaac came back into the room. "Someone already called."

Bethel. Who hadn't returned.

Isaac knelt beside Bishop Miah. "Stay still and rest, okay? Help is on the way. Three minutes out. The ambulance was parked in front of Gideon's store. I saw it when I passed by."

Gideon leaned back and surveyed the crowd that'd grown during the last few minutes. Amish and Englisch alike. Were they there for the drama or did they all truly care for Bishop Miah?

Gideon would have some big shoes to fill during the bishop's recovery. He refused to think of the alternative. The bishop *would* recover.

Gideon was beyond inadequate for the task. *Lord, help. Help him, help me. Help us.*

Flashing lights appeared outside the window. *Praise Gott.* Isaac's estimate of three minutes had been inaccurate. Sleigh bells jingled as the door opened again. "EMTs. Clear the way."

⁓

Bethel slumped down in the rolling chair in Naomi's messy office, clamping the cordless landline phone against her ear. The woman who had answered her call had told her to stay on the line and stay she would, even though she hadn't been able to answer most of the questions she'd been asked.

She could pray—and she did, her fingers cramping against the hard plastic of the receiver. She didn't know Bishop Miah at all, other than from the wedding ceremony he'd officiated for her and Gideon. But Isaac had spoken fondly of the man after having made his acquaintance. And if Isaac liked him, he had to be a gut man.

Bishop Miah's kind yet probing eyes seemed to see into her heart, even as he uttered words that made her uncomfortable. Jah, he was a gut man. *Gott, if You never hear another prayer of mine, please listen to this one. Take care of Bishop Miah—*

"The ambulance is at the destination." The woman's voice broke into her thoughts.

And then the line went dead.

At least, that's what Bethel assumed when she heard a click and then nothing. "Hello?" she said, just so she would know.

Nein response.

She returned the portable phone to its charger.

The light on the phone charger flicked on.

Bethel didn't move.

Silence filled the room and the effect was almost suffocating.

Bethel bowed her head, not sure what to do next. If the overwhelming quiet meant what she thought it did, she was still alone in the bakery, which had emptied soon after her arrival. When Bethel had informed Naomi of what was happening, Naomi had pointed her to the office before running to the front of the shop and shouting, "Bishop Miah collapsed! Next door at Sweet Treats!" Screams, cries, and general mayhem had followed for a minute and then... nothing. Blessed nothingness.

Bethel should pray more. That much was certain. But praying "Thy will be done" seemed dishonest when she considered that if the bishop died, that would put a lot more weight on Gideon's shoulders. Currently, Gideon was the only preacher. He'd told her that morgen that they were waiting until later in the year to call another preacher in the hopes that more of the wildfire evacuees would have returned by then.

She hadn't responded. What could she say? That she hadn't signed up for this?

It wouldn't do any gut.

The only preacher in the district....

With that in mind, she prayed, *Lord, if it is Your will, please heal Bishop Miah. Help him to recover fully from this.*

"Bethel." Gideon's voice broke into her thoughts.

She looked up, startled.

Gideon stood in the doorway, his furrowed brow making him look older somehow. "They're taking Bishop Miah to the emergency room. They think it was a heart attack." Gideon sighed heavily. "I don't want to go back to the hospital, but I have to."

There was a flash of pain in his eyes. Lizzie, of course. They must've taken her to the hospital when she was having problems during childbirth. And she'd passed there.

Bethel held out her arms toward Gideon, but he shifted out of reach.

His green eyes were stormy dark. "The people will expect to see me there. I'm sending you home with Naomi."

Gut. She'd been around enough strangers today.

"But you need to stop at the store first to tell Daed about Bishop Miah."

Bethel nodded. It was the least she could do. Maybe Naomi would give her directions. "I'm praying for him."

"Danki." Gideon expelled a loud breath. "And I'm sorry. I didn't mean to...I shouldn't have behaved inappropriately in public. That is private, between a man and his frau. I disrespected you."

But it felt so gut. Would he want to do such things when they were alone?

His gaze flickered upward, not quite meeting hers.

Her face heated and she glanced away.

"And, well, we are married...but we aren't. Maybe we shouldn't be."

The words were almost brutal as they stabbed her with their force.

Maybe we shouldn't be? Truth. Problem was, she didn't know what to do about it. Or what to do with the growing realization that she kind of liked him. Enough that she was open to the idea of a true marriage once he'd finished mourning Lizzie.

"I...well, I was wrong. Bishop Miah reminded me that I can't ride in all directions at the same time."

Apparently, Gideon didn't know what to do about it either, if he'd found a way to apply such an obtuse statement to their relationship. His mind was certainly riding in different directions.

He nodded, as if in agreement with the bishop. "So I won't be riding in *your* direction any longer." His voice was stern.

Her eyes burned.

Despite his earlier actions, he clearly didn't want her.

⌒

I won't be riding your direction any longer.

Gideon turned away, the weight of all of the loss weighing heavy on his shoulders. It hurt to stand up straight. He felt like an old hunchback as he shuffled along toward the candy shop. He might've resembled an old hunchback, too, but he hoped not.

Losing Lizzie had felt like losing his heart. His life. His reason for living.

Bishop Miah...Gideon wanted to cling to him. How would he ever manage without the bishop's wisdom and guidance? He loved Bishop Miah. Truly, he did. Most everyone did.

And Bethel...she'd always been his secret passion, but now she was becoming a big part of his reason for getting up every morgen. He wanted to see her sweet smile, hear her gentle voice, and watch her graceful, womanly body move about as she did her daily tasks. He wanted to kiss her. To love her. To possess her.

That was wrong, of course, with their relationship being what it was. He didn't really know how to describe it. Married but not. Married but complete strangers. Married, but in his heart—maybe even in hers—wanting to be with another.

Impossible, every which way he looked at it.

Except...he wanted to be *with* Bethel.

You can't ride in all directions at the same time.

He had nein idea what it even meant. But combined with Bishop Miah's comments about grieving what he had lost, maybe it meant he shouldn't pursue Bethel until he was finished grieving Lizzie. Which he would never be. Never. It simply couldn't be done.

Choose love. Not loss.

Lizzie's last words. He had nein idea what those meant either. Only what he wanted them to mean in his weakest moments—permission to love Bethel.

Now he'd lost both of them. Lizzie was gone. And Bethel....
Tears blurred his vision. Any hope of her ever loving him had been
killed by his own words.

I'll love you for always, Lizzie.

And Bethel....

Ach, Bethel.

Maybe someday he'd be free to love her.

Maybe.

13

Bethel listened numbly to the sound of Gideon's feet shuffling out the door. She felt detached and separate, a mere shell of herself. Her battered, lonely heart was in shambles on the floor of Naomi's office.

Minutes later, hoping he would change his mind, Bethel followed him. Only to find herself alone on the sidewalk outside the empty bakery as the EMTs loaded a stretcher into the back of an ambulance. Gideon climbed into the front passenger seat and the vehicle screamed off, lights flashing.

Across the street, Isaac stood with one arm around Agnes as she leaned into his side, crying.

The crowd began to disperse. Neighbors and locals talked loudly and ignored her, brushing past her to reenter the bakery. A few of them cast speculative glances at her waistline as they walked by. They could believe what they wanted. She wouldn't blurt out her truth to the world at large.

She pressed her hand against her breaking heart. If only she had something to do to occupy herself and keep her thoughts and tears away.

Naomi rushed past and ran into the bakery, muttering under her breath. Bethel followed the light-haired girl with the strange name who worked for Naomi—Paris, she suddenly recalled—through the bakery doors, then stopped and stood there, not knowing what to do. She ought to go find Ben and tell him about Bishop Miah, like Gideon had asked her to do, but she wasn't sure who to ask for directions to the salvage-grocery. Naomi was surely too busy to be bothered.

"Bethel."

She turned.

Paris looked at her with a friendly smile. "Flip the sign to 'Closed,' please? I could use your help. As soon as we get these people's purchases rung up, we'll close up for the day."

At least she had some direction now. She changed the sign on the door, then joined Paris behind the counter.

"Would you mind filling orders from the display case while I run the cash register?" Paris asked. "Disposable gloves are in here." She shoved a box at Bethel. "Fresh pair for every customer. Not sure why, but it's the law."

Bethel yanked on a pair of gloves, then turned to the Englisch woman standing before her. "May I help you?"

With two of them working, the line moved steadily, in spite of the extra time Bethel needed to locate certain items. Before long, the three women finished cleaning up and left the empty store, Naomi locking the front door behind them.

Bethel grimaced at the weight of the bag she carried containing all of the baked goods that hadn't sold. Too bad about the lost profits, but hopefully there'd be some raisin bread in there for Gideon. It might make him feel a little better.

Naomi paused on the sidewalk. "I'll see you Monday, Paris. Bethel, we'll stop at the store so you can run in and tell Daed what happened. I'll go get the horse unhitched." She walked away.

Remembering the shopping list from Reba, Bethel reached for her purse. It was gone. Where had she left it? Agnes's candy shop, probably, since she hadn't had it with her in the bakery. Her coat and mittens were missing, too. She hurried down the sidewalk to

Sweet Treats and, despite the "Closed" sign on the door, pulled on the knob. Locked. She pounded on the door and shouted Isaac's name. Nobody came. She peered through the front windows. She didn't see her purse or her coat on any of the tables. Maybe she'd left everything in Gideon's buggy, which was parked beside Naomi's.

Bethel hurried to the buggy and checked. Nein purse. Her heart constricted. Where had she left it? She was sure she'd taken it with her from the Kaisers' haus. Well, almost sure.

"I lost my purse and coat." And mittens, too, but that seemed obvious.

Naomi wordlessly returned to the bakery and unlocked the door.

Bethel's coat and mittens were in Naomi's office. Her purse was not.

A sick feeling washed over Bethel. She sagged. This day had just gone from bad to worse.

She watched Naomi lock the bakery door again. "Should I drive Gideon's buggy?" she asked.

"Just as far as the shop. Gideon will need a ride home to-nacht. There's a stable there and Daed can take care of it when he's ready to kum home." Naomi spoke with a curt tone and the sight of her frown twisted Bethel's stomach into an even tighter knot. "You *can* drive, right?"

"Jah." Bethel resisted her inclination to make a sarcastic remark. These people were under a lot a stress. A little rudeness could be excused.

"What did Mamm have on her list?" Naomi climbed into her buggy. "I could get started on the shopping while you talk to Daed."

Bethel cringed. "I didn't look at it. I just folded it and put it in my purse."

Naomi gave her a long, silent stare, as if Bethel wasn't worth her weight in manure. Then she sighed.

Bethel untied Gideon's horse, climbed into the buggy, and backed out of the parking space. As she drove the buggy onto the road, she tried to keep Naomi's buggy in sight so she wouldn't get lost while watching for Englisch cars. Hard to do with her vision blurred by tears. Her heart hurt. She'd somehow managed to undo all her progress in making friends with this family.

Maybe "friends" was the wrong word.

"Allies"?

Impossible.

Even Gideon had rejected her.

She'd been somewhat prepared for his rejection at the wedding, but after his flirtatious behavior that morgen, she'd begun to hold out hope of their getting past the hurdles in their path.

Nein more.

This marriage should've had a warning sign attached to it. "Wrong way. Do not enter." Or, "Danger. Enter at your own risk."

How could Daed have done this to her?

Bishop Miah wanted her to forgive Daed and write him. What would she say? *I forgive you—please let me kum home?*

Somehow she didn't think that would work.

"I'll do anything. Just get me out of here." She steered around a parked car and flicked the reins to catch up with Naomi's horse as it disappeared around a bend.

Prancer's ears flickered and he made a deposit on the road, as if he agreed about the condition of her day.

She needed to find her own path out of this place. Once she found her purse, she would be able to take the next step of getting a bus ticket to…somewhere.

Somewhere she was wanted.

Anywhere but here.

⌒

The EMTs whisked Bishop Miah out of the ambulance and into the hospital. Meanwhile, Gideon staggered inside as if he were carrying a buggy-load of bricks on his back. He stumbled and reached for the wall to steady himself, then dropped into a chair in the waiting room.

His stomach filled with dread. His pulse pounded so loudly in his ears, he feared he was having his own heart attack. And his eyes stung, as every single memory of the last time he'd set foot in this hospital washed over him in agonizing detail. Lizzie's suitcase, abandoned in the hall. A shrill alarm sounding. He glanced toward the very door the midwife had dragged him through.

It was a fight to force his face into an expression of calm as he settled into a different chair, close to the windows—one that Bishop Miah would've chosen—and tried to prepare himself to comfort and quiet the concerned Amish who would kum to the hospital for firsthand news of the bishop's condition. Scriptures swirled in and out of his mind in confusing succession and he wasn't sure which passage was meant for whom.

Not that it mattered. When the first carload of Amish arrived, they filed inside, glanced his way, and then, with wide eyes, scurried to the opposite end of the room. Maybe his services wouldn't be needed after all.

He started to stand when he spotted Isaac and Agnes strolling toward him. Isaac carried three soda bottles and Agnes had her hand tucked in the crook of his other arm like a proper lady.

"I brought you a pop." Isaac handed Gideon one of the bottles. "I hope root beer's okay. The girl behind the counter at your store said the delivery truck broke down and you were out of everything except root beer and orange pop."

"This is fine. Danki for thinking of me."

Isaac helped Agnes out of her coat, then removed his own jacket and dropped both garments on a nearby chair before sitting down in the chair next to Gideon.

Which made Gideon realize that he hadn't taken off his own coat yet. But he was still chilled to the bone, so he would keep it on for a while longer. He set his root beer on the end table and pulled his coat a bit tighter around him.

Agnes's eyes were red, as if she'd cried the entire trip into town.

How was Bethel holding up? Was she crying at the bakery after hearing him blurt out his uncensored thoughts—ones he already regretted? He shouldn't have spoken without taking the time to pray and consider what to say. Hadn't he just promised her he'd be a gut ehemann? He'd failed. Again.

Too bad he hadn't thought to bring her along to the hospital. Her calmness would have done a lot to comfort him. And as an experienced caregiver, she could reassure others—something Lizzie had never been gut at. In fact, the gift of mercy seemed to have skipped her entirely.

He needed Bethel.

Mamm needed her, too. She hadn't been feeling well that morgen—as evidenced by her choice to use the wheelchair—and yet she'd brightened, and even seemed to improve, when he suggested taking Bethel on a buggy ride. Of course, the prospect of more grosskinner would make her eager for him and Bethel to consummate their marriage.

A prospect that had him stressed over the risk of losing yet another wife in childbirth.

"*Be fruitful, and multiply….*" A Scripture he was pretty sure had been quoted at some point during the wedding service, though he couldn't be positive.

Ach, he was so confused. He dropped into his chair once more and bowed his head.

Maybe he owed Bethel's daed a letter. A note thanking him for the gift of Bethel—a treasure he never could have dreamed of, one that unfolded itself more and more to him each time they were together.

When he returned home to her, he would…what? Apologize for his apology and follow Daed's advice—both spoken and unspoken?

Take her by the hand, find that orange-bound New Testament, read it some more, and pray together—hoping to win back some of the admiration he'd seen in her eyes before he so royally messed up?

Tell her the truth about his emotions—how crazy strong they were, how he never felt this way about Lizzie, and—

The loudspeaker squawked and then a voice called out a code. And....

Ach. Ach, nein. Nein!

Tears flowed as he stood, turned, and fell to his knees on the floor.

⌒

Bethel had never felt more like a failure than while trudging around Ben and Gideon's salvage-grocery store, looking for Ben, while Naomi shopped for items she thought might've been on Reba's list. When the two had parted ways, Naomi had aimed another glare at Bethel that said, "You're worthless."

Where had Bethel left her purse? If someone had stolen it, he or she would be sorely disappointed. She had next to nothing in there. Fifty dollars Daed had tucked into her hand during their final gut-bye hug. Her ID card, now outdated since she was married and had moved. Reba's list. Some personal items....

Fifty dollars. She hadn't even thought of that until now. Had Daed been attempting to provide a way of escape from this nachtmare? He had whispered words of love and told her to stay safe.

What was going on that wasn't being said?

She would puzzle over those questions later. Right now, she had to find Ben and tell him...what? The message Gideon had given her to tell him?

Ach, she *was* worthless. Just like Naomi's glare had implied.

After peering down every aisle, she still hadn't found Ben, but she did find an Englisch clerk stocking shelves. Bethel paused a moment, then said to the girl, "Excuse me. I'm looking for Ben."

"Check the office." The clerk—Morgan, according to her name tag—pointed to a set of swinging doors in the back.

At the sight of Naomi coming around the end-cap of the aisle, Bethel hitched up her skirts and ran to the office. She couldn't fail at the only other job she'd been given besides shopping for items on a list she'd lost. Even if she didn't have a clue as to what message to relay.

Ben looked up from his desk and set down a pen when she dashed into the office. "Bethel. What's wrong? Did...is Gideon all right?"

She crossed her arms over her chest as if to hold herself together. And failed, blurting out a rush of words. "Gideon's fine, but Bishop Miah collapsed and they think it's a heart attack and Gideon told me to tell you something and I can't remember what it is and I didn't *know* he was a preacher and he doesn't want to ride my direction anymore and I don't even *know* what that means! And my purse was stolen and in it was fifty dollars from my daed and I don't know why he gave it to me and Naomi thinks I'm worthless and I feel like such a failure!" The words ended on a breathless sob.

Somewhere during her tirade, Ben had stood, kum out from behind the desk, and gently guided her to sit in a chair. "Breathe, Bethel. Breathe. And then start over. From the beginning."

"I'm worthless!"

14

Gideon prayed until he ran out of words. He still didn't feel peace. More of an unsettled uncertainty that made his stomach churn. As if something else, maybe something even worse, was in the works. Yet there were only so many times he could beg Gott for Bishop Miah's life. Either Gott heard or He didn't. Gideon was fairly positive Gott heard; he just wasn't sure the answer He would give was the one Gideon wanted to hear. Meaning that it might soon be up to him to lead these people through this trial. And that would be a case of the blind leading the blind.

Ach, Gott, help me to lead them....

He lifted his head. Isaac and Agnes knelt beside him. Across the room, several other Amish men and women had followed suit, bowing before their chairs. Unusual for them to do so in a public place such as this. It was sobering to realize that, even though he was a new preacher, he had such a degree of influence over others.

He wasn't worthy of such great responsibility. Without some serious help from der Herr, he would fail at leadership as quickly as he had failed with marriage to Bethel.

Of course, he could probably still make things right with Bethel, but he wouldn't try without first spending more time in prayer and Bible study. Maybe he wouldn't make so many mistakes.

In hindsight, he should've spent more time praying and less time reacting when he was married to Lizzie, too.

Ach, Lizzie. I'm so sorry I wasn't the ehemann I should have been.

And Bethel…just thinking her name tied him into knots. He wanted to touch the silky sunshine of her hair, to see if it was as soft as it appeared. He wanted to pull the kapp off, remove the pins holding it in place, and let it tumble, unhampered, into his hands. To run his fingers through it. He wanted to see it cascade across the pillow—

A spasm ran up his spine and his stomach muscles contracted.

He dipped his head again, partially out of shame for his lustful thoughts—especially while kneeling in prayer at the hospital, just yards away from the spot where Lizzie breathed her last—and partially as an outward sign of surrendering this matter to the Lord. Okay, maybe mostly the latter. *Lord Gott, help. You alone are my hope. I can't do this without You.*

"This." He snorted. He couldn't do *anything* without der Herr.

And while he might wish for Bethel's comforting presence for this crisis, even she wasn't necessary. He had to rely on Gott for that, too. Der Herr would have to give Gideon the words. The strength. The ability.

His head hurt. He wasn't capable.

But Gott.

Gideon straightened and stretched out his back, still aching from a nacht spent on that evil cot. If he ever went camping with Bethel, he would spring for a full-size air mattress.

And there went his thoughts again, spiraling into places they shouldn't be at this moment.

He shook his head to clear his mind, twisted his back to get the remaining kinks out, and then stood beside his chair a moment, surveying the other occupants of the room as he forced himself to focus on the matter at hand.

Katherine Brunstetter, the bishop's wife, hadn't arrived yet, nor had any of their sohns. Until that morgen, Gideon hadn't had any idea that Bishop Miah also had a dochter. Who was she? Where was she?

With so many Amish already gathered at the hospital, it was especially odd to see nein members of the bishop's family. Unless the Amish who had kum to the hospital had been in town when the heart attack happened. If Bishop Miah had really a heart attack. Although Gideon didn't know what else it could have been.

Either way, someone needed to get word to Katherine or their sohns. Gideon didn't have a cell phone or he would've called the phone located in the bishop's barn. He would buy a phone first thing tomorrow.

Isaac stood, stretched, and then reached over to help Agnes to her feet.

Isaac had a cell phone. Isaac, who could probably do far a far better job than Gideon of delivering the bad news.

Gideon cleared his throat. "Isaac. Would you call Katherine and let her know? I'm not sure if anyone's gotten word to her."

Isaac nodded. With a grim expression, he pulled his phone from his pocket as he left the waiting room.

Gideon turned to Agnes. She took a sip from her bottle of pop. The drink Isaac had so kindly offered Gideon waited, untouched, on the end table. Gideon's mouth was dry and cottony, so he twisted the lid off and gulped some of the carbonated liquid.

Agnes turned to him with a teary smile. "Bishop Miah will be okay."

Gideon nodded. He wouldn't ask how she felt so sure about that. Instead, he would cling to the hope she offered.

He turned to stare out the windows at the heavy gray clouds and the big snowflakes drifting down. Before moving to northern Michigan from his home district in central Illinois, he had nein idea it was possible to grow tired of snow. Now, he was more than ready to see clear blue skies and feel the sunshine warming him.

Maybe some warmer weather would help to defrost the ice that had taken up residence inside him.

Agnes stepped closer and touched his arm. "Have faith, Gideon. The sun will shine again."

He wouldn't ask how she'd known what he was thinking either. He forced a smile. "Danki, Agnes." He lowered his voice as he continued, "And danki for saying nein when I asked you to marry me. Isaac loves you. You deserved a wunderbaar man such as him. I'm so sorry for trying to dissuade you. Don't worry about me. Bethel and I will be fine." Eventually. He hoped. Once he got his head screwed on straight.

Agnes nodded but didn't smile in return. "Bethel *is* sweet. It's sad, what happened, but we were so glad you were available and willing to take her in. Her poor daed was almost in tears. I first met her in Mio when I went with Isaac to visit my family, you know."

What rumors had Agnes heard? He'd almost forgotten about having the Amish grapevine to deal with. On top of everything else.

Agnes was right in calling Bethel sweet. "I am so blessed." He echoed Bethel's words from the nacht before, except not her sarcasm. Because, really, he was. So very blessed.

He turned away as a nurse came into the room and sat down next to an Englisch man seated along the opposite wall. Gideon couldn't make out what she said to the man, not that it mattered. He was here for Bishop Miah and to be a source of consolation for any of the people who—

"Her poor daed was almost in tears"?

Wait. What?

❧

Bethel repeated what she'd just told Ben, going much slower this time and trying to make her words come out in proper sentences. Ben listened quietly before asking her to repeat her message for a third time. Then he sank down in the chair beside her, his face drawn. "Bishop Miah really had a heart attack?"

That was, of course, the most important part of her whole tirade.

"That's what they think, anyway," she remarked, just in case that detail hadn't made it into her thrice-relayed speech.

"You should go home with Naomi, as Gideon said. Reba shouldn't be left alone with Elam for much longer, considering how poorly she was feeling earlier. But I'm sorry your outing got cut short. You and Gideon spending time together was important to her…to us. Your relationship—your marriage—is so very important."

To them, maybe. Not to Gideon. *I won't be riding your direction any longer.* His words still stung.

There was nein relationship and any hopes for a future relationship had been all but eradicated by Gideon's statement before he left for the hospital. Still, Bethel nodded, not sure what else to do. She started to stand, but Ben held out his hand, his palm facing outward. She stopped and settled back into the chair.

"Don't worry about your purse. You need a new ID card anyway. And Gideon will provide for your needs, though it was nice of your daed to give you money as a wedding gift. Maybe he thought you needed it."

She nodded again. Maybe Ben was right. The money probably had been intended as a wedding gift. She'd read too much into it. Why would Daed give her money to fund an escape from a situation he'd forced her into in the first place? It made nein sense.

Nothing made sense today, least of all Gideon's complete turnaround from flirting to saying it had been a mistake to marry her.

"And, finally, you are far from worthless. You're still finding your footing. And Naomi is a bit…opinionated. But she likes you. She does. She barely tolerated Gideon's first frau."

Bethel's breath hitched and she blinked. What?

"Lizzie was as strong-willed as Naomi, maybe even more so. They clashed over so many inconsequential things. Gut thing they enjoyed doing different haus-hold tasks or there would've been plenty more disagreements. Gideon used to take Lizzie camping every other weekend. For privacy, he said, but we all appreciated it.

Our home was ever so much quieter when they were gone. Naomi had nobody to jangle with."

"*Tolerated*"? Perfect Lizzie had been "tolerated"? She and Naomi "jangled"?

"Naomi says you're peaceful."

Gut thing Naomi hadn't witnessed Bethel's meltdown just minutes ago.

Ben patted her hand. "You're doing great, all things considered. And it's actually gut to see Gideon showing some interest in—" He cut himself off with a shake of his head.

Naomi peeked in the office. "Are you going to the hospital, Daed?"

Ben shook his head. "Nein, I need to be here. Bills must be paid today. They're close to being past due because…well, I guess we haven't been paying close enough attention to them."

"Gideon needs to get his act together." Naomi snorted. "My office is a mess, too, Daed."

"He'll get there. In Gott's time. I'll pray and wait for updates on the bishop." Ben stood. "Go. I'll kum home as soon as I finish up here."

"We're leaving Gideon's horse and buggy outside so Gideon can get home later." Naomi blew out a frustrated breath. "Are you ready to go, Bethel?" She asked the question gently and even wore the hint of a smile.

Bethel nodded, but then she looked at Ben. If only she could stay here with this kind, understanding man. She'd had enough stress today. "Can I help you? I worked for years as a clerk and cashier for my daed."

Ben's eyes lit up, but then he glanced at Naomi with raised eyebrows.

Bethel turned and looked at her, too.

Naomi nodded. "It certainly couldn't hurt. You or me?"

Ben hesitated, glanced at his messy desk, then looked at Bethel. "We'll start with Naomi's books. Maybe you can help her get a handle on things until Gideon is able to focus on something other than his loss. I have a better head for numbers than Naomi does, so I'm staying afloat. It's just that we both relied too heavily on Gideon and when he lost his frau, we lost him as a focused bookkeeper." Ben returned behind his desk. "I'll bring home a couple of frozen pizzas, so don't worry about fixing supper. Just take care of Reba and then the haus and then, if there's any time, take a look at Naomi's books."

"We'll stop by the bakery to get them." Naomi sounded excited. Hopeful. "You may be a lifesaver, Bethel." Naomi's smile was a far cry from the barely-holding-on-to-patience look she'd given Bethel less than an hour earlier.

Of course, her use of the words "may be" implied that her judgment was being withheld until Bethel proved herself one way or the other.

After a brief stop at the bakery for a big stack of papers, which Naomi stuffed into a quilted tote bag while Bethel hunted fruitlessly for her purse again, they drove back to the Kaisers' haus. Bethel grabbed the bagful of papers and two bags of groceries, then headed for the haus, while Naomi went to the barn to take care of the horse.

At the sound of Elam screaming inside the haus, Bethel broke into a jog, though that was hard to do in the six or seven inches of snow that had accumulated. She really needed to shovel.

She twisted the knob, almost dropping a bag of groceries, and shoved open the door with her shoulder.

A red-faced Elam lay on his blanket on the kitchen floor, wailing.

Reba lay beside him. She reached a shaking hand toward Bethel. "Help me. Please, help me."

◠

Hours passed with nein word on Bishop Miah's condition. Agnes had made herself scarce after uttering that intriguing statement. *"Her poor daed was almost in tears."* When Gideon questioned Isaac about it, Isaac simply stated that they knew each other from

Mio, Agnes had spoken out of turn, and they had nothing else to say on the matter.

Agnes wasn't known for her ability to keep her mouth shut. If Gideon could corner her alone later on, he might get the whole story out of her.

Not to-nacht, for sure.

Katherine Brunstetter finally arrived, along with the bishop's sohns, dochters-in-law, and grosskinner. The oldest sohn, Micah, stood at the counter of the nurses' station for a few minutes, insisting on an update from the young woman sitting there. To nein avail.

Micah finally abandoned his post and plopped himself down on a chair next to Gideon with a huff. "'The doctor will be out in a moment.' Is that all they know how to say?" he muttered under his breath.

"I think it's all they're allowed to say." Gideon could identify completely with Micah's sense of frustration. He'd lived through it with Lizzie. Only worse because subconsciously, somehow, he knew the truth before it was spoken.

The door opened again and Daed and Naomi came in. Alarm worked through Gideon as he watched Daed approach the front desk and pull out his wallet. What was going on? And where was Bethel?

Naomi dropped into the empty chair on the other side of Gideon and expelled a noisy sigh. "Mamm fell. Bethel asked me to call an ambulance. She wasn't sure if she should try to lift her since Mamm couldn't even sit up on her own."

Daed joined them, his face grim. "Bethel made a gut call. The EMTs think your mamm broke her hip. Bethel might've done more damage if she'd tried to lift her."

Poor Mamm. How horrible for her to break her hip, on top of all her other health problems. He couldn't imagine. And how scared she must've been, lying on the floor, unable to get up or call for help. Gideon would need to thank Bethel for her quick thinking. "Where is Bethel?"

"At home with Elam. Nein sense taking the boppli out in this weather. We left my horse and yours in the stable outside the salvage-grocery. Besides Bethel was going to get started on cleaning up Naomi's books from the bakery."

Gideon winced. The bookkeeping was his job. But he hadn't done it since Lizzie's passing.

He owed Bethel. Big time.

And, sooner or later, she would collect.

He would make a down payment on the outstanding account when he got home.

He couldn't wait.

A hug. A kiss. Or maybe sleeping beside her in the comfy bed, even if nothing happened. He was done with that evil cot.

15

The hours crawled by as Bethel put away the groceries Naomi had bought, made the butter Reba had requested, sorted the paperwork from Naomi's bakery, and started to catch up on the bookkeeping. She separated the bills into two piles—paid and unpaid. She didn't have the checkbook or the authorization to write checks anyway. The work brought back gut memories of working with Daed. At auctions, there was always someone to talk to, conversations to overhear. Not to mention a level of excitement. This was just plain work. It would've been more enjoyable if she could have talked to someone other than Elam. At three-and-a-half months, he wasn't much of a conversationalist.

She took several breaks to feed Elam and take care of his other needs, giving him plenty of kisses and cuddles in between. When her stomach growled, she fixed herself a sandwich, though her appetite was hampered a bit by the memory of how upset Naomi had been with her for not helping Reba off the floor right away. But from taking care of her own mamm, Bethel had learned to err on the side of caution when it came to moving an injured person. While Naomi had called for an ambulance, Bethel had gotten down on the floor beside Reba and talked to her while checking Elam for injury. He was fine, just mad about a dirty diaper. And an empty stomach.

The numbers on the papers began to blur as daylight turned to dusk. To give herself a break and help clear her head, she prayed for Reba and the bishop. Then, after putting Elam to bed in his crib, she found a snow shovel and cleared the porch and front stairs. Not that it did much gut, with the white stuff still coming down. It was beautiful though. They didn't get as much snow in Mio. It helped her efforts if she pretended she was doing this for her own family. Pretended this was her home, instead of the reality—her being a stranger to both the family and the haus. Technically, what she pretended was true; it just didn't feel like it.

Darkness was falling by the time she propped the shovel against the outside of the haus. She took care of the evening chores in the unfamiliar barn before going inside. After unbundling, she checked the fire, added another log, and peeked in on Elam. Hopefully, he would sleep until the wee hours of the morgen, as he had done the nacht before.

She'd gotten up to care for him when he'd awakened, but Naomi was already in his room and she shooed Bethel away, whispering something about having to go to work early anyway.

Gideon, lying on the cot beside the crib, either had slept through the exchange or had pretended to. Bethel hadn't dared to do much more than peek at him in the dim glow of the lantern, though she did notice his navy-blue T-shirt stretched tight against his well-defined chest. His flannel-clad legs were visible from the knees up, the rest of him wrapped in the half-zipped sleeping bag.

To-nacht, Bethel would sleep on the hard cot. Gideon had indicated they would take turns.

She stayed up later than usual, but still nobody returned home. Nobody called either—or maybe someone did and she simply didn't hear the barn phone ringing over the howling wind. She added the biggest log she could find to the fire, banked the woodstove, and locked the doors. Being alone with a boppli in an unfamiliar haus, in an unfamiliar area, made her feel more than a little insecure.

When she climbed into the sleeping bag on the cot, she caught a piney scent mixed with a hint of cinnamon. She'd noticed the same aromas earlier that day when Gideon stood close to her, flirting. Pine and cinnamon. She breathed them in now, trying to imagine Gideon as her true ehemann—in more than name only—and herself wrapped in his arms.

She woke up the next morgen, sore from the hard cot, and ventured downstairs. Still nein sign of Gideon, Ben, or Naomi. She didn't expect Reba to return for at least a few days, depending on what kind of treatment she received at the hospital, but it was odd that none of the rest of the family stopped in. The day stretched by endlessly, a repeat of the evening before. Just caring for Elam and doing chores. All day.

There were nein words for how rejected and alone she felt.

That nacht, she went back to bed on the hard cot and again smelled Gideon's scent. Again tried to make believe he held her close. To pretend he loved her. That he wanted her. That she wasn't married to a stranger.

Imagined.

In her dreams, he enfolded her tenderly in his strong arms, lifted her from her uncomfortable sleeping-bag cocoon, and carried her to the soft pillow-top mattress in the other room. She wrapped her arms around him, her fingers feathering through his alluring red-gold locks.

Her imaginary lover tucked a few loose strands of her hair behind her ear and traced her face after gently laying her on the sheets, pulling the warm covers around her, and tucking her in. Cinnamon-scented kisses brushed her cheek, pressed against her eyelids, and touched the corners of her lips. Both sides. "Sleep well, precious."

The words were whispered, almost like another caress.

She moaned, turning into his kiss.

But there was nobody there.

It was a dream. Only a dream.

But it was a dream she wanted to continue.

~

"Don't leave. Stay with me."

Bethel's whispered words tore at Gideon's defenses. Her arm reached out for him with fingers splayed, as if to grab hold of him and pull him down to herself.

Ach, Bethel.

He was tempted. So tempted. She was desirable, after all. And he was a normal red-blooded male.

She would hate herself in the morgen.

He would probably heartily dislike himself, too, for taking advantage of her.

He backed away. She had nein idea what she was saying or doing. Her limp weight when he carried her to her bedroom was evidence that she was in a deep sleep. And who was she dreaming of? Nobody? Or Gideon? If only it were him.

He allowed himself one last touch of her hair, every bit as soft as he'd imagined, and then straightened.

She whimpered. This time, her hand snagged his.

What would it hurt? Just for a little while. Then he'd go back to Elam's room and lie down to sleep on that stiff cot again.

Either way, he would probably dream of her to-nacht. The wrong frau.

Nein, he couldn't think of her like that.

His frau. His.

His Bethel.

The fingers of his right hand entwined with hers.

With his left hand, he brushed his fingertips over her cheek again, his stomach muscles tightening.

"Please...."

He ducked away to quietly shut the bedroom door, even though they were home alone. Naomi and Daed were staying at the hospital again. Mamm had a broken hip and was scheduled to be prepped for surgery around six on Monday morgen.

Gideon had kum home to do the chores—which he'd thought had been neglected since Saturday morgen—and to share with Bethel the news that Bishop Miah would be all right. And also to say danki. He probably needed to apologize for his unkind words, too. *Not riding in her direction.* Even though he still didn't understand what the bishop had meant.

He'd found everything done, the lights off, and Bethel asleep on his cot...with her glorious hair down....

With all the extra work she'd done, she deserved the bed. Not the hard, uncomfortable cot.

And if she wanted to be held, he would hold her. Gladly.

Nobody would ever know.

Not even Bethel because he would leave before she awakened.

He slipped between the sheets and she rolled into his arms, her curves pressing against him.

He sucked in a breath and smoothed his hand down the length of her hair.

"My Bethel. Ich liebe dich." He whispered the words, just to try them out. "Ich liebe dich, Bethel."

They felt right.

She sighed, a contented sound, and her arm slid across his chest.

He stiffened. Nein. The words were wrong. Or maybe they were right but the timing was wrong.

Or possibly it was the woman that was wrong.

Nein.

He was wrong. When he slept with her, she should be awake, coherent, and completely aware of what was happening.

They wouldn't be sleeping.

And he would be able to hold her without stiffening.

He wasn't ready. He wasn't. And most definitely not in the room he'd shared with Lizzie. In their marriage bed.

Nein. Nein. Nein.

He slipped out of her arms, despite her sleepy moan of protest. Climbed out of bed. Went into Elam's room. And lay on the cot, feeling colder than he'd ever felt in his life.

Except maybe the day Lizzie died.

Or the nacht he married Bethel and "slept" in the basement.

He would nein doubt dream of the wrong frau again to-nacht.

Or maybe she'd be the right one.

Dash it all.

⌒

Monday morgen, Bethel woke up as the dawn sunlight spread its pink fingers across the eastern sky. She stretched, feeling warm and snuggly beneath the soft blankets and quilts.

She rubbed her eyes and glanced around the room she'd just spent her fourth nacht in. Nein, her third. She'd slept on the hard cot one nacht. This room was beginning to feel familiar to her, though she didn't dare touch anything in it beyond the contents of her suitcase. Gideon had boxed up his frau's belongings and moved them to the attic, but this still wasn't Bethel's room. She was still the unwelkum guest.

She made the bed, then frowned. How had she gotten here anyway? She'd intended to sleep on the cot again, next to Elam. In fact, she remembered going to bed in his room. She distinctly recalled drifting off to the scents of pine and cinnamon. She started to remember having dreams about Gideon—dreams that hadn't turned out as exciting as she might've hoped. A light kiss on the cheek, whispered words of love…. Pleasant dreams, to be sure, but her imagination was more active than that. Had she sleepwalked into Gideon's room?

She dressed and then checked in on Elam. He still slept. Beside his crib, the cot had been neatly straightened. Had she been so tired that she went to bed in the wrong room? Surely, she wasn't losing her mind. She went downstairs, peeking in on Naomi's open door as she passed her room. The space appeared undisturbed from the day before. Hadn't anyone kum home last nacht?

She made a side trip back to Ben and Reba's room. That door was open, too, the room undisturbed.

She headed to the kitchen to add a log to the fire and fix something for her breakfast. Hearing a creaking sound, she paused, startled. Then she peeked cautiously through the doorway.

Gideon crouched in front of the stove as he added a couple of logs.

She smiled. "Gut morgen." Maybe her dreams weren't just dreams.

Then her face heated. Had Gideon seen her in her nacht-gown?

And which Gideon would he be today? The flirt? The loving ehemann of her "dreams"? Or the harsh "I'm riding in a different direction" man?

He closed the stove, straightened, and turned to her. "Gut morgen, beautiful. I refilled the firewood after I did the chores. I came home to do them last nacht, but found them already done. Danki for everything you did. I really appreciate it. Mamm has a broken hip and will be having surgery sometime in the next few hours. You made an excellent call, not lifting her when she fell."

Bethel smiled and opened her mouth to say something about how she was praying for Reba, but Gideon approached her and briefly touched one of her kapp strings, then slid his hand behind her neck and fingered the loose strands of hair too short to be pulled into a bun.

He was the loving Gideon from her dreams. She shivered.

His gaze focused on her mouth. "Do you mind...that is, may I kiss you?" His brow furrowed as if he were uncertain, or maybe afraid she might refuse.

She moistened her lips. Tilted her head upward. A flutter of excitement worked through her. Her first kiss from her ehemann.

Her first kiss *ever*.

He cupped her face with his hands and pressed his lips to hers. Softly. Gently.

Her mouth quivered slightly in response. Embers flared to life. She started to lean into him.

And he pulled away.

His thumbs skated over her cheeks and down the curve of her jaw, then he dropped his hands at his sides.

It was over? It couldn't be over. Not when she wanted more.

She wrapped her arms around his neck, tugged him back toward her, and kissed him. His soft whiskers tickled her face, he tasted of the cinnamon breath mints she'd found in the bedroom.

And after a moment's hesitation, he kissed her back. He tasted of desperation and gathered her closer into his arms as he deepened the kiss.

She surged against him, kissing him with the same level of passion. With all her hopes. All her unfulfilled dreams. Maybe, just maybe, everything she'd ever longed for was finally within her grasp.

He picked her up and carried her into the living room. Started up the stairs.

Her heart pounded. This was finally happening? The stuff of her dreams last nacht? Had he changed his mind and decided to ride in her direction, after all? Hallelujah, praise der Herr! She tightened her grip around his shoulders. Toyed with his hair. Leaned in a little to press a kiss against his shirt-covered shoulder. Excitement pulsed through her.

He stopped halfway up the stairs. Set her down.

"I can't. I just can't." Tears beaded on his eyelashes. Dropped down his cheeks.

He gave her one last, hard kiss, with tears streaming down his face.

And then he spun on his heels and started back downstairs.

An answering sting burned her eyes.

He didn't want her.

16

Gideon stood by the barn doors, ready to pull them shut and go back to the haus, but he couldn't. Bethel was in there. His pulse pounded just thinking about her. The way she'd responded to him seemed to indicate she wanted him, too.

But now wasn't the right time. He couldn't consummate the marriage on the same bed he'd shared with Lizzie. In the same room. It'd be like having Lizzie standing there looking over his shoulder the whole time, condemning him.

He supposed he could swap bedrooms with Elam, but he still needed a new bed to share with Bethel.

He sighed heavily and blinked back the burn in his eyes. It was better to distance himself from Bethel for the time being. He wanted her more than he should, all things considered, but it definitely wasn't the opportune moment. At least she seemed open to the idea of....

His blood heated again. He glanced at the haus, mentally and emotionally reliving every moment of their passionate embrace. He had noticed her lack of experience though. Further proof that the story he'd been told was all lies.

But...they weren't even friends yet. They really didn't know each other.

Was it too early to be in love? Or was love at first sight truly possible? Even his heart had taken notice of her as they walked side by side to the haus following their wedding ceremony. And the following evening, he'd vowed to be the ehemann the Bible commanded him to be.

A promise he'd broken repeatedly since then.

And now, with the haus empty—excepting his sleeping sohn—he couldn't bring himself to consummate the marriage.

She was going to suspect something was wrong with him.

Maybe something was.

Daed would say he was overthinking things.

Was he? Hmm. That was probably true, too.

But he would know if it was right. And married or not, it wasn't right.

Lord Gott, I've tried, but I'm failing at this second marriage thing. I know I need to court her, but I had to go and complicate things by flirting, by whispering those declarations of love last nacht, by asking to kiss her. Help me to untangle the mess I've made of things and to slow things down so that we can truly and earnestly fall in love and have a gut marriage.

If the bishop weren't in the hospital, Gideon would have gone to him for advice. Maybe he should talk to Gabe Lapp. He needed to visit him sooner rather than later, anyway, to see about finding new furniture for his bedroom.

Maybe he would stop by Gabe's after Mamm was out of surgery, unless he saw Gabe at the hospital visiting Bishop Miah. The bishop's sohn had told Gideon that the doctors had deemed the event a "warning heart attack," or just a mild one. Nein bypasses needed. Though he would need to make some drastic lifestyle changes. Like giving up those fried pies he'd mentioned.

Gideon had forgotten to tell Bethel the gut news about the bishop. He should go back inside and let her know.

But with things being as they were between them right now, he couldn't quite find the courage to face her again in all her tempting glory.

He let out a breath of frustration and went back into the barn to hitch up Prancer for the drive to town. He would make sure the store was unlocked for the employees, grab something for his breakfast while he waited for a trusted worker to show up, and then head to the hospital.

Breakfast…another way he'd failed Bethel. He should've eaten breakfast with her and then offered to take her and Elam with him to the hospital. But she would be better off at home rather than at the hospital with nothing to do but hold Elam for endless hours during Mamm's surgery and recovery.

"Better off"? His thoughts mocked him. The only way to make things better for her would be for him to explain his reasons for repeatedly backing off instead of slinking away silently like the coward he was. Or to let her make a choice like a true partner instead of a "hired" helper.

He bowed his head in shame and regret.

He would explain himself later, when there were other people around to help him keep his hands and lips to himself.

He steeled his heart and, without another glance at the haus, climbed in the buggy and headed for town.

Bethel watched him go, the buggy a fuzzy blur in the early-dawn light because of the moisture clouding her eyes. She'd started oatmeal for their breakfast, with apples, raisins, cinnamon, and walnuts. Evidently, she would be enjoying it alone.

Was she so repulsive that he couldn't even say gut-bye?

Why was he sending such mixed messages? Hot and then cold. Flirting like he meant it and then withdrawing completely. And that kiss…. Well, kisses. Plural. They still warmed her. Not to mention his heated look when she caught him staring at her.

Granted, his initial kiss had been little more than a controlled peck until she took over. It'd taken him a moment to respond, too, so maybe she repulsed him with her eagerness, her inexperience. Men liked to be the hunters, ain't so? How many times had she heard that phrase during her teenage years?

And, well, being handed to an ehemann hardly equaled being pursued. An ehemann who'd had to be threatened to take her.

Nein wonder he didn't want her. However, he'd talked about wanting to court her. Had even initiated several courtship activities. He might consider those to be a sort of pursuit.

The boppli wailed, a welkum distraction to her thoughts. The sound also served as a pointed reminder that she was there as a caregiver and not a true frau. Gideon only wanted her to take care of his sohn and his mamm.

Bethel grabbed a bottle of prepared formula from the refrigerator, set it on the coolest part of the hot stove, and transferred the pot of oatmeal to a different burner before dutifully stomping upstairs.

Lying on his back in his crib, Elam smiled up at her and waved his arms. Her heart melted. Gideon may not want her, but this sweet boppli welcomed her love. She cooed at Elam as she laid out a fresh, clean diaper and unsnapped his sleeper to change him out of his wet one.

Her movements slowed.

Elam, whose mamm had died giving birth to him not even four months ago.

Nein wonder Gideon didn't want to do more than kiss her. Besides, he'd openly said he wasn't ready. Multiple times. She was the one who'd read more into his flirting than he'd intended her to. Shame filled her. Daed had mourned Mamm for six months before he started courting a widow in their district. And he'd known Mamm was dying for years before she passed.

Gideon had been taken by surprise, losing his Lizzie to an event he'd anticipated with joy, and had been forced to wed Bethel—a stranger—when he was still mourning.

Love wasn't in the forecast at all. Not the short-term one and probably not the long-term one either.

But maybe passion was. Sometime. Eventually. It was already present on her part. Her lips tingled. Her waist burned at the memory of his touch.

He might eventually learn to care for her.

The thought left open a tiny window for hope that might enlarge with prayer and time. She would try to do her best to take care of his haus and family and she would ask der Herr to give her patience. She would also pray to somehow learn to be content with her lot in life—a lot that was forced upon her by Daed's refusal to believe her.

Bethel forced a teary smile as she scooped up the clean, dry boppli and kissed his terry-cloth-covered belly. She was rewarded by a boppli chortle that made her laugh, so she kissed him again and again. Then she carried him downstairs, retrieved his bottle, shook it, and tested the temperature of the liquid on her wrist. It felt just right, so she grabbed a nearby flannel blanket, laid it across her shoulder, and settled into the rocking chair to feed him.

Elam was the one person in this haus who accepted her without judgment or comparison.

If she were to find the fifty dollars Daed had given her, she would…. She would…nothing. The boppli needed her. Even if she did leave, where would she go? And her departure would change nothing. She would still be married to Gideon. Forever.

It'd be better to stay, to hope for a glimmer of affection to develop. She'd pray for that, too, if there was even a smidgen of hope Gott heard her. Or cared about her.

But there didn't seem to be. Gott hadn't granted her pleading request that Daed would believe her, that he would desist in forcing the marriage.

But maybe, with the fifty dollars, his words of love, and the hug before he left, he had reasons he couldn't share.

Forgive him. The bishop's words replayed in her mind.

Could she? She considered it again. Then shook her head. Nein. She wasn't ready.

After feeding the boppli, she burped him and laid him on a blanket on the kitchen floor. She ate her breakfast alone, then went back to work on Naomi's books, which were still spread across the kitchen table.

Sometime later, a knock sounded on the back door. She opened the door to a blond-haired, blue-eyed man who walked with a slight limp. Beside him stood a woman with honey-colored hair and brilliant green eyes.

"I'm Gabe Lapp and this is my frau, Bridget," the man said. "We were at the wedding, but I'm not sure you'd remember us."

Bethel didn't remember them from the wedding, but she recognized their names. Gideon and Isaac had mentioned them several times. She tilted her head. "Nice to meet you. I'm Bethel. Kum in."

"Bridget wanted to visit with you, but I need to look around some. I saw Gideon and Ben at the hospital while I was visiting Bishop Miah—"

"How is he?" Bethel spun away as they entered. She hadn't even prayed for the man or asked Gideon about his condition. She'd been too interested in his gaze and his kisses. And that reminded her that she hadn't prayed for Reba either. Her face heated and she tried to mask it by busying herself with being hospitable. She moved the bookkeeping aside, then put water on for koffee or tea. Too bad there weren't any cookies to offer them. Well, basic chocolate chip cookies were quick and easy. She started gathering the necessary ingredients.

Gabe cleared his throat. "His sohn says he'll be fine. Still not making much sense when he starts sprouting random verses or proverbs."

So Bethel wasn't the only one who found the man utterly confusing? She glanced at Gabe.

"Which I suppose is a gut thing. Keeps us guessing." A crooked, dimpled smile flashed. "Anyway, I saw Gideon and Ben. They are talking about listing the haus for sale because...."

He kept talking, but the words sounded like a low buzz. Bethel stopped working and turned to stare at him. "What?"

Gabe's smile was patient. "Selling the haus. Apparently, with the projected decline in Reba's health, it will leave this one unsuitable for her future without an extensive remodel. That's what Ben said, though I'm fairly sure he was quoting a doctor verbatim. It sounds rather like medical-ese, don't you think?"

Bethel continued to stare, not sure what to say. The doctors had told her parents the same thing and Daed had remodeled portions of their haus. She could see the practicality of the Kaisers' moving— but why wouldn't they consult her? Then again, she wasn't a true partner in this marriage. Why would Gideon ask for her opinion?

Gabe chuckled, but his gaze was serious. "Gideon wants to start fresh with nein old memories marring the ones he hopes to make."

What? A surge of joy made her catch her breath. Did that mean what she thought it did?

She'd take a lesson from Ben and address this situation one step at a time. "So are you interested in buying?" She measured flour into a mixing bowl.

Bridget giggled. "Nein, we're happy where we are. But Gabe knows of a family looking to relocate, so he's checking it out in order to tell them about it."

"According to Bishop Miah, a preacher who used to live here is returning to the area with his large family," Gabe added. "They lost their home in the fire and the preacher is considering trading land for land and buying the haus and outbuildings."

None of that made sense to Bethel. Was it possible to trade land for land? Apparently so.

"If they decide to buy—and I imagine they will—they'll want to take possession as soon as possible. That means I'll have to move construction of the Kaisers' new home to the top of my job list.

When I left the hospital, Gideon, Ben, and Naomi were working on a list of features they wanted or needed. I imagine they'll ask you for input."

Or not. Her wants and needs weren't important in this discussion. Reba's well-being would be the top consideration.

But it warmed Bethel's heart to know Gideon wanted to start fresh with her.

She would give him another kiss when he returned home.

If he didn't avoid her.

⌒

Gideon stopped by the bakery with Naomi so she could gather the rest of her bookkeeping papers and her checkbook. It bothered him that Bethel was doing the job he'd promised to do for his sister. He would need to figure out a way to check Bethel's work without hurting her feelings. He'd seen the papers spread out on the kitchen table that morgen but hadn't taken the time to even glance at them.

As he stood in the doorway of Naomi's office, he pictured Bethel sitting there after calling for an ambulance for the bishop. Watching Gideon walk away after he uttered those hurtful words. Struggling to contain a sob.

The pain in her eyes had haunted him for hours.

She'd been there for him in so many ways, while he'd hurt her without thinking about the pain his words would create.

If only he could have a do-over. Or make things right.

But he didn't know if that was possible.

Daed was planning to stay at the hospital with Mamm another nacht. So sweet that even after almost thirty years of marriage, the two of them couldn't bear to be separated. Gideon hoped that if he and Bethel made it thirty years, they would feel the same way about each other.

"If you and Bethel can get this mess whipped into shape, I'll bake a loaf of raisin bread just for you and whatever her favorite treat is just for her," Naomi said as she finished loading the papers into another tote. She raised her eyebrows as she looked at him, as if she expected him to spout off Bethel's favorite baked good.

He hadn't a clue as to what it might be. Another thing he needed to find out. At least he knew of her fondness for white chocolate raspberry ice cream.

Then he remembered the gift of candy Agnes had promised him. Or rather, that Isaac had mentioned to Bethel. Bethel had mentioned something about milk chocolate filled with caramel. Maybe there was something like that in the candy shop. He didn't carry any similar products in the salvage-grocery store.

"I'm going to run down to the candy shop while you finish up in here."

"Finish up for today, you mean. I need to be open a while tomorrow." Naomi sounded a bit defensive.

"Right." Gideon turned on his heel, left the bakery, and hurried down the sidewalk to the candy shop.

The sign on the door read "Open," so he went inside. If Isaac wasn't around, perhaps Gideon would question Agnes a bit about what she'd said at the hospital. Wrong of him, probably, but she would never talk with Isaac present and her words indicated she knew something.

A realistic-sounding "moo" came from the corner of the shop where Agnes kept her indoor garden of house plants and herbs.

Gideon glanced in that direction and saw Isaac's young nephew, Timmy, playing with a colorful collection of plastic farm animals amid the indoor foliage.

That meant Isaac was likely here.

Gideon sagged, even as he smiled at the young bu. "Hi, Timmy."

"Hi, Preacher Gideon. My daed has a doctor's appointment today and teacher's sick with the flu, so Onkel Isaac and Aenti Agnes are taking care of us."

Sure enough, Isaac emerged from the kitchen area with a welcoming smile. "Agnes is at a critical stage with her candymaking, so I'm the server today. May I help you?"

"I hope so. Bethel mentioned something about her favorite candy being milk chocolate with caramel filling and...."

Isaac was already reaching inside the glass display case. "Agnes made it especially for her. Bethel likes it with a caramel filling, but this one has a layer of caramel and sea salt. Really gut. Bethel will absolutely love it. You might want to order another slab. The first one is free, a wedding gift from us."

It bothered Gideon more than it should have that Isaac knew more about his own frau's preferences than he did.

For now. That would change.

He reached for his wallet. "I saw Gabe at the hospital this morgen. I'm headed to his place now to see the furniture pieces he has stored and ask if he'll hold any I'm interested in. Daed and I are trying to design a haus Mamm will be able to get around in easier as her condition worsens." And one that would give Gideon and his bride a little privacy, but he wouldn't mention that.

Isaac nodded. "Bishop Miah said something about Preacher John returning to the area and needing a home. I haven't met him yet, but I know he'll be helpful around here."

It seemed Isaac had his finger nearer the pulse of this area than Gideon did. Was it because Isaac liked to talk to people? Or because Gideon had been drowning in his grief and had shut out everyone and everything? The pile of paperwork for Naomi's bakery was evidence of how much his family had suffered while he was simply trying to survive.

He hadn't heard a word about Preacher John's imminent return until Gabe mentioned it to him and Daed, knowing Preacher John might be a potential buyer. Premature excitement filled Gideon at the prospect of a bedroom—an entire home—that wasn't filled with memories of Lizzie. He planned to design his portion of the haus as a special gift for Bethel, if she was willing to share her input. And if he was brave enough to ask her. Whatever she wanted, if it was in his power, he'd do for her.

His Bethel.

It was funny how those two words twisted his insides and warmed him at the same time. The woman he'd always dreamed of marrying, but never would've dared pursue, handed to him like a gift. *Danki, Gott, for the gift of Bethel.* She'd stepped into the role of caregiver for Mamm and Elam so naturally. She seemed willing to step into her role as his frau. And with her experience as an auction clerk, she ought to be able to help him get caught up with the book-keeping for both Naomi's bakery and the salvage-grocery store.

What was her favorite meal? Maybe he could buy the ingredients so she could fix it for him. He hesitated to ask Isaac, though he probably knew.

Isaac boxed and bagged the fudge, then handed it across the counter to Gideon. He waved away the cash Gideon held out for a second slab. "One of them is a gift. If she likes it as much as I expect, you can order more. But listen." Isaac leaned closer. "There's an auction this weekend in Indiana. I hear rumors a micro-camper is being auctioned off. Agnes mentioned that you and your first frau liked to camp and I thought of you."

A micro-camper? Gideon frowned. It would be different from the musty tent and hard cots he and Lizzie used. "I have nein way to tow or drive a camper."

"It's light enough to hook onto a trailer hitch on your buggy." Isaac shrugged. "You can kum along with me and take a look, if you want."

It couldn't hurt to check it out. If the price was right, maybe he'd buy.

"I'll clear it with Daed and Bethel and if it's okay with them, I'll go along. Danki for the offer and the fudge." He lifted the bag. "Tell Agnes hi."

Isaac nodded. "Will do."

Gideon took his candy and, with a wave at Timmy—who ignored him in favor of driving his colorful plastic cows deeper into the window-garden forest—went back to the bakery. Naomi stood outside the door, looking his direction with a disgruntled expression.

He picked up the pace a little. Why did he find it so easy to upset the women in his life?

"Sorry I took so long," he said.

Naomi grumbled something under her breath as she turned and tugged on the knob of the bakery door to make sure it was locked.

Gideon decided to ignore her sudden bad attitude. "I need to stop by Gabe Lapp's to take a look at some furniture. And if you wouldn't mind watching Elam, I'd like to attempt to court Bethel again. Our last try was interrupted by...medical drama." Both Bishop Miah's and Mamm's.

That brought a half-smile to Naomi's face. "I think it is so romantic how you are courting Bethel. If I ever marry, I hope my ehemann will court me."

"Hopefully, before the wedding." Gideon started down the steps to the road.

"I also think it's romantic how you and Bethel married. It's as if Gott said, 'I want you to be happy, Gideon. Here's a new frau. Love her and treat her well and have a happy marriage.'"

That comment sent a jolt of anticipation through Gideon.

Did Gott truly have his best interests in mind when He brought the girl of Gideon's long-time dreams—dreams he always assumed would go unrealized—into his life?

Suddenly, he was in a hurry to get home and find some place private to court his bride.

And possibly steal a few more kisses, after apologizing for his hasty departure that morgen.

17

Having finished sorting the papers Naomi had given her the day before, Bethel now had nothing to do except take care of Elam—who was sleeping—or run downstairs and do some laundry. If she did a small load, it shouldn't take too long and she could check on Elam frequently.

She'd sorted the dirty clothes earlier, so she chose the smallest pile, ran the water, added detergent, and then quickly folded the garments she'd left hanging on the line last time. They were cold but dry.

She ran upstairs with the folded clothes and peeked in on the sleeping boppli before she went back downstairs. It didn't take too long to run the load of towels and washcloths through the wringer washer. She dropped the wet towels and washcloths into the basket. Overhead, the kitchen floor creaked. She stopped to listen but didn't hear any more sounds. Probably the haus settling. She started the water draining from a hose connecting the drain in the machine to the sump pump nearby. She was midway through the task of hanging up the wet laundry in the basement when heavy footsteps pounded on the floor above.

"Bethel!" The male voice sounded panicked. Gideon? She hadn't expected him home so soon. But why would he be scared? Was something wrong with Elam? Or, worse, had someone snuck in while she was downstairs and kidnapped him?

She dropped the clothespins into their bag and hurried toward the stairs.

Gideon appeared at the top of the staircase and ran down to her, his eyes wide. "Ach, you're here. Naomi said she didn't see you. I was afraid you had gone. I'm so sorry for the way I left this morgen." He pulled her into his arms, his hands roaming down her back, and then moving upward again. "I thought I'd lost you. That you'd left me." His hands flattened, drawing her against him.

Were those tears glittering in his eyes?

She instinctively wrapped her arms around his waist, then awkwardly patted his back. His cinnamon-scented breath teased her senses. She started to pull away. She shouldn't be brazen and chase him. "I was doing laundry. Elam was asleep and I finished the book—"

His fingers pressed against her lips, silencing her. He stared down at her a moment, a strange light filling his eyes. It heated her through, despite the cold in the basement.

And then he tugged her back into his arms. She shivered and he pulled her closer, maybe in an effort to warm her. A second later, his mouth covered hers with kind of hungry desperation. While his initial kiss that morgen had been reserved, cautious—a mere peck—now he held nothing back. He kissed her with a passion she never could have imagined. Moaning, she arched against him, her lips parting.

He made an answering sound deep in his throat and the next thing she knew, she found herself lying on a soft pile of quilts. Probably where Gideon had spent their wedding nacht. He landed on top of her, his kisses intensifying. His soft beard tickled her face. She wrapped her arms around his neck and dug her fingers through his hair.

"Gideon?" Naomi's muffled call, from somewhere upstairs, was an unwelkum intrusion.

Gideon stilled, breaking off the kiss. But he didn't move. Instead, he buried his face against her neck, breathing heavily. "Ach, Bethel." Frustration lined every syllable.

"Gideon? I can't find her anywhere." Naomi's voice sounded louder as she came closer. The floor creaked overhead.

Bethel shoved at Gideon. They couldn't be caught like this. Her face burned.

"I found her," he finally shouted, somehow managing to sound normal. As if completely unaffected by their stolen moments of passion. But he didn't roll off her. Instead, he toyed lazily with her kapp strings. With another groan, he nuzzled her neck with his lips. Nibbled at her ear. Followed her pounding pulse down her neck.

She shoved at him again. She didn't want an audience, nor did she want him getting her hopes up, only to turn cold once more.

His lips swallowed the rest of her objection.

She whimpered. Ach, she wanted his affection. His love. She was parched for whatever passion he wanted to give her. Was this part of the fresh start Gabe had referred to? If only they didn't have to worry about getting caught. She squirmed and he made another growling sound in the back of his throat.

"Where are you?" Naomi's voice intruded again. Nearer still.

"Go away," Gideon grunted with irritation as he rolled to his feet, then held out a hand to help Bethel up.

"Ach!" Naomi stopped halfway down the stairs. She abruptly turned and started back up them, giggling.

Gideon sighed. "She's more effective than a cold shower." Then he gave Bethel a much less passionate kiss. "To be continued."

And with that delightful promise, he turned and followed his sister upstairs.

Leaving Bethel to try to extinguish the resulting flames with the cold, wet towels she had yet to hang on the line.

Gideon paused halfway up the staircase. "Since Naomi is here to babysit, may I take you on a walk to-nacht?"

"I'm all yours." Her voice cracked. Her face flamed.

So much for not being brazen.

⌒

If only.

Gideon trudged up the final step and into the kitchen. Naomi stood at the table, holding Elam against her shoulder. While the boppli tried to shove his fist inside his open mouth, she appeared to be studying the work Bethel had done with the bakery's books. Naomi looked up with a smirk. "I didn't expect to see you so soon."

"Seriously?" Gideon rolled his eyes. "Just wait, Sis. I'll get you."

Naomi's lips settled into a frown. "He's back."

Gideon stared at her. "Who?"

But before she could answer, he knew. If Preacher John was returning to town, it stood to reason that the entire Troyer family would be joining him—including his oldest sohn, Kish, who'd somehow landed a contract to play minor-league baseball.

Though, if Kish lived and worked in the Grand Rapids area, he was unlikely to hang around their district any longer than he had to.

In the weighty silence, Naomi walked to the stove, where a bottle of formula warmed. She tested the temperature of the liquid against her wrist and then settled on a chair to feed Elam. "She appears to know what she's doing."

It took Gideon's mind a moment to switch gears. "Bethel. Right. I'll look over her work in a moment." He cleared his throat. "Did you, um, see him?"

She frowned. "He actually had the gall to stop by the bakery and say hi. As if he expected me to be all smiley and giggly and happy to see him."

"If he expected that, he doesn't know you very well," Gideon teased. He got out a mug and filled it with koffee, added a dash of cream, and sat at the table.

"I should've chased him out of the bakery with a towel," Naomi stated bluntly. "Instead, I told him to go back where he came from and leave me alone. And he acted shocked and hurt." She huffed. "I don't want to talk about him anymore. And if I ever see him again, it'll be too soon."

That explained Naomi's disgruntled look at the bakery. Gideon grimaced. "Sorry. Didn't expect him to kum up with his daed."

Bethel came upstairs then and Gideon's heart rate increased at her appearance. Her cheeks were stained pink and her lips appeared swollen and well-kissed. She avoided Gideon's gaze as she reached for Elam. "I'll feed him."

Naomi shook her head. "Danki, but I'd like to do it. I need to de-stress and there's nothing better than boppli snuggles. You can start our noon meal, if you want. I was thinking tuna casserole."

When Bethel disappeared inside the pantry, Naomi glanced at Gideon. "I've known about Preacher John's plans to return, but I guess I never dreamed *he'd* return, too."

Bethel returned moments later with a small plate of chocolate chip cookies. Gideon's favorite.

Gideon glanced at the cookies, then looked at her, arching an eyebrow. "When did you make these?"

"Earlier today when Gabe and Bridget Lapp stopped by to look over the haus. I had nothing on hand to offer them, so I baked some fresh." Bethel put a kettle of water on the stove to heat.

Naomi frowned at Gideon. "Gabe and Bridget are thinking of buying our home?"

Gideon reached for a cookie as he glanced at Naomi. He shook his head. "Not them."

Naomi raised Elam to her shoulder to burp him. She huffed as he belched. "Well, if that doesn't beat all. They—*they*—are the ones who want to buy our haus?"

"Maybe," Gideon said cautiously. "Gabe was going to meet with Preacher John later today. If they're interested, they'll return to look it over."

Which, now that he thought about it, might hinder his plan to take Bethel for a walk. He ate his cookie in three bites. Wow, it was delicious. Maybe even better than the ones Naomi made. He sighed as he reached for another cookie. "Danki."

Bethel grinned. "Don't spoil your appetite."

"Not a chance." All he'd eaten that day was a granola bar he'd grabbed at the salvage-grocery that morgen. His own fault. He hadn't been able to bring himself to buy any of the unappetizing-looking food in the hospital cafeteria. And he'd left home before breakfast.

Because....

He glanced at Bethel as she busied herself making tuna casserole. Jah. Well.

They *were* married, but they wouldn't have any privacy until.... Well, he would work on that.

Until then, he would court her. For real. The puzzle they'd started still waited in the living room. They could get to know each other while assembling it.

Much better than being alone. Especially since he needed to fall in love with her for real and not just because she was his frau. Not just because she was lovely. Not just because he decided he would. Not just because he suspected she was the girl who'd caught his attention over ten years ago.

He reached for the paperwork Bethel had organized. It'd be better to look it over now to avoid gawking at her while she fixed the meal.

Naomi laid Elam on a flannel blanket on the floor, then joined Bethel at the counter. "I'll wash your baking dishes." She dipped her hand in the water. "Ach, it's cold. I'll empty the dishpan."

"Gut thing I have plenty of cookies left in case the new preacher stops by to see the haus," Bethel said cheerfully.

Gideon looked up. "He isn't a new—"

"That man's sohn is not getting a single one of those cookies," Naomi spat with a glare.

Then, dishpan in hand, she stalked over to the door, opened it, and sucked in a breath.

And slung the water with greater force than Gideon had ever seen her use.

 ‿

Bethel jerked around at the very loud, very male gasp and stared at the tall Englisch man standing there, his open black coat, blue T-shirt, and jeans dripping with cold, dirty dishwater. In his hand was a drenched ball cap. Behind him stood an older, slightly damp Amish man.

Gideon rose to his feet. "Kish. Preacher John."

Naomi dropped the dishpan on the floor at her feet, spun around, snatched up Elam, and ran from the room.

Bethel grabbed a kitchen towel and hurried over to the doorway. She handed it to the younger man—Kish, presumably—and picked up the plastic pan. "I'll be right back with a bath towel," she said to anyone who might care, then retreated after Naomi.

Bethel hurried to the small bathroom on the main floor—one of the areas that wouldn't accommodate Reba's long-term needs—grabbed a navy-blue towel from the tiny closet in there, and returned to the kitchen. Preacher John and Kish had kum inside and now stood on the mat. Gideon was hanging their wet coats on the hooks beside the door.

"Bethel, this is Preacher John Troyer and his oldest sohn, Kish. They've kum to look at the haus." Gideon glanced at her with a half-smile, then turned his attention back to the men. "This is my frau, Bethel."

Both men looked at Bethel and frowned. "I hadn't heard…" the older man began, then shook his head. "Nice to meet you."

The younger man smiled, but the expression seemed rather pained. He plucked at the wet fabric of his shirt where it clung to his chest. "Hi, Bethel." He took the towel she held out to him as his attention flickered to Gideon. "When did Naomi have a boppli?"

"Elam is my sohn from Lizzie," Gideon said simply. "Bethel and I married Thursday."

"Congratulations," both men said at the same time.

"Danki." Bethel stood there awkwardly for a moment before pivoting on her heel and heading for the kitchen counter. Whatever Naomi's reason for not wanting to set out cookies for these men, it was the polite thing to do. She added several cookies to the plate she'd prepared earlier, then set it at a clear place on the table. "Would either of you like something warm to drink?"

"Koffee would be great, danki," Preacher John replied. "Do you mind if we take a tour while you're getting it ready?"

"I'll show you around." Gideon led the way out of the room.

Kish handed Bethel the towel as he passed. "Danki."

Bethel smiled. The towel really hadn't done much gut. "Should I get you a set of Gideon's clothes to borrow?"

Kish glanced down at his soggy Englisch clothes and shook his head. "Danki, but I'm fine."

At least she'd offered. It was the best she could do.

When did this sohn of an Amish preacher turn Englisch, anyway? Ach, wait. Now she was putting two and two together. Kish must've been Naomi's fiancé. The one who'd been discovered by a talent scout for the minor leagues when his family evacuated to escape the wildfire.

As the koffee brewed, she returned her attention to the noon meal. What should she do? Double the recipe for tuna casserole so she could feed their guests? Or delay lunch until they'd left? She peeked in the other room, hoping Naomi would be in there to ask. But she wasn't.

It probably didn't matter. Judging by the way Naomi clearly felt about Kish, she would be opposed to feeding him and his daed.

But offering lunch would be the right thing to do. And from the frau of a preacher, such hospitality was likely expected.

Okay, then. She would make enough food for the two men. If they declined to stay for the meal, then so be it. At least she would have tried. She cleared off the table and got to work.

The tuna casserole had just kum out of the oven when the men reappeared, both preachers—John and Gideon—chuckling over something. Kish wore a sober expression. There was nein sign of Naomi or Elam.

"I hope you'll join us for lunch." Bethel gestured toward the table, set for six. The hot casserole bubbled on a trivet in the center, flanked by bowls of home-canned peaches, cottage cheese, and green beans with onions.

"Bethel is an amazing cook." Gideon's smile warmed her. "We'll be glad to have you stay."

Naomi appeared in the doorway, her lips pursed and arms crossed. She must've put Elam down for a nap.

"Well, we do need to talk, but I think Ben should be here." Preacher John glanced at his sohn. "Will he kum home this evening?"

Gideon shook his head. "Nein. Tomorrow, maybe. Depends on how Mamm is. But you can talk to me and I'll relay the message when I see him."

Preacher John nodded. "Then we'll stay."

Kish glanced at Naomi with a smirk, then grinned at Bethel. "We'd be delighted."

Bethel met Naomi's ice-cold glare and shivered. She may have just invited her first major jangle with her sister-in-law. And this had been Naomi's home first. But Naomi had been conspicuously absent when Bethel was trying to figure out whether to issue an invitation. And someone needed to do the right thing. To act like a grown-up.

Whatever the history between Naomi and Kish, Bethel didn't want to be in the middle of it.

Too late. She was.

Naomi stomped into the kitchen and sat in Reba's place. Her sour expression didn't ease. "I'm going to be included in this conversation."

Preacher John glanced at Gideon, waiting for his nod of approval before he said, "Sure, sure."

Naomi settled into the chair beside Preacher John.

Kish, seated on the other side of his daed, smiled at Bethel. "The meal looks great."

Naomi scowled. "I hope it gives you indigestion."

18

Gideon glared at Naomi and slashed one hand across his throat, warning her to tone it down. He understood that Kish had hurt her deeply when he broke off their engagement to play in the minor leagues. But Daed was concerned, and rightly so, that Naomi would never find an ehemann unless she changed her demeanor and came across as sweet and docile, as Amish women were supposed to be, rather than aggressive and outspoken.

This anger was new and not welkum. Whatever the deeper issue with Kish might be, forgiveness was key and the door needed to be left open for reconciliation. Naomi especially needed to act civilly in front of Kish's frowning father, with whom Gideon would be working closely in his efforts to meet the spiritual needs of the community. If she didn't, Gideon might eventually be asked by Preacher John to vote on a suitable punishment for his own sister. Naomi was putting him between a rock and a hard place. He'd need to have a talk with her about her attitude.

Not that he expected Naomi to be open to the idea of reconciliation.

For now, while her frosty demeanor didn't soften, she gave him a nod of acknowledgment and then bowed her head for the silent prayer.

"Let's pray," said Gideon from his seat at the head of the table. He'd assumed the patriarch's spot in Daed's absence. Bethel sat to his right and he took her hand, making circles on her soft skin with his calloused thumb. Then he bowed his head and silently recited the Lord's Prayer, adding a prayer for guidance, wisdom, and favor.

And maybe some privacy—sooner rather than later.

If Gott willed it.

Please will it. He tightened his grip around Bethel's fingers and squeezed.

She squeezed back.

It almost seemed as if they'd shared a delightful secret.

Lord, danki for the gift of Bethel. I love her.

He meant it. Really. Or he really meant to mean it.

Nein, he did mean it.

Preacher John cleared his throat, indicating he was long done with his prayer and ready to eat.

Gideon wasn't willing to be pressured. He went on praying, for Bishop Miah, for Mamm, for Daed in the face of this new medical issue of Mamm's, and for Naomi.

Then he raised his head. "Amen."

"Amen," the other two men parroted.

"Okay, we're interested," Preacher John began. "The haus is definitely big enough for our family, especially if we remodel the third-floor attic and add two bedrooms. How much do you want for the haus and outbuildings?"

Gideon took a deep breath. "Daed and I haven't discussed it yet. The decision to sell was made just this morgen, in light of the doctor's grim tone as he explained the potential impact of Mamm's broken hip on her disease."

Learning of the Troyers' imminent return was the icing on the cake and a confirmation that it was time to let go of the old and embrace the new. In more ways than one.

Bishop Miah had been right.

Preacher John furrowed his brow in a show of sympathy. "We're praying for Reba. That must be so difficult. May the will of der Herr be done. But regarding the haus, here's what we're prepared to offer." He reached in his pocket, pulled out a piece of paper, and slid it across the table to Gideon.

Gideon blinked at the paper, fighting to hide his surprise. He hadn't thought that their property might be worth that much. And the preacher had probably made what he considered to be a low offer, expecting to haggle. Gideon scratched at his beard. "I'll let Daed know." There was nein way he would venture to guess what Daed might give as a counter-offer, but Gideon would be more than willing to accept the "low" offer.

As Preacher John talked about how much he looked forward to returning to the area, Gideon daydreamed of home designs. He and Daed had already agreed on the importance of having a dawdi-haus, which would serve as the hub of the residence, located at the center. Arranged around it would be a one-bedroom apartment for Naomi and a three-bedroom apartment for Gideon, both of which could be enlarged when—or if—needed.

With their own, private apartment, he and Bethel would have some much-needed privacy.

Gideon's face heated and he busied himself eating the delicious meal.

Although Kish and Naomi glanced frequently and furtively at each other during the meal, they remained silent. Overwhelmingly so. Almost painfully so. The tension in the room was thick enough to cut with a blunt butter knife.

What had happened between Kish and Naomi other than the broken engagement? Or was that enough of an explanation for this tension? Gideon released a sigh of frustration. Daed would remind him that courtship was a private matter and he shouldn't get involved. Gideon would honor that. For now.

When Preacher John quieted, Gideon glanced at Kish. "How's life in the minor leagues?" He really wanted to know if Kish planned to play indefinitely or return to the Amish.

Kish glanced in Naomi's direction and shrugged but remained quiet.

Naomi made a derisive snort.

Kish's expression turned slightly defiant.

Ach. Kish might not feel comfortable talking about his Englisch career in front of his daed, or in front of Gideon, since he was a preacher, too.

Or maybe he just didn't want to talk about it with Naomi present.

He glanced at Bethel to see how she was handling this awkward exchange.

She looked confused. A little uneasy, maybe. Moments later, she bolted up from her chair and set about serving cookies and koffee.

"These cookies are fantastic, Bethel," Kish said after he tried one. He didn't look at Naomi.

Naomi glowered.

An awkward silence prevailed until lunch ended and Bethel and Naomi started the dishes.

"Ach, I didn't show you the farm equipment we're prepared to sell." Gideon stood. It'd probably be wise to separate his sister and Kish before the poor guy ended up taking another bath in dirty dishwater.

The three men bundled up, but before they left, Kish turned and looked directly at Naomi. "If Daed buys this haus, I know exactly which room will be mine."

A pregnant silence fell. Naomi froze, her gaze fixed on him, a strange light in her eyes.

"The one I used to throw pebbles at after dark." He added a wink and made a noise that was probably supposed to be a chuckle. Instead, it sounded rather sick. His mouth transitioned into a smirk that quickly became a grimace. Then he left the haus.

Naomi half snorted, half sobbed.

Gideon rolled his eyes. "Drama? Jah, we've got that."

Preacher John nodded. "In several varieties, it seems."

Jah. His sohn and Gideon's sister.

Or was he thinking also of the cot in Elam's room, proof positive that he and Bethel weren't yet one?

Gideon's stomach churned. That would definitely mean marital counseling.

Naomi thrust the stack of soiled dishes she'd gathered at Bethel and, for the second time that day, ran from the room.

⟿

Left alone to do the dishes, Bethel made quick work of them. She'd just finished and was drying the last dish when she looked out the window and saw the preacher and Kish drive away in their borrowed buggy.

A door slammed and Bethel turned around as Naomi reentered the kitchen, her eyes red-rimmed.

Bethel bit her lower lip and pretended not to have noticed. Gideon's sister was likely embarrassed and probably didn't want to explain why she'd run from the room or why she'd been crying. Or why she'd been beyond rude in her treatment of their guests. Or maybe Bethel was about to be drawn into the jangle she'd worried about all afternoon. She gave the table a final wipe-down, then hung the dishcloth beside the sink to dry.

"How dare you..." Naomi growled. "How dare you invite *that man* to join us for lunch?"

Bethel sighed. So, it was just as she'd thought. Time for her first argument with her new sister-in-law. She kept her attention on the floor as she slowly turned. She took a deep breath. And silently whispered a prayer for wisdom. Then she raised her gaze to meet Naomi's eyes. "It was the polite thing to do. And you had the option of saying nein, but you weren't in the room for me to ask."

"Nein, I didn't!" Naomi flung out her arms. "This is my haus. Not yours."

Ouch.

"Mine, mine, mine." Naomi reiterated, sounding more like a spoiled two-year-old than a grown woman.

Bethel opened her mouth to speak but heard a quiet click behind her. Then a heavy, warm, comforting hand grasped her shoulder. Mind-numbing tingles raced through her and what emerged from her mouth was a squeaky whine, not the half-formed retort that had danced on the tip of her tongue.

"It's her haus, too," Gideon said calmly.

His thumb rubbed her shoulder, heating her all the way through her dress and turning her brain to mush. She could've moaned and leaned into his touch.

Naomi gave her an odd look.

"And she's right," Gideon added. "It was the polite thing to do. You know it was. Mamm would've done the same thing." He stepped away, winking at Bethel as he walked by.

Bethel wobbled and swayed, wanting to move back into his embrace.

Naomi glared at him. Without another word, she snagged a cookie, then grabbed the bookkeeping records Bethel had set aside and dropped them on the table.

Bethel wasn't quite inclined to help with accounting right now. Gideon might've managed to defuse the anger lurking just below the surface, but now Bethel wanted to take him by the hand and lead him to that bed of blankets in the basement. After she figured out some way to lock the door.

With that course of action out of the question, she fixed herself a mug of peppermint tea, poured another cup of koffee for both Gideon and Naomi, and carried all three mugs over to the table. She sat down across from Naomi—who, oddly, had chosen the seat Kish had occupied during the noontime meal—and next to Gideon.

Gideon shuffled through the papers Bethel had organized earlier, then set the pile down and pulled at his beard with the fingers of one hand. His other hand rested on Bethel's knee beneath the table. Her muscles tensed and sparks shot up her leg, swirling into a whirlpool of emotion in her stomach. "Great job, Bethel. Naomi brought home some more receipts and bills today if you want to start sorting those. I'll add this information to the ledger." He glanced at his sister. "Naomi, you can pay the bills. Unless you'd rather I pay them while Bethel does the ledger and you sort."

Naomi groaned. "Bills distress me. You can pay. I'll sort." She reached for the tote bag on the floor beside her chair.

He raised an eyebrow. "Distress? You mean de—"

"I mean distress. Cause extreme anxiety." She glared at her brother.

"Ah. Gut enough." Gideon shook his head, patted Bethel's knee, then stood and went over to the hutch, where he retrieved a pencil, a pen, and a roll of stamps. He handed the pencil and the ledger to Bethel before sitting down and snagging two chocolate chip cookies. "These really are sur gut."

Naomi grunted, but she helped herself to a second cookie and ate it without comment.

Bethel decided to take it as a compliment. She slid the ledger closer to herself. She'd started working on it earlier, but then, afraid she might be overstepping her boundaries, she'd set it aside. But it was wunderbaar to hear Gideon praise her help, her cooking, her baking, and now, her bookkeeping skills.

The three of them worked together yet independently for about an hour, until Elam's wail split the silence. Naomi glanced at the wall clock. "He shouldn't be hungry for another half hour yet. I'll get him. I need a boppli break anyway." She stood and hurried from the room.

Bethel looked at Gideon. His hair was messy from his raking his fingers through it as he paid the bills.

He glanced up with a smile and set his pen down. In the next second, he was on his knees beside Bethel's chair.

Her lips tingled in anticipation.

Instead of kissing her, he grasped her hands in his. "Five questions. First: What is your favorite baked treat?"

She blinked. "Apple fritters." Should she ask the same question of him? She was almost certain his was raisin bread. She wanted to bake him a loaf or two if Naomi didn't bring any home soon.

"Those are great. I love them with apple cider." His thumbs rubbed circles on the backs of her hands. "Favorite dish?"

"Shrimp alfredo." She'd had it only once actually. Isaac had prepared it for her and Daed.

His brow furrowed. "I've never heard of it."

Maybe she shouldn't have named a dish associated with Isaac. "It's a pasta dish of noodles like spaghetti and a creamy, garlicky sauce with shrimp."

"Hmm. Make me a list of ingredients you'd need and I'll get them—or order them—for you. I've ordered seafood for other customers before. My favorite meal is chicken spaghetti. It's a little spicy. I like foods with heat. And barbeque…I love that."

She could barbeque, although she generally didn't when there was snow on the ground. She glanced out the window. Drips of water fell from the eaves. The snow was melting at least. In the meantime, she would try to find a recipe for chicken spaghetti.

"Favorite color?" He turned her hands over and pressed a kiss against each palm.

She shivered. Her mouth dried. "Um, periwinkle blue?"

His attention moved away from her hands. "I don't know what that is either. But I love just about every shade of blue." He nibbled her pulsing wrist, his gaze holding hers.

"It has a note of lavender to it." Her words sounded breathy, but she couldn't help it.

When a step creaked, he was off his knees and back in his chair one second before Naomi reentered the room carrying a grinning, slobbering Elam.

Gideon stood and reached for his sohn. He gave Elam a kiss, then tossed him into the air. Elam squealed with glee. Laughing, Gideon repeated the game twice more before handing the boppli back to his sister and returning his attention to the bills.

Seeing Gideon with his sohn made Bethel long to give him more kinner. How was it possible she already felt that desire? It seemed his apparent determination to work his way into her heart was paying off.

Five questions. The way he'd asked her the first three was enough to set her heart to pounding.

She could hardly wait for questions four and five.

⌒

Gideon wrote the check for the last bill, then stood and stretched his aching back. He missed his bed. He hadn't had a gut nacht's sleep since his wedding nacht, almost a week ago. Of course, another barrier to sound sleep, besides the discomfort of the cot, had been all his dreams about Bethel.

He deliberately looked away from her to Naomi, who sat on the floor, playing with Elam. "I'm sorry I got so behind on your bookkeeping, Naomi. I'll do better from now on."

"You still have to catch up on the store's books, too. Daed was working on them yesterday." She looked up, her demeanor almost peaceful. "Elam is a gut stress reliever," she liked to say. "Except when he cries and cries and nobody can figure out why. Then he's a stress inducer."

Gideon cringed. "Jah. I'll go to work tomorrow." His gaze shifted to Bethel.

Nobody would expect him back at work yet. Not with a still-new bride and not with Mamm in the hospital. But if he hid in the office, nobody would know except for his employees. And he could tell them that Mamm needed Daed, so he had to show up at the store. And that he and Bethel would finish their honeymoon later.

Start it, rather.

Maybe he'd better not mention the honeymoon at all.

Did he dare mention to Bethel his feelings for her? How, when the youthful Gideon dreamed of his future frau, this shapely blonde beauty he'd seen at auction was the one who filled his dreams? Not the petite, dark-haired tomboy he'd eventually married. He and Lizzie were drawn together through their common interests in volleyball, camping, fishing, and their ability to talk about anything and nothing. They were friends first, lovers second.

The best sort of marriage, he was told.

Except she didn't get along with his family and resented having to leave hers. How many times had she pointed out that a man should leave his family and cleave to his wife?

But she'd known for years about the salvage-grocery store he owned with his daed. And while her parents' move south to a warmer climate hadn't been part of the plans, she hadn't insisted on going with them. At least, not exactly. She had hinted blatantly at her interest, of course.

He shook his head. Friendship. He and Bethel didn't have that. Yet. But they also didn't have any of the typical teenage ways of developing it. He couldn't take her to any frolics—except maybe to work frolics—or to volleyball games, or any of the other activities the youngies did.

He could court her. He could show her kindness.

She shifted, set down the pencil, and closed the ledger, then started making circles with her shoulders and neck, as if to work out kinks.

That was something else he could do.

Without putting any more thought into it than that, he moved to stand behind Bethel and started to massage her shoulders.

She moaned softly.

Which sent his thoughts spiraling in a different direction. He licked his lips.

"Elam will need a little brother or sister sooner or later." Naomi didn't look up as she dangled Elam's favorite stuffed frog for him to grab.

"Honestly, Naomi, do you have nein filter?" Gideon jerked his hands away from Bethel and glared at his sister.

"I don't give voice to every thought," Naomi groused. "But really, wouldn't the world be so much better if people said what they were thinking? Go ahead and tell Bethel how lovely she is and how much you want her. Tell her she's nothing like your first frau."

Bethel sat completely still. She seemed in suspense. As if wondering whether he would confirm or deny his sister's words.

Gideon's mouth worked, but nothing came out. His face heated to what felt like a dangerous level. He squirmed, hating how close his sister had kum to blurting out his secrets. These things needed to be said, but shouldn't he be the one to voice them?

"Tell her how much you love her. How much you've always loved her."

He sucked in a gasp. His secrets were out.

Bethel slowly turned around and gave him a strange look. Then she stood, walked over to Naomi, and crouched down beside her. Gave her a hug.

Naomi hugged her back.

Had Lizzie and Naomi ever embraced? He was almost certain they hadn't. They'd made their dislike of each other more than plain.

Bethel whispered something before she released Naomi, stood, and turned to him with a smile that reached her eyes. "Do you want to go for a walk?"

"Nein…jah…maybe." His face burned even hotter.

And both women giggled.

19

Bethel walked to the door, lifted Gideon's coat and hat off the hook where he'd hung them, and handed them to him. He shrugged on his coat, then reached for hers and dangled it out for her.

She backed away, shaking her head with a smile. "Naomi and I need to talk."

His shoulders slumped and her heart nearly broke.

She didn't mean to play with his emotions, but she wanted to speak with Naomi in private about her issues with Kish. "I'll walk with you later?" She spoke it as a question, leaving room for him to say he didn't want to. Though she really, really hoped he would want to.

"Go with him now," Naomi urged. "We'll talk this evening while Gideon does his chores. I'll watch Elam now. When you get back, we can all go to the hospital to check on Mamm and Daed."

Bethel nodded eagerly. Naomi's desire to include her warmed her heart almost as much as Gideon's earlier assertion that this was her haus, too. "I'd love to go visit. I don't want your mamm thinking I don't care about her. And seeing Elam will lift her spirits."

"Mamm was worried that she hurt him when she fell. It will make her feel better to know he's fine." Gideon held out Bethel's coat again. "Please, Bethel, kum with me now." His voice had lowered to a husky plea.

It felt so gut to be wanted.

"Alright." She turned and allowed him to help her into her coat. As he did, his fingers brushed her neck multiple times. Was his touch deliberate, as when they stood in front of the candy shop?

"At least the sun is shining now. Temperature is above freezing." Gideon grabbed the stack of envelopes containing bill payments and then opened the door for Bethel. "We'll mail these on our way past the mailbox. Did you write your daed yet?"

"Um, nein." She didn't know what to say. Especially after Bishop Miah told her to forgive him. She thought of her last exchange with Daed, when he had hugged her, whispered that he loved her, told her to stay safe, and gave her fifty dollars. Money that was still missing, along with her purse. Should she mention that to Gideon? Or had Ben told him about it?

A letter was probably in order.

Tomorrow. Not today. Or maybe to-nacht.

Gideon grasped her hand, tugged her outside, and shut the door. "I have to tell you a story."

"A story of how you've always loved me?" Bethel hitched an eyebrow and giggled.

If only it could be true.

But there was nein way. They'd never met before their wedding day.

Naomi was clearly confused. Either that or she was trying to stir up conflict between Bethel and Gideon. As if she wanted to spread the misery Kish's presence had caused her.

Bethel supposed she would have to wait for that story. In the meantime, she was curious about the tale Gideon would tell.

So Bethel had heard Naomi's remark. It would be a gut starting place for their conversation. He'd have to thank her later for breaking the ice.

Gideon nodded. "That's exactly the story I have to tell." He rubbed his thumb over her hand as they walked toward the road.

Her brows drew together. She stared at him. "Are you joking?"

"Not a joke. At least, not if you're who I think you are. Ten years ago, more or less, my parents began talking about starting a salvage-grocery business. I was about sixteen or seventeen at the time and Naomi and I went with them to the auction. There was this girl there, with hair the color of sunshine." He wouldn't mention how he'd also noticed her curves. "She was so pretty—the prettiest girl I'd ever seen. Ever. She worked at the auction, somehow, and I stayed as close to her as I could get. We didn't talk, not that I remember, but I gave her my heart. Love at first sight. Not something I ever believed in, but…well." He shrugged.

"I'm not sure I believe in it either." Bethel smiled softly. "If you didn't talk to her, you can't be sure it was me."

"I always thought her name was Beth. But they might've said 'Bethel' and I just misunderstood."

Her eyebrows shot up. "A lot of people did call me Beth. And I started working with Daed at the auction when I was fourteen."

His heart skipped a beat at this affirmation of his strong suspicions. "I came home and, well, the auction girl had my love. I told everyone I was going to marry her someday. I didn't court, didn't date. I did hang out with the youngies and once, during a game of truth or dare, I chose the dare. It was to ask out Lizzie. Nobody wanted to date her. She was…well, better at sports than most guys. And she liked to rub it in. I was obligated to ask her and I went, somewhat grudgingly, and feeling like I was cheating on the girl I loved. But to my surprise, Lizzie and I clicked. We talked. We couldn't stop talking. And I asked her out again and again. We became friends and then sort of fell into love. Which is how I would normally recommend people do it. Friendship first. Not the blind handing off of a heart to a stranger like I did with you."

Bethel smiled. "I'm glad for you. Though I will admit to being somewhat jealous of what you and Lizzie had."

She didn't need to feel jealous. He'd never had the passion for Lizzie that he had for Bethel. Nor the strong urge to make her happy.

He couldn't tell that to Bethel. It was bad enough coming clean about his truth-is-stranger-than-fiction story. "The only womanly job Lizzie was gut at was sewing. She loved that. She was more than willing to let Mamm and Naomi do everything else. If she was supposed to do something she didn't enjoy, she would do a slap-happy job, upsetting both Mamm and Naomi enough that they'd tell her they would do it themselves. She didn't want to live with my family. She wanted to live with hers. And it got worse when her parents decided to move south to Pinecraft, Florida. Then we discovered we were expecting and you know how that ended. But I loved her. I did." His voice broke. It seemed kind of disloyal to speak of Lizzie this way...but at the same time, it was *loved*—past tense—and now he was free to love again.

Bethel's hand tightened around his. "I know. I'm glad you have Elam."

They'd reached the mailbox. Gideon slid the letters inside, shut the door, and raised the flag. He looked around, then started left down the road. Away from town. Toward the pond where the youngies hung out on the weekends. Since it was a weekday, maybe they would find some privacy at a semi-romantic location.

They walked in silence for a while, him sneaking glances at Bethel while she apparently mulled over what he'd told her. Her brows were drawn, her forehead creased. "You shouldn't speak ill of her," she finally said.

Gideon winced. "I didn't mean to. Really. I just thought you needed to know she wasn't as perfect as I might've made her sound. She was human. She made mistakes. Like me."

"Danki for that." Bethel moved a little closer to his side. He caught a whiff of boppli powder. He loosened his grip on her hand enough so he could entwine their fingers together. Wow, he loved holding her hand. And the sparks....

"Anyway, I need to continue the story. Your daed called. I have nein idea how he got my name or number or anything. I *was* in Mio in the fall sometime before Lizzie passed, looking for boppli stuff, and medical supplies for Mamm. But I didn't cheat on my Lizzie. I loved her." Gideon shook his head. "I wasn't real happy when your daed called with his accusations. I mean, I didn't even know who you were. I'm sure your daed mentioned your name, but I didn't catch it, and honestly, I never imagined you might be my auction girl, my Beth. Not that it would've mattered, though I probably would've thought a little harder about it. Then we married and I got my first gut look at you when we walked back to the haus after the wedding and, well, I knew who you were. I recognized you."

Bethel's breath caught. "But—"

"My daed and Naomi recognized you, too. And they'd heard all my teenage declarations of love and my boldly declared intentions to marry you."

"Really?" she whispered. A look of longing appeared in her eyes.

"Really. And...and I want you. I do. Just in case there's any doubt. I think I still love you. Or at least, I love the idea of you. But I want to be sure. It seems like some elaborate joke Gott is pulling, forcing me to marry the woman I always said I someday would. But I want to do it right. I want to be your friend first. Your best friend. Your lover second."

He couldn't wait to get to that point.

She made a sound he couldn't identify. He turned in time to see her rub her eyes with the back of her free hand.

As they entered a more densely populated residential area, he decided to take her out of the public eye by pulling her off the road and leading her into the woods, till they reached the remains of a stone fence. He picked her up, set her on the sturdiest part of the fence, and wiped away her tears before he wrapped his arms around her waist. "Don't cry."

"I can't help it. You are amazingly sweet." She sniffed.

Gideon leaned in, kissing her eyelids. Her cheeks. "You are amazing."

"Lizzie was a blessed woman."

He chuckled. "Lizzie was jealous of my dream girl, Beth."

"She knew about me—her? Your Beth."

"You. I'm certain of that. And jah, of course. I told her on our first date that I'd already found the woman I intended to marry."

⌒

Bethel's heart pounded and her eyes teared up even more. His story was too amazing. Had Gideon really imagined himself in love with her since she was fourteen or fifteen? Too young to be courted, yet old enough to help Daed at the auction. She remembered her foolish dreams of romance at that age, though she didn't remember Gideon specifically. She'd liked being useful and meeting people. She'd dreamed of being chosen and claimed and pursued. Well, two out of three wasn't bad, since Gideon seemed to have chosen and claimed her…and now, with his courting, seemed to finally be doing the pursuing. But part of her heart still doubted. After Lizzie, would he have chosen and claimed her if Daed hadn't….

"But Daed forced you to marry me." That was a fact and nothing would change it.

He wiped away the fresh round of tears from her eyes. "Even if I'd known who you were, I would've denied the accusations, though I might've been open to the idea of courting you. But your daed threatened a mud campaign. Said he would destroy me for putting his dochter in the family way and not taking responsibility for my actions. I know I've said this before, but honestly, I've never been with anyone except for Lizzie. I told your daed I was willing to take a paternity test to disprove his suspicions. Your daed refused to allow it. That's when I hung up on him. And then my daed pointed

out all the ways we needed you and how badly your daed's false-
hoods might hurt us and…well, I caved in. I called your daed back,
though I was determined to hate you for naming me when I didn't
have the vaguest idea who you were."

A gust of wind shook the branches overhead, releasing a shower
of slushy snow. Gideon leaned protectively over Bethel. He shook
off his hat and glanced up, only to get another glob of the white stuff
on his face.

Bethel couldn't help giggling.

Gideon gave a playful growl as he scooped up a handful of slush,
grinning deviously.

She squealed and started to squirm away, causing the stones
she sat on to start to crumble. Gideon dropped the wet snow and
grabbed her, pulling her against his chest, right where she wanted to
be. To stay. "Careful, there."

She looked up at him. "I didn't name you. I told Daed the truth.
I wasn't—"

He leaned in and kissed her tenderly. "I know."

"Daed refused to tell me any details about the man I was marrying. I didn't know your name until our wedding day. I actually
thought I might be marrying—" She coughed in order to keep the
name unsaid, lest she wreck the intimacy they were working toward.

But then, she knew she ought to be completely honest with him,
the way he'd been honest with her. Or at least let him know she'd
thought her courting days were past and nobody would want her
unless it was as a caregiver. Probably shouldn't say that either. And
yet, shouldn't Gideon be aware of how betrayed, blindsided, and
"used" she'd felt coming here?

"Isaac."

Gideon winced.

Should she say more? She hunted for the right words.

"Speaking of whom…." Gideon drew in a breath. "Isaac invited
me to go along with him this weekend to an auction in Indiana. He
said there were supposed to be some micro-campers available and

while I'm not sure exactly what those are, I figured they'd probably be better than a tent for camping."

Her face heated. "Do you think we'll be best friends by the weekend?" The words slipped out before she realized their brazen implication. Her cheeks burned even more.

"I'm going to the auction this weekend. And I think we're already halfway there. I've told you my biggest secret"—he winked—"so now it's time for you to get real with me and share your biggest secret. Because I intend for us to share a bedroom in our new haus and Gabe tells me that if Preacher John buys our current home, he'll have the frame up in a day, weather permitting. Which means we could move within the next week or two."

She reached up, tugged his head down to hers, and kissed him to let him know she was ready when he was. She felt she was more than halfway to becoming his friend and lover. A family man who loved der Herr. Who stood up for Bethel. Who complimented her gut qualities and relied on her help with such tasks as bookkeeping. Who kissed like a dream. And who'd admitted having been in love with her since he was a boy.

Maybe she would write a letter to Daed to thank him and express her forgiveness.

Forced to marry or not, Gideon was amazing. She couldn't have dreamed up a better ehemann. And she would serve as caregiver all day, every day, for even just another moment in his arms. For the chance to be in his life.

He deepened the kiss, tugging her closer to himself.

And then Gott interrupted them with a shower of cold, slushy snow.

20

Gideon hurried through his chores without taking the time to change out of his cold, snow-dampened shirt. To change seemed pointless when he would have to put on clean clothes to go to the hospital anyway. It wasn't fair that his "date" with Bethel was cut short by his wet clothes, but with all the passion simmering beneath the surface, it probably was for the best. All his words about wanting to be best friends first would've been for naught and they both would've been wet, cold, and miserable. Except what did best friends look like? Partners in life. Sharers of faith. Often having similar interests and skills, such as, in their case, bookkeeping and boppli. As long as he talked freely to her and listened to her opinions and ideas, friendship would build quickly.

Lord, help me to do it right.

And that reminded him of another area where he'd need help from der Herr. Even though he'd received word that Bishop Miah would make it, the man would need to watch his diet in addition to cutting back on his workload—meaning Gideon would have more responsibility, more stress. He would have to spend more time in prayer and Bible study, that was sure. And he would need someone like Bethel telling him when he was out of line. Someone who would help him to do the right thing, like invite Preacher John and Kish to share a meal, even if doing so made Naomi mad.

Gott, I can do nothing without You. I feel so inadequate for this task.

My grace is sufficient.

Philippians 4:13 came to mind: *"I can do all things through Christ which strengtheneth me."* Once Gideon had finished feeding and watering the horses—he would need to care for Daed's horse at the store's stable at some point during the hospital outing—he went to find that orange New Testament. He thumbed through the pages until he found the fourth chapter of Philippians.

He started reading at the beginning of the chapter and was struck by verse 11: *"For I have learned, in whatsoever state I am, therewith to be content."*

Another lesson he needed to learn.

Danki, Gott, for expanding my boundaries.

He didn't feel truly thankful, but encouraged himself with the realization that if Gott was stretching him, it probably meant Gott was planning to use him for something. Maybe Gott had a job that only Gideon could do, with His help.

Ach, that was a sobering prospect.

Lord, help me to lean on You. To trust You with every aspect of my life.

A fresh round of tears stung his eyes. He fell to his knees, propped his arms on a bale of hay, and prayed about everything and everyone Gott brought to mind. Himself. Mamm. Bishop Miah. Naomi. Kish. Preacher John. And Bethel.

A heaviness descended on him. Bethel. Ach, Bethel.

Bishop Miah's recent allusion to something sinister in her past flashed through his mind. Was the bishop just talking things through, or was he actually hitting on the truth?

And how should Gideon go about finding out?

Whatever it was, it went beyond the need to be a gut ehemann. He also needed to be willing to do whatever was needed to protect her.

∿

While Naomi went downstairs to check on whether the clothes were dry, Bethel packed a mid-afternoon snack for them to tide them over till dinner in case of a longer-than-expected visit at the hospital. She filled a tote bag with four oranges and a small baggie of peanut butter cookies Naomi had brought home from the bakery. Naomi had devoured the few remaining chocolate chip cookies Bethel had made.

It was overwhelming and beautiful to imagine a teenage Gideon noticing her and then publicly declaring his intentions to marry her. His family members had probably stopped what they were doing and turned to check out the girl who'd made him forget all about propriety. Would they have gone so far as to have her vetted? Or would they have chalked up his off-the-wall comment to overactive teenage male hormones and promptly forgotten about it?

Though, if they remembered her now, a decade later, it seemed they must not have dismissed it. Either that or Bethel hadn't changed very much in ten years.

The fact that Daed had contacted Gideon directly and demanded he marry her—evidently knowing deep down that Rodney's claims were false—seemed to suggest that either Gideon or his daed had reached out to find out who she was. They must've contacted and communicated with Daed. Which would explain why Ben had encouraged Gideon to go along with the marriage. He'd known all along who she was.

But if that were true, then why did Daed have to threaten Gideon? Why not just tell him that the girl he'd imagined himself in love with ten years ago was in desperate need of an ehemann?

Bethel shook her head as if to dispel the dull ache forming in her temples.

That scenario brought up all kinds of questions she'd asked a dozen times over. Why had she found herself in desperate need of an ehemann? Why couldn't Daed have simply stated so? Time would've proved she wasn't with child, even without a pregnancy test.

She would ask Ben about it sometime. Maybe when they were working on the books for the salvage-grocery. Gideon would be there, too, and he must be a little curious about how she'd kum to be his bride.

Nothing made sense. Even so, it was all too amazing for words.

Gideon loved her.

And, more important, he'd loved her first. Before Lizzie.

Love at first sight.

Bethel smiled and shook her head.

Unfathomable. Inconceivable.

The door opened and Gideon came in, his hat in his hand, his hair unruly. He paused long enough to remove his outerwear and shoes, then strode past her with a glance. "I'm going to shower and change. I've called a driver to pick us up. He'll be here in fifteen or twenty minutes. We'll stop in town long enough to care for Daed's horse and return Naomi's books to her shop. And then, after we've visited Mamm, we'll have the driver let us off at the salvage-grocery and we'll bring Daed's horse home."

He was out of the room before he'd finished talking.

Fifteen minutes?

Bethel prepared two bottles of formula and added them to the tote, then went to the top of the basement stairs. "Naomi?" she called down.

Nein answer.

She glanced at Elam, lying on his blanket and playing with his stuffed frog. She had just changed his diaper, so he should be fine for a while. And his diaper bag was filled and hanging on a hook by the door, ready for church on Sundays or a quick trip to town.

"Naomi?" she called again as she crept down the stairs. The space was lit only dimly by the bit of daylight that filtered through the small, dirty window. The flashlight Naomi had carried down there either was turned off or had burned out.

None of the clothes had been taken down from the line or folded. And there was nein sound in the basement. Not even a sniffle.

Bethel touched the nearest towel. Still damp. And cold. She walked around to the bed of blankets Gideon had made up. There, huddled on the floor, was Naomi, her head buried in her folded arms, which were wrapped around her knees.

Bethel sat down beside Naomi and gently touched her shoulder. "Do you want to talk about...him...now?"

"I'm not sure I want to talk at all." Naomi didn't lift her head.

"Okay. Gideon said the driver would be here in about fifteen minutes." Bethel shifted her weight.

"He evacuated during the wildfire last year. Without a gut-bye, but that's acceptable when you're running for your life. Then I get a postcard from some baseball training camp somewhere. He broke up with me by postcard! Everyone who read the address knew what it said. And thanks to the grapevine, even those who didn't actually see the card also knew exactly what it said."

Ach. That was pretty low. Bethel settled beside her sister-in-law again and rubbed the area between her shoulders.

"Nein explanations. Nein nothing. I threw it away."

And nein closure. That probably explained Naomi's attitude.

Bethel sighed. "That's rough."

Naomi's expression was hard, yet there was devastation mixed in. "Don't tell me I have to forgive him. I know. And I'll say the words, if he asks. But they won't be real. Anyone who breaks up with his fiancée by postcard when the whole community can see it doesn't deserve to be forgiven."

Bethel could sympathize. She harbored the same feelings toward Daed. She didn't know what to say, so she rubbed Naomi's back some more.

Something creaked. She started to turn.

Naomi turned into her arms and hugged her. "You really are the sweetest thing."

"I agree, she is." Gideon's voice intruded. "But you need to take grace into consideration."

Bethel peered up at him.

"What? Who?" Naomi asked.

"The grace of der Herr. His infinite mercy forgives us for all our sins, even when they are worse than the greatest offense you've experienced. Bethel's daed. Kish."

Bethel nibbled her lower lip.

Naomi huffed. "You don't have to be a preacher at home. Can't you just let us wallow together in our misery?"

Gideon smiled. "Sorry, but preaching isn't a part-time job. You need to hear His truth, too. But I didn't kum down here to preach, only to find Elam's car seat."

"The one you haven't used since you brought him home from the hospital?" Naomi unfolded her body and stood. "I think it's in the attic."

"Of course." Gideon grimaced. "Maybe Gott sent me down here first so I could hear you say why you think Kish needs to remain unforgiven."

"He didn't tell me he was sorry either."

One corner of Gideon's mouth curved upward. "Forgiveness is more for you than for the other person. When you harbor a grudge, it poisons you. *Vengeance is mine; I will repay, saith the Lord.* Remember?"

"Jah, as if you weren't angry about being forced to marry Bethel." Naomi planted her hands on her hips.

Bethel stood, hugging herself.

"I heard you raging about it for a week." Naomi's chin jutted out.

Gideon nodded. "I'm not perfect. Gott is still working on me, too. And I'm thankful I married Bethel. My problem is not with her, even if I still have issues with the one who's responsible for this situation."

Daed. Bethel agreed.

A horn sounded outside and Gideon jerked around. "I still need to find the car seat. Tell the driver we'll be right out." He ran for the stairs. Naomi followed. Bethel grabbed the flashlight that lay unlit on the floor beside the bed of blankets and climbed the stairs at a slower pace.

Naomi was splashing water on her face at the kitchen sink when Bethel reached the kitchen. Judging from the continued honking of a horn, nobody had spoken to the driver. Bethel opened the door and went outside. "One moment," she told the man behind the wheel. "We're looking for a car seat."

"Okay." He nodded and held up a book. "I've got plenty of reading material." He laughed.

Bethel went back inside, climbed the stairs to the second floor, and ascended the wooden ladder that Gideon had pulled from the ceiling in the hall. She poked her head through the square hole. "Would you rather I stay here with Elam?"

"Nein, I'd like you to kum. Mamm will want to see you both." Gideon emerged from the far corner of the attic. "I found it. A bit dusty, but I knocked off the worst of it."

Bethel backed down the ladder, then reached up to take the car seat as Gideon stepped onto the first rung as if descending a staircase.

"I've got it. You get Elam bundled up and ready to go, if Naomi hasn't done that already."

Bethel nodded but stayed put a moment more, watching as he effortlessly maneuvered the steps.

He winked. "Like what you see?"

Her face heated. "Maybe."

Gideon's gaze slowly slid down the length of her, then rose again, his eyes darkening. "I definitely like what I see."

Ach, Gideon. Tears stung Bethel's eyes.

She was in love with the man.

Gideon chuckled as Bethel turned and fled downstairs. He really shouldn't tease his frau like that.

He carried the car seat downstairs and into the kitchen.

Naomi stood over the table, trying to wrestle Elam into his tiny black boppli coat, which was spread on the table. Elam wasn't being particularly cooperative, continually kicking his legs, flailing his arms, and pulling his hands out of the sleeves.

Bethel came back inside, already wearing her coat and black bonnet. "I took the diaper bag and a tote bag of snacks to the car. Told the driver we'd be right there."

"If we can get Elam to cooperate," Naomi muttered.

"Here, let me." Gideon handed his sister the car seat. "You can get this buckled in. Facing backward. The hospital said he should ride rear-facing until…well, for now, at least." He didn't know at what age it was safe to switch the seat to front-facing. One of those questions a grieving father didn't think to ask. "The seat belt goes through these little holes," he said, pointing. "Ach and he's supposed to ride in the middle of the backseat. Not sure why."

"Just to make it difficult, I'm guessing." Naomi frowned as she carried the car seat to the door, where she set it down to put on her outerwear.

"I'll do it. I think I know how it works." Bethel grabbed the seat by its handle and carried it outside.

Naomi hurried after her. "I'll help on the other side."

"Okay, sohn of mine, you cooperate." Gideon made a playful growl at Elam.

Elam grinned and let out a full-belly laugh of his that made Gideon laugh, too. And when he flung out his arms, Gideon whisked both sleeves over them, then quickly buttoned the front.

As he carried Elam outside, he noticed that the driver had kum in a sedan, not the large van he usually brought, probably because Gideon had mentioned only three adults needing transportation.

Bethel was on her knees in the back, her feet dangling over the edge out the door. Her bottom hovered slightly above the seat and it wiggled in an intriguing way as she tried to wrangle the seat belt through the designated holes of the car seat.

Something strange swirled in Gideon's stomach. He forced himself to look away and opened the front passenger door. "Do you need help?" His voice came out husky.

"Nein, I think we got it." On the other side of the backseat, Naomi shoved, and a click sounded. "Buckled." She scrambled into the car the rest of the way with a sigh.

Bethel somehow twisted in the seat and sat down, then reached for Elam.

Gideon handed him to Bethel, who lifted him into the seat and hooked the harness around him. Then she lifted a tote bag for Gideon to take. "A mid-afternoon snack," she explained. Gideon set the bag on the floor by his feet.

"This is more entertaining than a three-ring circus," the driver said with a grin. "Listening to them talking in your German language while attempting to thread that seat belt through...."

It was Pennsylvania Dutch, not exactly German, but Gideon nodded. There was nein need to explain why they were so inexperienced with car-seat installations. The driver didn't know this was only the second time they'd used it, that they generally didn't... well, actually, this *was* Elam's first time out of the haus since his birth. Someone had stayed home with him on church Sundays and the midwife had kum by often to check on him and make sure he was thriving. Though Gideon suspected her visits had had more to do with her worry over him as a grieving daed to a newborn than Elam's growth. Once she'd determined Elam wasn't in danger of being abused and was actually loved, she had stopped coming.

Elam made a frightened-sounding whimper and Bethel murmured to him softly, soothingly. He quieted.

She was a gut mamm.

Except.... Gideon dug his fingernails into his palms.

What if the birth of his second child ended in the same tragic way as that of his first?

21

Bethel let Elam grip her finger with his slobbery hand. His eyes were wide, taking in every inch of the unfamiliar backseat, and he babbled away, as if telling her all about it. Whenever his babbles took on a tone of uneasiness, she murmured words of comfort. If only she could do the same for Gideon, who'd withdrawn into himself almost before they left the driveway. Slumping in his seat, he didn't answer or even acknowledge any of the driver's questions. So Naomi did.

Was it just too hard to go to the hospital where Lizzie had breathed her last? Even though he'd been there a lot in recent days, for Bishop Miah and then for his mamm, that didn't mean it was getting easier for him. Bethel had been so wrapped up in her budding romance with Gideon, she'd nearly forgotten he was still mourning Lizzie. He might call Bethel his "dream" girl, but he wouldn't be as upset as he seemed about going to the hospital unless those emotions for Lizzie were still fresh and raw. Bethel sighed, earning a sharp glance from Naomi.

If he'd wanted to bring her along as a source of comfort for him, she was failing miserably. But nein, his main reason in inviting her was to assure his mamm that Elam wasn't injured. And her main reason in wanting to go, she supposed, was to get a sense of the degree of care Reba would need from her once she returned home.

Taking care of her own mamm had been one thing. They'd loved each other. And Bethel had immediately fallen in love with sweet, cuddly Elam. But Reba could be every bit as prickly as her dochter, for whatever reason. It could be the disease she had. Bethel frowned as she tried to remember what Gideon had told her on their wedding day about his mamm. She couldn't remember. That day was mostly a blur of negative emotions. Fear. Betrayal. Hurt.

At least they caught up on Naomi's bookkeeping. It was nice to be needed for something she actually enjoyed doing. Numbers were lovely because they made sense. People, with their emotions, didn't. She was beginning to understand Naomi though. She'd had a terrible hurt and her bristly demeanor seemed to be a way of protecting herself. She responded harshly to any perceived attack, whether or not it was justified.

Elam was asleep by the time they reached the hospital. The driver pulled up to the main entrance. "Do you want me to park in the lot and wait for you?"

"I don't think we'll be here long. Maybe an hour, more or less." Gideon glanced at the sky, then grabbed the tote of snacks.

"Okay. I'll run a few errands and return in an hour or so. Just give me a call if you're ready for me sooner."

"Thank you." Gideon traded with Bethel, the tote bag for the still-sleeping Elam, while Naomi grabbed the diaper bag and her own purse.

Bethel slipped the tote bag over her shoulder where she normally carried her purse. If only she could find it. Although Ben was right in saying that nothing she carried in it was all that important. Except for the money, but she hadn't had need for that. Yet.

She followed Gideon and Naomi as they strode confidently though the hospital without even stopping at the front desk to ask directions. When they reached Reba's room, they found Reba staring glumly at her lunch on the bed tray before her: a slice of gray meatloaf, a pile of grayish green beans, a sad-looking slice of bread, and a puddle of what was probably supposed to be orange gelatin. A plastic mug of very dark liquid—koffee?—sat nearby. The clock on the wall said it was half past two. Bethel wondered how long the poor woman had been trying to muster up an appetite for this poor excuse for a meal.

"They set it in front of me with a perky 'Doesn't this look good?'" Reba poked at the meat with her fork. "I was tempted to ask them to wheel me to the kitchen so I could give a cooking lesson."

"I was rather glad she didn't." Ben winked at Bethel. "But I'll admit, almost anything would be more appetizing."

"I brought some oranges and cookies." Bethel lifted the tote.

"Danki, but she's supposed to eat only what the hospital provides. Something about making sure all systems are functioning and all that. Last nacht, I offered to go to the restaurant down the street and get her a fish dinner. The nurse snapped at me. This was supposed to be her lunch, but...well, a couple of hours later and we're still encouraging her to eat something."

"I'll pick up a smoked fish for you when you're released," Gideon promised his mamm.

"Tomorrow." Reba looked up with a smile. "The therapist came in to evaluate me and mentioned wanting to send me to a nursing facility for rehabilitation, but I insisted on going home. I have Bethel."

What? Bethel stared at her mother-in-law. "I'm not a therapist."

"Nein, but they'll train you. And since we're so rural, they'll come to our haus for therapy anyway. You'll just have to help me with the exercises." Reba hurried through her explanation as if she sensed that Bethel wanted to refuse.

Gott must be sitting up in heaven, howling with laughter. Hadn't Bethel prayed not to be a caregiver, married to a widower, or an instant mamm?

He'd given her all three unwanted situations.

But Elam was a sweetie. Gideon was amazing. And Ben was an unexpected blessing, a safe harbor in the storm she'd been thrust into.

She would look for the rainbow with Reba, too. "You up for that, Bethel?" Ben asked quietly. His gaze probed hers, as if searching for the truth.

She squirmed. If any of these people could lure her into a meltdown, it was Ben. He was a true haven in this storm-tossed sea. She blinked, trying to hide the truth.

It was nice to be asked, even though there was only one acceptable answer. She found a smile, though it might not have been very bright. She tried for a tone of excitement. "Absolutely."

Her word choice earned her a glance from Gideon. His eyebrows rose.

Maybe she'd sounded too excited. Too fake. She fought to keep her smile in place as she looked at Reba.

Ben murmured something that sounded like "Gut girl," but the words were mostly lost in the sudden brightness that appeared in Reba's eyes.

"Danki." Reba nodded at Bethel, then grabbed her ehemann's hand and patted it. "You eat the oranges and cookies, if you're hungry. I'll make an honest attempt at my meal. First, though, I want to hold my gross-sohn." She reached for Elam.

"If you eat most of your food, I'll give you a cookie." Gideon winked at his mamm as he lowered Elam into her waiting arms. Then he walked around the end of the bed, leaned closer to Bethel, and whispered, "You are a treasure."

His breath tickled her ear and warmed her all the way through. The sacrifice of helping Reba was worth it.

⌒

Gideon hovered close to Mamm's side, ready to relieve her of the wiggly boppli when she'd had enough of holding him. He wasn't hungry, but he accepted the orange Naomi handed him, hoping to encourage Mamm to eat something.

Once Elam was back in his arms, he retreated to the wall opposite the bed and carefully slid down till he was sitting on the floor. He pulled in a breath. It wasn't so hard to be here with Bethel beside him, though he did feel a little unfaithful to Lizzie, bringing another woman to the place where she'd died.

Should he take Bethel to the cemetery on their next buggy ride? Introduce her to his late frau? But then, why do that? Lizzie wasn't really there. And that might make Bethel more than a little uncomfortable.

It would even make Gideon uncomfortable.

Naomi took the seat beside the bed and tried to get Mamm to eat some of her meal, so Daed sat in the chair beside Gideon, then reached down to lift Elam into his lap. "Bishop Miah was released a few hours ago. He said to tell you to stop by and visit him as soon as you can."

Gideon nodded. "Will do." But he wouldn't make it top priority. The bishop needed to recover, not focus on Gideon's relationship with Bethel. Especially when he was giving advice that made nein sense, such as the admonition not to ride in two directions at the same time. Listening to his "wisdom" had only muddied the waters between Gideon and Bethel. He could still see her shocked, hurt expression as she sat there in Naomi's bakery.

He didn't want to hurt her again. Ever.

He wanted to spend the rest of his life making her happy.

The bishop could keep his advice.

However, there *were* a number of items the two men needed to discuss, not least of all being how to address the spiritual needs of their community while Bishop Miah recuperated.

Bethel retrieved an orange from the tote bag and sat on the floor beside Gideon. Bethel began to peel the fruit but stopped when Elam reached out his arms and lunged for her.

Gideon chuckled as he took the orange from Bethel and filled her arms with Elam. "You want your mamm?" he asked his sohn in singsong.

Bethel's gaze rose to meet his, but he barely met it before a voice inside him said, *She's not his mamm. Just the only mamm he'll ever know.*

The voice was Lizzie's. The one she used when she was spouting accusations. And it hurt like a stab wound.

He looked down, staring blindly at the half-peeled orange in his hand.

The bishop's confusing advice came to mind once more. *You can't ride in two directions at the same time.*

He truly was trying to go in two directions. The bishop was onto something, even if his delivery of the message was a bit enigmatic. Gideon mentally wrestled with it until he started to understand which direction he needed to stop going. He didn't know how to do it, but he knew it was time—past time—to release Lizzie.

Gideon rose to his feet. Handed Bethel's orange to Daed. "I'll be back."

He just didn't know when.

He stumbled out of the room and turned right, headed to he-didn't-know-where.

⌒

Bethel clutched Elam closer to her as she watched Gideon until he disappeared from sight. The light in his eyes had dimmed at his murmured comment about Elam wanting his mamm. And even more so with the unspoken, but heavily implied, statement that accompanied his abrupt departure.

You're not his mamm.

Gideon might've loved Bethel first—or imagined he did—but he loved Lizzie more. Still loved Lizzie. Which was how it should be, since he'd married her. But it didn't bode well for Bethel. She would always be the replacement. Or maybe not even the replacement, for how could you replace a person?

The impostor.

She couldn't even tell Elam about his mamm because she'd never known Lizzie. Well, she supposed she could relay what she did know: Lizzie was petite, athletic, and apparently looked like Elam with his dark hair and eyes, since none of the Kaisers had those features. Naomi's hair was flat-out red. Reba's must've been red at one time, but now it was more an auburn with strands of gray mixed in. Ben's was a golden color. Gideon's a lovely golden-red, a mixture of both his parents.

His personality was a mix, too. Hot, then cold. Calm, then impatient. Wise and…not so wise.

Somehow, Bethel's presence here with these people was the will of der Herr, even though she was far from understanding. But if this was the path she had to walk, she desperately needed His help and wisdom.

Elam felt heavy against her chest. Bethel glanced down. His little eyes were shut, his fist in his mouth. She gently pulled it away. He rooted in his sleep. It wouldn't be long before he would be screaming, hungry again. She glanced at the tote, glad she'd thought to pack a couple of bottles.

"I've finished eating," Reba said, shoving the tray away. Plenty of food remained, but at least she'd forced down a few bites. "Naomi, I'll hold Elam if you'll bring him to me. Bethel, go find my sohn and remind him that he's married to you."

Ben glanced at the clock on the wall. "But be back soon. The therapist will be here in less than an hour. They'll want to see you, to explain how to care for Reba after we get her home."

Naomi gently lifted Elam and laid him in the crook of Reba's arm.

Bethel stood, took her half-peeled orange from Ben, and left the room, turning right, as Gideon had.

She hadn't a clue where to look from there.

Maybe it didn't matter. She needed to find the chapel and talk to der Herr, whether he was laughing at her or not. There was nein way she'd get through this unless He and she were on the same side. Maybe, if she knelt in surrender to His will, He'd be a little more inclined to make her path smooth.

She located the chapel on a map on the wall and soon entered the quiet room of pews. Soft music played in the background, sounding similar to a tune she recognized. The effect was peace, comfort, like a warm hug from...

Well, she would've said "from Daed," but right now, Daed's hugs were among the least comforting things she could imagine. Back before all this trouble started, though...she used to be able to go to him for anything. The way she now felt about Ben.

At the front of the chapel stood a statue that was supposed to be Jesus. His arms were outstretched, as if He were prepared to draw her into His warm, loving embrace. At His feet were chiseled the words "Cast all your cares upon Him, for He cares for you."

She certainly had a heavy load of cares to cast.

Right now, if she wanted to wave the white flag of surrender to Gott, she needed to assume that He did care.

She stumbled forward, landing on her knees in front of a small bench at Jesus's feet.

Bowed her head.

And cried.

22

Gideon wandered the halls, aimlessly, blindly, until he ended up in the maternity ward. Just inside the big window of the nursery were three bassinets. The middle one was empty. The one on the left held a petite boppli girl, judging by the pink knit hat she wore, while the other was occupied by a more robust boppli bu wearing a blue hat. The bu looked to be almost double the size of the girl, reminding Gideon of how huge Elam had appeared in contrast to the boppli beside him—also a tiny girl. Maybe Lizzie wouldn't have died if Gott had seen fit to grant her a smaller boppli.

If Lizzie's child had been a girl, she would've been named Elizabeth, according to Lizzie's wishes. Though, he probably would've shortened the name to Beth, which would've made him think of....

He bit back a guttural sob and turned away from the nursery window.

Had that been Lizzie's intention all along—to name their child Liz, after herself, and Beth, after the girl he'd imagined himself in love with for years? Both of the women he'd loved, represented in one name.

The first woman, he had lost. And if he didn't get his act together and release Lizzie to the past, he'd lose Bethel, too. Maybe she wouldn't walk away and leave him, but she would never love him. The admiration would fade. She would barely tolerate him, at best.

"Do you have a baby in the nursery, son?" A voice broke into his thoughts.

Gideon blinked and stared at the man standing beside him—a rather nondescript older fellow with gray hair. His flannel shirt was a dark, almost-black, shade of green and he wore navy-blue slacks.

"Nei—no. My son, he's with…." Was it really any of this man's business? Well, maybe it was, if he happened to be with hospital security. Gideon had heard of people stealing newborn boppli. "He's with his mamm. I'm just…well, I needed to think."

"Babies are a huge responsibility. It's common for new moms to feel overwhelmed. Some of them fall into a deep depression." The man looked at Gideon, not the boppli, as he spoke.

Jah, that might be what he was afraid of—Bethel getting depressed. But not because of Elam. More because of Gideon. Or his needy mamm or his bossy sister. Or all three. Gideon frowned.

"These women sometimes require medical intervention."

Gideon shook his head. He'd never heard of that. Depression, jah, but after the birth of a boppli—a blessing from the Lord? Maybe this man was speaking of depression in general, not depression due to a boppli. Besides, the Amish were usually encouraged to turn to der Herr rather than to medicine for their ailments. If anyone in the community chose to consult a doctor for depression, he sure didn't hear about it.

"The husband and father bears a lot of responsibility as his wife's support, both physical and emotional. Pregnancy and childbirth cause the woman some serious changes—physical, emotional, and mental, not to mention hormonal—and it can be extremely overwhelming. Serving and loving one another is very important and the verse in the Bible about husbands loving their wives may mean, in this season of life, that wives need a little extra attention once there's a new baby in the house. Might be wise to hire a babysitter and take your wife out on a date. Let her know you still value and cherish her. That's important to a woman. Give her frequent mental-health time."

"*Mental-health time*"? Maybe he meant "breaks." Gideon nodded. This conversation was a bit overwhelming for him. But the man spoke truth. Bethel had been through a lot of changes. Getting married, becoming an instant mother, and finding herself inserted into a family that, while it wasn't very big, was still considerably larger than the haus-hold she'd left behind. Moving away from her friends and community. Not to mention having to care for Mamm's needs and cater to Naomi's moods. There was also his grief intermingled with desire for the woman he'd always loved. Wanted to marry.

Had married.

Gideon moved away from the nursery window to let another man peer inside.

"Let her know, son. Tell her how much you love her," the stranger said, keeping pace with Gideon as he started to walk away. "The Good Book says that a man should love his wife as he loves himself. How would you want to be treated if you were in her place? Suddenly, she finds herself responsible for the life of a little person...."

The man rambled on, but Gideon stopped paying attention because his reality was far removed from what this other man spoke of. He only half-listened as the man said something about an older woman, about trouble coming from unexpected places, about listening to concerns that might be warnings. The man had quickly gone from friendly and helpful to unsettling and agitating.

When they reached an intersection of hallways, Gideon stopped, intending to turn, even though he didn't know where the new direction would lead him. "Nice talking to you."

The man's serious gray eyes fixed on him and something in their depths held Gideon's attention. "Pray lots, son. God knows. He knows and He cares. He sees you. He wants you to be blessed. Happy in Him. He has plans for you. Plans for good and not for evil, to give you a hope and a future. In that day, you will call upon Him and He will answer."

Gideon's heart rate slowed, then galloped on, at the unexpected recitation of Scripture, almost as if it were a prophecy. The man's words had turned from friendly and inquisitive to rambling and now to direct. Knowing. A rock settled in Gideon's stomach. The hairs on the back of his neck stood on end and his feet turned to stone. He couldn't have moved if he'd wanted to.

"As someone you know has already said, you can't ride in two directions at the same time."

Gideon blinked. Was this man related to Bishop Miah? Did they know each other? Had the bishop sent an Englisch stranger to give him more marital counseling?

Okay, Gott. I'm listening, but I don't understand.

"Set aside that which is past. I know you heard what I said, even if you tried not to listen. You'll recall later what you need to know. You've been warned."

The words had turned ominous. Chilling.

"What?" Gideon found his voice. "Warned about what?"

And blinked.

There was nobody else around.

Bethel lost track of all time as she prayed, cried, complained to Gott, and then prayed some more. Her eyes hurt from the tears, both shed and unshed, and her knees ached from kneeling so long. She'd probably been gone longer than the not-quite-an-hour Ben had said she'd have before the therapist came to talk to her.

The whole situation was terribly overwhelming.

When her grossdaadi had a hip replacement, he'd been incapable of even putting on his own socks and shoes. Walking past his room one time, Bethel had heard him calling for her grossmammi to help. Bethel had gone in and assisted him and he'd called her a blessing for helping an old man. She'd hugged him in return. And that was the extent of the care she'd given at that age. She'd probably been about fourteen.

The same age as when Gideon claimed to have fallen in love with her.

She sniffled and swiped the backs of her hands across her eyes. Then she looked up at the stone figure of Jesus. "Can we call a truce? I need peace. Not more drama."

It would've been nice to have some kind of confirmation that He'd heard her. A feeling of peace that passes understanding, or something of that nature.

"I surrender, okay? I surrender."

She wasn't quite ready to add, "Do with me as You will." That would only be asking for more trouble.

But something inside her seemed curled up in self-defense, as if her spirit sensed that Gott had heard that last part. And realized that was the portion of her prayer that He would answer.

Peace? Right now, she experienced just the opposite. An anxious, panicky sense that Gott was going to ask something really big of her. Something as big as laying down her life, or being prepared to do so.

Why had she bothered asking for anything?

She stumbled to her feet, reached for a tissue from the box at the end of the pew and dried her eyes. She somehow managed to find her way back to Reba's room without having left a trail of bread crumbs.

At the sight of the therapist, her shoulders sensed an additional weight.

Gideon still wasn't there. She must've really hurt him, not correcting him when he'd referred to her as Elam's mamm, though she hadn't had time to say anything in that moment. That was why she'd left the room in the first place—to remind him that she was his frau, even if she wasn't Elam's mamm.

Naomi was gone, too. And Elam was screaming as Ben jostled him on his hip.

"Gideon came back," Ben told her, raising his voice to be heard above the boppli's wails. "He and Naomi both went looking for you. You didn't happen to pack him a bottle, did you?"

"It's in the tote." She reached inside the bag, grabbed a bottle, and handed it to Ben. At least he was willing to feed his gross-sohn.

She'd left the chapel feeling almost as burdened as when she went in and this just seemed too much. Screaming boppli. Frowning mamm-in-law. Whatever hope she'd had left now shriveled up even more. She blinked her bleary eyes and took a deep breath, preparing herself for going through the motions. She turned to the therapist. "I'm sorry I'm late."

The therapist gave her a sympathetic smile. "You have a lot on your plate, don't you, honey?"

If she only knew.

⌒◞

After returning briefly to Mamm's hospital room, only to find Bethel missing, Gideon had gone looking but still couldn't find her. A couple nurses reported having seen her and one said she thought Bethel had gone into the chapel, but she wasn't there when he checked. Shoulders slumping, he finally made his way back to Mamm's hospital room, ready to admit defeat.

He was cursed. Not only had he lost Lizzie in this awful place, but he'd also lost Bethel. He would never be able to hold his head up in public again.

Okay, perhaps he was being a bit melodramatic. But after his conversation with a disappearing man, he had resigned himself to the apparent fact that melodrama was the norm at this hospital. All he wanted was to hold Bethel in his arms and know he wasn't alone. To keep her by his side and never let her out of his sight.

Melodramatic? Jah. But how else did one say gut-bye to the past?

Gott, help me let go.

He blinked again, half-expecting the flannel-clad man to reappear. Instead, it was Lizzie who came—his beloved best friend—leading Bethel by the hand.

Lizzie gazed at Gideon with eyes full of warmth and also sadness.

She glanced at Bethel, put Bethel's hand in Gideon's, and then, with a watery smile, a firm nod, and a look of peace in her eyes, she released Bethel's hand. *Choose love. Not loss.*

And with that, Lizzie turned and walked away. Vanished at the end of the corridor.

Gideon took a deep breath for the first time in ages, or so it seemed. Especially in a hospital. It was freeing. So freeing. He'd loved, he'd lost, and now he loved again.

He turned, ready to walk into his future and find Bethel.

He plowed into something—someone—in the hallway. He looked up and saw a woman in scrubs carrying a folder. She held out one arm to shake hands. "Hi, I'm Angela, the physical therapist. Your wife is in there." She nodded behind her, at Mamm's room. "Your sister went to buy coffee and call the driver. Your mother will be released tomorrow when the doctor does his morning rounds, if she's still doing well."

Three pieces of gut news.

After imagining Lizzie and the confusing warning from the disappearing man in the hallway, Gideon had halfway expected to hear the worst upon returning to Mamm's room. He wouldn't dare mention the exchange between himself and the man, or himself and his late frau, because everyone would believe he'd gone off in den kopf. And maybe he had. There was nein way to be certain, one way or the other.

You've been warned.

About what, specifically? Not loving his frau enough? Allowing Bethel to take on too much responsibility with the boppli, Mamm, the bookkeeping, and almost all the haus-work? Naomi helped here and there, but the demands of her job at the bakery meant Bethel did the lion's share of the chores. And Bethel did the work as if effortlessly, without notice. It was just done. And while Gideon truly appreciated it, had he ever really thanked her? Or had he treated her like a hauskeeper who earned room and board by all her work?

That needed to change.

As he entered Mamm's room, he glanced at Bethel, who didn't notice him because she was refilling Mamm's glass with water from the pitcher beside her bed, and smiled. *We are so blessed with Bethel. Danki, Gott.*

He reached for Elam with an appreciative smile at his daed. "I'll get him ready to go." It was the least he could do.

That and maybe try to take Bethel on another walk to-nacht after they got home. Though it was now just after four and he had chores to do and….

Well, he should definitely give her the slabs of fudge from the candy shop. He'd forgotten about them, sitting abandoned in his buggy.

With the fudge, he should add a whispered, "Ich liebe dich."

And maybe a kiss or two.

Ach, yeah. His heart pounded.

He could treat his frau tenderly. That old man had nothing to worry about.

Not a single thing.

Even if he had quoted Bishop Miah.

And there, the worry returned.

23

The farmhaus was cold when Bethel walked inside carrying Elam and the diaper bag. The haus smelled different. A strong floral aroma permeated the air. Roses? Odd. She looked around but didn't see any flowers.

Naomi followed her inside with the car seat, where she'd tucked her purse and the empty tote bag. "Wow, it smells like roses in here. I wonder why." Naomi wrinkled her nose as she set her load down just inside the doorway, then went to check the fire.

The fire was almost out, but there were still some glowing embers. Hopefully, it wouldn't take long to heat up the haus. One of them needed to start supper soon.

Gideon had stayed in town, saying he needed to talk briefly with Bishop Miah before stopping by the store to pick up Daed's horse and buggy on his way home.

Bethel laid Elam, still in his coat, on a blanket on the floor, then hung her outerwear on a hook by the door. She picked up the car seat. "Should I put this back in the attic?"

Naomi added a log to the fire, then flapped at the embers with a piece of cardboard. "I think the basement would be handier. But you can store it later, unless you want to go down there now and wash another load of laundry while you're at it."

Bethel shook her head. "It won't dry. The towels were still wet when we left after lunch."

"We could string up a clothesline here in the kitchen. Or in the living room." Naomi straightened, apparently satisfied with the fire she'd started. "Do you want something to drink? A slice of pie?"

Something warm, maybe. But Bethel only shrugged. The haus was cold, her heart was cold, and with Naomi already having been upset with her for inviting Kish for lunch…. Maybe Naomi was over it though. Bethel opened her mouth to suggest a slice of pie with warm milk, but then she pressed her lips together, deciding to surrender. "Whatever you'd like is fine with me."

"I think hot chocolate, since it's almost suppertime. I'll string a line and watch the fire and Elam while you get started washing our unmentionables, since we'll need those."

Bethel's face heated. "But…your daed. Your brother." The laundry didn't need to be done right now, did it? This surrendering thing was hard.

"If you hurry and we hang them up here, they should be mostly dry by the time Gideon gets home later this evening. Besides, it isn't as if he and Daed have never seen women's underwear before." Naomi rolled her eyes.

They hadn't seen Bethel's.

But there was nein point arguing with Naomi.

A trip to the cold basement was in her immediate future.

Bethel grabbed a dark gray sweater off the back of a kitchen chair and tugged it on. It reeked of roses, intense and overly sweet. And it was too large. She started to roll up the sleeves but quickly stopped, frowning. It was too large for every female in this family. And she didn't remember seeing it there when they left for the hospital.

She glanced at Naomi, who knelt beside Elam, unhooking his coat. "Whose sweater is this?"

Her sister-in-law looked up. "Where'd you find it?"

"On the back of this chair."

Naomi huffed. "If someone was here while we were gone, seems they could've added a log to the fire."

Bethel took the sweater off, folded it, and laid it on the seat of the chair. "May I borrow yours? Mine's upstairs, still packed away in my suitcase." Naomi's sweater hung on a hook beside the door and Bethel knew it smelled like fresh-baked bread. Definitely preferable to roses. That strong scent would give her a headache in nein time.

"Sure."

Bethel put the sweater on, then grabbed the car seat and carried it down to the cellar, where she set it against the wall.

Next, she started to run the water for the laundry tub. The tub was almost full when she heard Naomi scream. The sound was angry, not pained or surprised. Bethel turned off the tap and ran upstairs. Where was Naomi? Had she gone to the second floor? Bethel scooped up Elam and dashed up the stairs.

Naomi stood in the doorway of her bedroom, shredding a red rose. The petals fluttered to the floor at her feet.

Someone had left Naomi a rose—a lovely gesture, a statement of love—and she was destroying it?

Bethel stumbled to a stop and stared at her sister-in-law. "What are you doing? Are you off in den kopf?"

"I guess we know who the sweater belongs to." Naomi kicked at a petal, then tossed the naked stem in the trash. "I found that on my pillow. He—" The word came out as a hiss.

"He," Bethel parroted. Then it hit her. "Kish? The sweater belongs to Kish?" That didn't make sense.

"Nein. His mamm is quite large." Naomi stomped toward the stairs, leaving the mess of rose petals behind. "They must've brought her to see the haus while we were visiting Mamm. The second tour in one day. That means Preacher John liked it and figured Rachel would approve. And since Rachel left her sweater, they'll return. Hopefully, they'll kum when Gideon or Daed is here, because I don't want to see them. I should've realized it when I smelled roses. Rachel takes her baths in rosewater, I think."

Okay, then. Bethel glanced at the mess of rose petals.

"He was in my room," Naomi groused as they descended the stairs. "I found it on my pillow."

Jah, she'd said as much. Bethel would love to find a rose on her pillow. A lavender one, symbolizing love at first sight. From Gideon. Not that she would ever get one. Most Amish men didn't give hothaus flowers to their fraus. If they gave flowers at all, they were wildflowers and there weren't any of those around here this time of year.

Bethel sighed. "I think he still likes you." She didn't know why she felt the need to point out the obvious.

"He's the one who broke up with me by postcard. He's the one who left me to join some baseball team. He doesn't get a second chance."

"But he gave you flowers." Well, one flower. Still, it was sweet. "I'd love to get a rose someday."

Naomi ignored her. Either that or she hadn't heard. But Bethel wasn't going to repeat herself. She didn't want Naomi telling Gideon to buy her flowers. She would rather receive unsolicited romantic gestures.

"I guess Preacher John must really be interested in the haus." Bethel sagged at the realization that she would be responsible for packing up the contents of this entire haus.

Naomi didn't respond. Apparently, she wasn't in the mood for conversation.

Bethel was more than happy to leave her alone, lest she stir up more of her wrath. "I'll go back to doing the laundry." She handed Elam to Naomi.

After removing Elam's coat, Naomi headed for the rocker. "I do need some boppli cuddle time."

Mamm always said that cuddling a boppli should take top priority. But maybe Bethel would like to have some snuggle time, too. Instead, she would be hanging wet laundry and preparing hot chocolate.

And daydreaming of Gideon, thanks to the memories evoked by the sight of the pile of soft, fluffy quilts in the corner of the basement.

To be continued.

Had he meant it?

⌒

Even though most people just walked right in, Gideon knocked, as always, on the bishop's door. He didn't want to disturb the Brunstetters without warning.

Bishop Miah's frau, Katherine, opened the door and invited him in. The bishop sat at the kitchen table, staring glumly at the mug of steaming liquid before him. Isaac sat beside him, sipping from another mug, while Agnes puttered around as if she still lived there, setting out a plate of…what were those? Not cookies. They looked like rice cakes.

Gideon glanced at Katherine and raised his eyebrows.

"Agnes made him some sort of herbal tea that's supposed to lower his blood pressure," Katherine explained.

"Tastes like grass," the bishop muttered.

"You shush. It's gut for you," Agnes scolded. "I need to keep you around for a while."

Gideon chuckled. "My daed said you wanted to see me?" He would wait until Isaac and Agnes had gone before bringing up the strange man he'd met in the hospital. He didn't want them questioning his sanity.

"I'm glad to see you. Saves me a trip by your place." Isaac took another sip of his drink. Hot chocolate, if Gideon's nose wasn't failing him. "We need to catch the bus tomorrow afternoon for the auction in Indiana. They need me there a bit early. You won't need to stay for the whole thing unless you want to, but I know you wanted to look at that micro-camper."

"Micro-camper?" The bishop frowned. "Whatever for?"

Gideon squirmed uncomfortably. "Privacy," he muttered. His face burned.

Agnes set a mug in front of Gideon.

Hot chocolate. He smiled in relief. "Danki."

"Privacy." Isaac chuckled.

Gideon glowered. The man shouldn't find too much humor in his situation. He was also a newlywed, after all.

Isaac glanced at his new frau and winked. "I understand it's really nice. You open up the back and have a tiny built-in kitchen. Rather pricey, though. The micro-campers are quite popular with the Englisch."

"Pricey?" Gideon frowned. "I can't do pricey. Not with the expenses of building a haus and medical bills for Mamm. Not to mention the money I still owe the hospital for Elam's birth."

Bishop Miah scowled. "You have a tent and a camping stove. Just buy an air mattress."

Gideon had considered that option. It would certainly be a lot less expensive. Besides, an air mattress would kum in handy during the move.

"Gabe has an air mattress in storage that I got at an auction," Isaac said. "New, with tags. Stop by after you leave here."

Gideon nodded. "Danki."

"Preacher John took his frau on a walk-through of your haus today, since she'd previously seen only the main living area. She liked what she saw and, given the size of their family, I'm sure they'll want to buy."

Bishop Miah picked up his mug and swirled the contents. "You sure this won't kill me, Agnes?"

"Absolutely positive. I bought a book about herbs to replace the one I lost in the fire and—"

Bishop Miah grunted. "Never mind. I don't want to know what's in it."

Gideon glanced at Isaac. "I think the air mattress might be my best option. I guess I won't be going with you to Indiana after all."

He felt immense relief. Not only would he be saving money, but he hadn't looked forward to leaving Bethel for several days.

Isaac nodded. "Agnes and I were over at Gabe's overseeing the delivery of some more auction furniture I picked up and he showed me the preliminary plans he drew up for your new haus." He rubbed the beginnings of his beard. "After sharing a one-room cabin with his bride and brother-in-law, he designed something I think should work for you. It has an apartment in the center for your parents, with handicap access to everything, and entrances on both sides, one of which would be a private apartment for Naomi that could be added on to when she marries. The other side would be a two-story haus for you and your family. And the first-floor walls slide open for church Sundays." Isaac drained his cup. "Agnes has given it her stamp of approval."

"It's really cute." Agnes sat down next to Isaac and slid the plate of rice cakes toward him.

"None for me, danki." Gideon waved away the plate as he turned to the bishop. "What did you want to talk to me about?"

Bishop Miah glanced at Agnes before shaking his head at Gideon. "Since you'll be here, you can be the opening preacher Sunday. I'll see if Preacher John will preach, too. My family members—Agnes included—think I need to take it easy a bit longer." His sigh was one of long-suffering.

"You do, definitely." Agnes bobbed her head.

The preaching schedule wasn't what Bishop Miah had wanted to discuss with Gideon. Whatever the real issue was, he apparently didn't want to speak about it in front of Agnes. Gideon could work with that. At least there were nein confusing marital counseling sessions in store.

Gideon drained his hot chocolate and stood, thankful he hadn't bothered to shed his coat. "I'll go see Gabe, then. I'll stop by to see you another time soon."

"Or I'll visit you when I'm released from haus arrest." The bishop's tone was serious, but his eyes twinkled with humor. "I need to talk to Bethel, too."

Isaac frowned at the bishop. "Maybe this is something you need to leave alone. She needed an ehemann. He needed a frau. Gott provided. Simple as that."

"And she's the same girl I fell in love with ten years ago," Gideon added. "But she didn't need an ehemann. She's not…in the family way." He wasn't sure whether Isaac had heard that rumor, but Isaac at least knew she wasn't a widow.

Isaac shrugged. Did he not believe Gideon?

Gideon should probably try to find out what rumors were circulating so he could put a stop to them. A carefully worded comment in the presence of the biggest gossip would soon put any lies to rest.

The truth was, he'd fallen in love with Bethel ten years prior. And Gott had reunited them.

A nice, romantic story, even if their relationship back then was real to him alone.

Even if Bethel hadn't known he existed.

Bethel hung the unmentionables in the basement, out of public eye. If there was a chance that Preacher John and Kish would return before the items dried, she didn't want to embarrass Naomi by having undergarments strung around the haus. Since it was evening, that chance was slim, unless the men wanted to stop by and see Ben to discuss final details. Ben should be returning from the hospital soon. He had planned to stay there long enough to get Reba to eat something. Laundry hung, Bethel went upstairs and decided to start supper, since Naomi was still snuggling Elam while feeding him the last of his bottle.

"I'll put him down for a nap as soon as I finish feeding him and then I'll kum back down to help," Naomi assured Bethel. She sounded a lot less stressed than she had earlier.

The kitchen was heating up nicely. Bethel set the kettle on the stove, then turned to the pantry. She remembered seeing a few cans of cream of chicken soup in there.

Hearing the kitchen door opening, Bethel turned. Gideon entered and his gaze latched onto hers. He crossed the room in three huge steps, not bothering to take off his coat. He tossed a large envelope on the table as he passed. In the next second, his arms were around her, engulfing her in his embrace, as his lips claimed hers with a kiss that made her blood heat. She burrowed into him, returning his kiss with matching passion. Maybe to-nacht? The chill in her heart began to thaw.

Too soon, he released her and stepped back. Looked around. "Where's Naomi?"

Bethel glanced at the now-empty rocker where she'd been sitting. "She's putting Elam down for a nap."

Just then Naomi came into the room. "How can I help?"

"I want to show you the design Gabe's suggesting for the new haus. Apparently, a lot of the inspiration came from his Bridget and from Agnes." Gideon picked up the envelope and pulled out a large folded paper, which he laid out on the table before stepping back with a flourish and a big grin. Bethel hung back, but Gideon motioned her nearer and wrapped an arm around her waist. "You need to see, too."

Naomi frowned at the blueprint. "Three kitchens? And even so, it looks smaller than this haus."

"That's because it's three different residences built into one. The walls between your apartment and ours will open so the whole downstairs area—excepting the bedrooms and bathrooms—will be available for use on the Sundays when we host church. We'll all have our privacy and we'll be right there for Mamm when she needs us."

Bethel leaned closer and smiled when she saw only two bedrooms on Gideon's side.

"You have only two bedrooms," Naomi pointed out. Her sour tone caused Bethel to deflate a little.

"That's all we need for now. And the haus is designed to make additions easy if and when you marry, or if our family grows." He gestured to the center of the drawing. "Mamm's living area will be entirely handicap accessible. Gabe will make the doors extra wide to accommodate a wheelchair and he's putting grab bars in the bathroom."

"Nice. But what about Bethel?" Naomi persisted. "Are you going to make her share a room with Elam? Or will you do what I overheard Daed suggesting?"

Which was…what? Wait. Gideon had discussed their sleeping arrangements with his daed? Bethel's face heated.

Gideon frowned at his sister. "None of your business, Naomi." Then he reached into his coat pocket, pulled out a crumpled white bag, and glanced at Bethel. "From the candy shop. I'm sorry I forgot to give these to you, but I got distracted. They're from Isaac and Agnes." Bethel opened the bag and removed the two rather crumpled boxes inside. "Danki." It was sweet that he'd thought of her. Or had he remembered her fondness for chocolate only because Isaac had said something? But remembering the snow ice cream of a few days ago, it did seem as if he was trying, even in his bumbling way, and this gift was as sweet as any rose she would never see.

Gideon tapped the lid of one of the boxes. "I forget what Isaac said it was called, but he mentioned milk chocolate, caramel, and sea salt. And he guaranteed you'd love it."

"Ooh, give me." Naomi looked on eagerly as Bethel set the boxes on the table and opened the lids. "I taste-tested this one," she said, pointing. "It is so gut."

Gideon shook his head at Naomi. "It's for Bethel."

"I'll share, of course." Bethel went to get a knife to slice the treats. She needed to keep the peace with Naomi. Besides, sharing was the nice thing to do. And it went along with the surrendering thing.

"Would you mind watching Elam for a couple of hours to-nacht?" Gideon asked Naomi. "I have another wedding gift I need to give Bethel."

Bethel's heart skipped a beat. Her lips tingled. More kisses?

Naomi was silent for a moment. She finally nodded as Bethel returned to the table. "Courting her again?"

"Courting. Jah." Gideon winked at Bethel.

Her heart pounded. Courting, wedding gift, two bedrooms, and fudge—

A car horn honked in the driveway.

Gideon frowned and went to the door. "What's the driver doing here again?" He went outside and returned a minute later with a big wrapped package Bethel recognized. It was the smoked fish he'd bought to celebrate Reba's homecoming.

"Guess I left it in the car." He put it in the refrigerator.

Sweet of him to take responsibility when the fault was really Bethel and Naomi's since Gideon had been left off in town.

Bethel sliced the fudge and then waited for Gideon and Naomi to try some before she popped a piece into her mouth. The flavor was heavenly. "Mmm, this is so gut." Almost as sweet as Gideon's kisses.

Naomi nodded. "Agnes is the best candymaker. It's probably a gut thing Gideon didn't marry her or I'd have gotten so fat from eating all those extra sweets."

The bite of fudge Bethel had just swallowed turned into a heavy lump in her stomach. She looked at Gideon as acute pain filled her. "You courted Agnes?"

Gideon shook his head and then shrugged before meeting her gaze. "I didn't want to. Daed wanted me to because of Elam's needing a mamm and Mamm's needing a caregiver occasionally. I did ask her on a sleigh ride. She said nein. Isaac was already in the picture. It would've been a marriage of convenience."

Right. Just like his marriage to Bethel. Bethel winced.

"Then, after your daed called, Daed said Gideon should marry you," Naomi added. "Especially since all the threats your daed made would ruin us." She reached for a bigger slice of fudge.

Bethel choked back a sob. She glanced from Naomi to Gideon. While she'd known Daed had threatened the man he called, she hadn't realized just how serious the threats were.

Gideon caught his breath. "Naomi, just hush."

"That's why he won't—"

"Naomi! Enough." It was almost a roar.

The pain worsened. Bethel's eyes stung. She hugged herself and took a step back. Something inside her died.

Gideon took one look at her, his eyes showing concern, then grabbed her coat and bonnet off the hook by the door and held them out to her. "Let's go."

"Gid, stop," Naomi pleaded. "Don't be foolish and send her away. She's nice and ever so helpful and we'd be lost without her. Daed was right, you know. We need her. What are you going to do with her? Besides, what if *he* comes back?"

"I told you what I was going to do when I asked you to babysit Elam." Gideon made a growling sound. "Don't wait up."

24

Gideon helped Bethel into the buggy, then retreated toward the haus. "I'll be right back," he called over his shoulder. "Need to grab a few things. Like those packages of fudge. Naomi's liable to finish it herself and you might need the chocolate fix."

Her lips parted and she sucked in a breath. There was a flash of fear in her eyes that almost, but not quite, obliterated the bleakness that had spurred him into action. She definitely needed some "mental-health time," as the stranger at the hospital had suggested. "Are you sending me aw—"

He held up a finger. "I'm *courting* you."

The bleakness faded as a tiny flicker of hope ignited in her eyes.

"I'll explain after we get on the road, okay? I don't want to risk a derailment of my plans. Wait here. I'll be just a second." He ran into the haus and raced upstairs to his bedroom. He found Bethel's suitcase, still packed. That hurt. He'd really failed her. He dumped the contents on the bed, rifled through them, and repacked a few things he thought she might need. Then he grabbed a few things of his and stuffed them alongside hers in the suitcase.

When he went back downstairs with the suitcase, Naomi followed him to the door. "Gid, nein. You can't send her away." Her voice sounded panicked. "I like her. When Kish leaves town again, I'll be less moody. I promise."

"I'm *courting* her. Danki for watching Elam. Daed said he *will* be coming home to-nacht, after all, so he should be here *if* Kish returns, but I doubt he will to-nacht. Don't wait up for us. I'm not planning on coming home to-nacht."

"Not…?" Her eyes widened as the implication of his statement apparently sank in. "It's about time." Naomi half-smiled. "I'll be ever so happy to watch Elam over-nacht. I owe you and Bethel, anyway, for all that work you did for my bakery. I might even bake you some raisin bread."

"Danki, Sis, but do something nice for Bethel instead. Maybe bake some apple fritters." Gideon snagged the boxes of fudge and shoved them into his coat pocket once more. "And maybe try to think before you talk."

There was at least one proverb in the Bible about that very thing, but his mind was too befuddled to recall it right now.

He attempted a smile at Naomi before scooting outside and jogging to the buggy.

When he tossed the suitcase in the backseat, Bethel looked at him with wide eyes. The hope was gone, replaced with a deadness, a look of defeat. Gideon was about to explain when he remembered something else he needed. He held up one finger, asking her to wait once more, and ran into the barn to grab the orange New Testament. They would need Gott in this if they had any hopes of surviving.

He climbed into the buggy and put the New Testament/Psalms between them on the seat. Grinned at Bethel. "There's a Bible between us."

She didn't smile in return. Instead, tears beaded on her eyelashes.

"You *are* sending me away." Her voice broke.

"Nein, I'm not. I…I just…well." He moistened his lips. "It was supposed to be a surprise."

"Sending me away was supposed to be a surprise?" There was a hardness to her tone.

He turned the horse in the opposite direction from town. Should he tell her? He had said something about courting her, right?

She fidgeted. "I tried to get along with Naomi. And what about your mamm? I'm supposed to help her."

That was definite fear in her voice. He needed to explain.

He released the reins with his right hand and reached for her left hand. "I'm not sending you away. Okay? I *am* courting you."

Her eyebrows rose. "With a suitcase?"

His face heated. "I'm also giving you some mental-health time."

"Mental-health…what?"

She sounded as baffled as he'd felt upon hearing the term.

He shrugged. "Something I was told you needed. Along with a bunch of other stuff I can't say at home."

"Ach, that clears it up *so* nicely." The gentle sarcasm was back.

He squeezed her hand. "I guess it means time to yourself. I don't know. Trust me, okay? It's gut. It's all gut."

She fell silent, her hand trembling in his. He hadn't meant to alarm her, but he supposed she feared the worst when she saw her own suitcase. What was he thinking, bringing it along? Well, there was the matter of his own suitcase, still packed from the nacht Elam was born. He hadn't been able to bring himself to open it and deal with the contents.

He puffed out a breath as he stopped the buggy outside small log cabin, the last in a line of five identical structures. "These are some guest cottages Gabe bought and has been renovating. He told me about them when I stopped by to see him today. Something about wanting to use them for prophet quarters, or for visiting Amish families, or for the families returning after the fire and waiting for their homes to be rebuilt. He said we were welkum to use one for some much-needed privacy. He gave me the key, but he also said Bridget would fix it up a little and she would leave it unlocked. Preacher John and his family are in the far cabin. I'll build a fire and bring in the suitcase."

He knew he was rambling, but he wanted to put her at ease. Now he was eager to get inside with her. Once they'd built a fire and warmed up, they could finally have the talk they needed. And then he'd be able to kiss her without worrying about someone walking in on them.

He jumped down from the buggy, then turned around to help Bethel out.

She didn't move but only stared at the cabin. A long moment later, she turned and met his eyes. "Are...are you leaving me here by myself for this...mental-health thing?"

He stilled, suddenly unsure of himself. He'd planned to have long-overdue conversations with her, sprinkled with apologies for his many failures, and well-seasoned with explanations about his actions or the lack thereof, depending on the case. And then maybe, just maybe, he would actually start their honeymoon. "Do you want me to stay?"

Her face turned a lovely shade of pink as she nodded.

A glimmer of relief warmed his heart. "Let me start a fire, bring our stuff in, and take care of the horse. Then I'll kum in and we can...talk." Jah, they needed to. With each other and with Gott.

"About my mental health?" Her tone was one of alarm.

He was beginning to regret voicing the term. "We'll touch on it. Along with my own." Because he was the one who'd talked to a disappearing man and also saw his dead wife in the hall of the hospital.

Her brow furrowed, her lips parted, and she stared at him. Wordless. Then she climbed out of the buggy, grabbing the orange New Testament as she did. "May I have the fudge?"

He chuckled as he handed over the boxes, smashed even more now than before. "It's that important?"

"It is. If we're talking mental health, I'll need chocolate for sure." She wrinkled her nose at him.

Was she making a joke? He studied her eyes. The bleakness was gone. There was hope.

He chuckled again and reached for her. His intentions were a simple hug and maybe a kiss. Or two.

She darted away and raced up the porch steps to the cabin. Then she opened the door and went inside, leaving the door ajar.

At least she intended to let him in.

He grabbed the bags and followed.

~~~

Bethel stopped in her tracks just inside the door and surveyed the interior of the cabin. It was plain, of course, but it was cute. An inviting loveseat was positioned in front of the woodstove, one armrest draped with a crocheted granny-square throw in shades of lavender and blue. Bethel set the boxes of fudge on the nearby end table and lit the lantern that sat there, appreciating its cozy glow.

Looking around once more, Bethel realized this was better than a rose on her pillow. This was a cabin just for her. For them. A wedding gift.

She surrendered again. She would listen to what he had to say. And forgive him for the hurt.

She wandered past the kitchenette down a short hallway and found a small bathroom and, just beyond it, a bedroom with a four-poster bed, a thick comforter of red and black plaid, and—

Gideon's arms closed around her, his hands locking just above her waist, and tugged her backward a step until she rested against his chest. He nuzzled her neck and nipped her ear. She gave a contented sigh and leaned against him.

"I lit the fire. I still need to take care of the horse, but I'll be back soon. We can lock the door and talk in front of the fire, maybe sip some hot chocolate? I brought the ingredients."

She stared at the comfortable-looking bed, center-stage in front of them. "My mental health is fine. Just so you know." That statement had sounded a bit breathier than she'd intended.

Gideon's kisses trailed down the pulse line on her neck. Then he stopped, raised his head, and chuckled. "I'm more worried about my mental health at this point. Wait for me." He kissed the side of her neck again, released her, and started down the hallway.

She turned to watch him go.

He stopped and glanced over his shoulder. "Ach, you should know. That isn't Lizzie's bed."

What? Ach!

"That bed is yours. I told Gabe I wanted to buy it. For you. For us."

One corner of his mouth crooked up and he hesitated, as if unsure of himself.

She moistened her lips. "Hurry with the horse, ehemann."

His eyes widened and his grin spread. Slowly.

His gaze slid over her. "I like the sound of that."

⁓

The next morgen, they rode home hand in hand, snuggling against each other the entire way. Gideon parked in the shadow of the barn and pulled Bethel close for a few more kisses before he lifted her down from the buggy. If only he could've kept her at the cabin longer. Maybe he would be able to spirit her away again soon. At least they wouldn't have to sleep apart any longer, thanks to the queen-sized air mattress in the back of the buggy, courtesy of Gabe.

Finally, they separated themselves and strolled toward the haus, still holding hands. He would go back later to retrieve the suitcase and the new air mattress.

Gideon's daed greeted them at the door. "I'm glad to see you. Naomi has already left for the bakery and Mamm should be released soon, so I need to get to the hospital. I already called the driver and was trying to think of someone I could get to babysit on such short notice." He glanced from Gideon to Bethel, then back again. A small smile flickered on his face. He'd probably noticed Bethel's heightened color.

Gideon's face burned, too. If he could have, he would have whisked Bethel back to that cozy cottage and stayed there indefinitely. At least, until their private quarters were completed in the new haus. But he had a sohn and a business and other responsibilities.

Speaking of which....

"Did Preacher John kum by last nacht?"

Bethel stiffened beside him.

Daed nodded. "Late. I'd finished the evening chores and Naomi and I were having evening devotions. He decided to buy and we settled on the fair price he offered. I notified Gabe this morgen. Gabe's going to see if he can get started on the new place this week, since Preacher John has already cleared the land of burnt rubble. They won't construct the barn first this time but will start with the haus. He said the barn could be up in a day, anyway, with the help of the community."

Barn raisings were always fun. Gideon nodded.

Bethel stepped away from his side. "I should start packing, then."

Wow, he hadn't thought of that. Sorting through all their belongings would be a big mess. And what should he do with Lizzie's stuff? It seemed wrong to just get rid of it. On the other hand, Bethel didn't need any of it and Gideon had already decided to let go of the old.

Just as Bishop Miah had advised him to do. The man was a font of wisdom.

Gideon had a lot to learn.

And a lot of work to do today.

Including moving Elam's crib into Gideon's old room and setting up the air mattress in Elam's room for Gideon and his bride.

That would be a pleasant task.

But what about Lizzie's sewing room? Even four months after her death, no one had dared to enter that space. Yet it would need to be cleared out.

Maybe he could arrange a moving frolic and the women of the community would handle that room and Lizzie's belongings. Give everything away. He didn't care.

Well, he cared, but he wasn't worried. Lizzie had given him permission to choose love. Not loss.

His gaze went to his new frau as she crouched down and lifted Elam into her arms, then whispered something in his little ear. The boppli smiled and snuggled into her embrace.

Gideon smiled.

He was so blessed.

25

One week after she'd become Gideon's frau in the fullest sense of the word, Bethel leaned against the kitchen counter and watched as Reba made laps with her walker around the main floor of the haus. Her physical therapist followed closely behind, holding one end of the colorful belt that was fastened around her waist in order to steady her as she maneuvered the uneven flooring between the kitchen and the living room.

The therapist glanced back at Bethel. "You'll need to make sure the floor is level. She should have the least possible number of trip hazards. And the doorways should be widened for when she eventually uses the wheelchair more often."

Bethel straightened and stepped away from the counter. She'd heard those same pointers three times already that week. "My father-in-law assured me that the new house will have all those things." If only she could see for herself. Gideon wouldn't even allow her to help Naomi paint. He'd hinted at a surprise he had planned, but whatever it was, nothing could be better than being in his arms.

The therapist nodded. "She should have grab bars in the bathrooms, too."

Bethel nodded, though she'd already notified Ben of that detail, too.

"Okay, one more lap around the house and we'll take a break. Come on, Mrs. Kaiser. You've got this. You're doing great today," the therapist said, his voice sounding encouraging.

Bethel followed them into the other room, noting the bare spots due to furniture that had already been moved out to the new haus in preparation for the official move-in date on Monday. Just two days away. Reba's pedal sewing machine was gone, as were her crates full of serviceable material and her thread collection. She had an enviable collection of black, navy blue, gray, pine green, and maroon. Not the brighter, lighter colors that were allowed in some districts. But it was pointless for Bethel to wish for such vanity. The darker colors were more serviceable.

The other women of this district were supposed to kum today to sort through Lizzie's sewing room and the attic and take whatever they could use. Bethel figured she ought to go upstairs and open up those areas so they could air out. Nobody had been brave enough to venture into Lizzie's sacred sewing room, which probably smelled musty and stale after being shut up for five months now.

Bethel headed for the stairs. Now would be a gut time to go, while the therapist was working with Reba.

"Okay. Sit in your wheelchair. We'll rub some lotion on your legs to get the circulation moving better. That'll feel good," the therapist was saying.

Bethel winced. She should've thought to try that, but she'd been overwhelmed with trying to stay on top of packing, childcare, laundry, cleaning, and baking, since almost everyone else had been focused on finishing the new haus.

The therapist produced a small white bottle from his bag, squirted some lotion on his hands, and reached for Reba's legs. "It might feel cold at first."

"Nein!" Reba's voice was sharp. "Bethel will do it. Or my husband. Or my daughter. Not you."

Bethel watched as Reba pulled her legs back and tucked her dress more tightly around herself.

"Okay." The therapist calmly wiped his hands on a towel he'd pulled from his bag, then rose and handed the bottle to Bethel.

She sucked in a breath while shaking the small bottle. According to the label, the lotion was unscented. Bethel would talk to Ben about getting some lotion with a lavender fragrance, the kind Mamm had loved. Maybe Reba would find the scent soothing, too. At the very least, it would calm Bethel's nerves. "I should wash my hands first." Bethel set the bottle on the table and headed for the kitchen sink.

"Rub her arms and legs once or twice a day," the therapist advised her as she started the warm water. "Maybe when you help her with her shoes and socks in the morning and again when you're getting her ready for bed."

As she lathered her hands with soap, Bethel nodded, intending to relay all of this to Ben. He had been giving his frau what little help she needed with dressing for as long as Bethel had lived with them. Surely, Reba would prefer being rubbed down with lotion by her ehemann. If Bethel were to find herself in Reba's place, she would want Gideon to administer the caring treatment.

Her face heated as she recalled their time together at the cabin and, more recently, upstairs on the big air mattress, now set up on the floor in Elam's former bedroom.

And if the lotion application was punctuated with words of love....

Words Bethel hadn't heard yet, except in her dreams. Granted, Gideon maintained that he fell in love with her years ago, but that was in the past. And he said he'd made the decision to love her, which sounded like a future act. But the actual words "Ich liebe dich," in present tense? Nein.

That would be something to look forward to.

Of course, she hadn't yet dared say the words to him either. But she'd given him her heart in its entirety. Moving past friendship had been so sweet.

As Bethel dried her hands on a towel, Gideon came into the haus, whistling a tune. She enjoyed seeing this new, happier Gideon.

He'd started smiling more, humming and whistling, and even singing in the shower. Things he hadn't done before they became friends. More than friends.

Gideon winked at her before greeting his mamm and the therapist.

Bethel's insides fluttered. She'd gladly do just about anything all day long just to spend her nachts in his arms. Jah, she loved him. She tugged Reba's socks down, then squirted some lotion on her hands.

The therapist presented Gideon with an electronic clipboard that Bethel had kum to hate. Signatures were made with a fingertip and Bethel's handwriting on the screen looked like a preschooler's scribbles.

Gideon took the clipboard and frowned down at it. Then he made a quick mark before handing it back.

The therapist chuckled as he glanced at the screen. "You could just sign your initials or even a smiley face. No one ever sees this except me. But while you're here, I'd like to talk to you about a few things...." And he launched into the same spiel he'd given Bethel earlier.

Bethel focused on Gideon's shoulders. On his strong arms. How would it feel to have him rub lavender lotion on her...?

Reba's hands came to rest on Bethel's shoulders.

Bethel's attention jerked back to her mamm-in-law.

Reba smiled. "I know my sohn is handsome, but you'll get the lotion applied ever so much faster if you stop gawking at him."

Bethel's face heated. She dipped her head and rubbed the lotion around between her hands to warm it a little.

"I'm so glad he married you." Reba leaned forward enough to pull Bethel into an embrace. "We all love you."

Tears burned Bethel's eyes. She blinked them away and began gently rubbing the lotion on Reba's shins. "I feel the same about you." Not exactly, but she was at least learning to appreciate her mamm-in-law. And if she said it enough times, maybe she'd start believing it. Reba was Gideon's mamm and the only mother figure in Bethel's life now.

Bethel finished applying the lotion, then wiped her hands on her apron and stood. Through the window, she watched the therapist get into his car. Gideon had vanished. She looked at Reba. "I'm going to check on Elam and open the windows in the upstairs sewing room to air it out a little before the women arrive."

Reba pursed her lips. Implied criticism? Or was she just thinking? "I'll watch Elam if you want to bring him in here. I know you still need to pack. I wish I could do more to help, but at least I can watch my gross-sohn as long as you're nearby to lift him if needed. You've made enough cookies made to feed an army and Naomi prepared over a hundred sandwiches at work Saturday."

They also had picnic jugs full of iced tea. When it came to the hospitality-related demands of a work frolic, they were ready. But Gideon had invited the women of the community to help themselves to Lizzie's things in the attic and her old sewing room. Was he really prepared to part ways with everything she'd owned? To have it all erased, as if she'd never existed? Maybe Bethel should keep something of Lizzie's for Elam. But what to choose?

Bethel ran upstairs and tested the knob of the sewing-room door. It was unlocked and the door opened soundlessly. Bethel took a deep breath, inhaling the strong odor of neglect mixed with a weaker floral scent, and tiptoed across the room. She tried not to gawk at the stacks of colorful fabric, the projects started and abandoned. Half-finished boppli dresses. Tiny boppli trousers. A quilt stretched across a small frame. She took a quick glance out the nearest window. Who knew when Gideon would return...and he might be upset if he caught Bethel snooping in Lizzie's private haven. She unlocked the window latch, then gave it a shove upward as far as it would go.

The second window was trickier. It didn't want to budge. Finally, with some work, she managed to open it an inch. That would have to do.

She hurried out of the room, leaving the door wide open, and crossed the hall to Gideon's old room, now Elam's. The large bed had been stripped of its bedding and on it was a note in Gideon's handwriting that said, "Bed stays." Preacher John must have purchased the piece.

The new bed for Gideon and Bethel still waited in the cabin Gabe had let them use. Gideon hadn't wanted to move the bed twice and so, for now, they spent every nacht on the air mattress.

Elam rolled over in his crib and reached for Bethel. She scooped him into a hug and then kissed his cheeks. "Ich liebe dich, you little bundle of sweetness."

He cooed and smiled in a way that warmed her heart. She snuggled him closer.

Female voices drifted up from downstairs. The women were starting to arrive for the work frolic. Hopefully, someone she knew or at least recognized had showed up early. *Please, Gott. I could use a few friends here.*

She quickly changed Elam's diaper and headed downstairs.

Ach, gut. Agnes was here. And then Paris, the sweet woman who worked for Naomi. Bethel didn't recognize the other young woman standing near Agnes or the older woman on the other side of Paris. She was about to introduce herself when the door opened and a larger woman charged in, bringing with her the strong fragrance of roses.

"Gut morgen, Bethel." Agnes smiled. "This is my sister-in-law, Jenny, and I think you know Paris. This is her mamm, Jane. And this"—she motioned to the larger woman—"is Rachel, Preacher John's frau."

Bethel smiled and nodded at each of the women in turn. Looking again at Rachel, she remembered the sweater that'd been left behind, as if Rachel had been already staking claim to the haus. Had she volunteered for the frolic in a desire to possess the haus sooner? Or maybe to scope out more furniture pieces to keep? Bethel winced at her own unkind thoughts. *Sorry, Gott.*

"Danki for coming," Bethel said to the group. "We really appreciate the help."

"We're thankful for what you're doing for us," Rachel told her. "Really too bad about Reba's condition, but with Gideon and you married and—if my wishes kum true, Naomi marrying soon—they'll need the new haus."

Paris frowned at Rachel, then reached for Elam. "Let me hold that little cutie."

Bethel handed him over. "Take him to Reba when you're ready. I'll be right back; I'm just going to carry the trash to the burn pit. The sewing room is open if you want to start in there and Gideon opened the attic, too." He'd intended to carry the stuff down but he hadn't gotten around to doing it. She hesitated, feeling suddenly overwhelmed by the amount of work left to do before the move.

Agnes touched her arm in a reassuring way. "We can get anything we want to keep that's up there. Anything we can't lift or carry, Isaac can help with. He's outside now talking with Gideon. And giving him something that came in the mail for you, delivered inside an envelope addressed to him."

"Something for me?" Nobody from home knew where Bethel was, except for Daed. Could it be that he'd written her back? Her smile grew. Sending that letter of forgiveness had been so freeing. Gideon had been so wise to suggest it.

"Isaac was going to give it to Gideon." Agnes quickly pursed her lips, as if stopping herself from saying more.

Bethel grabbed the trash. "I'm going to find Isaac—"

"Preacher Gideon, you mean," Paris said between kisses to Elam's cheeks.

"Right. Gideon. And get my letter. I'll be right with you. Go on upstairs and get started without me." Bethel hurried toward the door.

"Maybe you should wait until Gideon gives it to you." There was a touch of worry in Agnes's voice.

Was it improper not to wait for Gideon to bring her the letter? That seemed odd. And Gideon knew how much she missed her daed. He wouldn't mind if she came to him and asked for the letter.

Bethel waved her hand dismissively and headed outside. A circle of men stood just inside the open barn doors: Gideon, Ben, Preacher John, Kish, and Isaac, who held an envelope.

Her letter?

She started that way.

~

Gideon alternately clenched and relaxed his fists as he stared at Isaac. His jaw had tightened. "So you're saying Elijah Eicher asked *you* to marry Bethel first and since you were marrying Agnes—"

"The day that he called, jah," Isaac said.

"You refused. And told Elijah Eicher to call me and see if I'd marry her?" Which meant that Gideon was the second choice—not just from Bethel's perspective but her daed's as well. Rejection stung. He wasn't picked for his qualifications, but in an act of desperation when Plan A didn't work. And Bethel's daed still thought highly enough of Isaac to send a letter to Bethel through *him* instead of mailing it directly to her ehemann. Gideon had been considered solely because of Isaac. So much for Bethel's referring to Isaac as "nobody," if her daed considered Isaac the better man for her.

Isaac gazed steadily at Gideon, his expression sober. "You're forgetting the most important part. Who he called first is not the issue. Bethel is in danger. Recently she lost her purse. The person who found it sent it to her daed, but someone else intercepted it. Her daed was beaten and left for dead and the man stalking her has at least a vague idea of where she is."

Beaten and left for dead? Isaac had to be exaggerating. But he sounded serious. Gideon tried to summon sympathy for the man. How would he tell Bethel?

Preacher John tugged at his beard. "You said he believes she's in the Soo."

Isaac scoffed. "How long will it take him to realize she isn't in Sault Ste. Marie? The next-closest Amish community is this one. He'll look here and any Amish person will point to Gideon when asked. His Bethel is the only Bethel in this community."

Gideon frowned as he recalled the sneer in Elijah Eicher's voice the only time they'd talked. Gideon's hands clenched as his rage grew. While he'd been tempted to shake a few answers out of Elijah himself, Isaac was closer. "You gave Elijah Eicher my number. You're the reason he threatened a mud campaign against me and my family. You're the reason I was forced to marry when I wasn't ready." His voice grew steadily louder.

"Calm down, Gid," Daed murmured. He reached for Gideon's arm. "All things work together for gut—"

Gideon shook Daed off. "Did it ever occur to you that I'd want to pick my own frau instead of being forced to marry a stranger? Did you take that into consideration at all?" Gideon roared. "That maybe I never would've chosen Bethel…?" He would've chosen her, but that wasn't the point.

"Uh, Preacher Gideon." Kish jerked his head sideways.

"What?" he snapped, then turned and glanced in the direction Kish was looking.

Bethel stood there, one hand pressed against her mouth, with tears streaming down her face. An open bag of trash sat beside her. The wind picked up some papers and blew them around.

Ach, nein! Horror filled him. All the work he'd done to court her, to win her love, thrown away in a fit of anger. His stomach ached. What had he done?

He opened his mouth, searching for words to undo the damage. "Beth—"

She spun on her heels and ran.

26

Bethel ignored Gideon's calls as she staggered into the forest at the back of the property. She had to get away. Had to.

She'd given herself, heart and body, to a man who never would've chosen her.

So much for being friends first. So much for anything. She was done. Done!

Done with living in a home that wasn't hers, caring for a family that didn't want her except as a caregiver, being married to a widower who resented her, and being shut out of rooms like Lizzie's shrine sewing room. And being shut out of Gideon's heart. Hence the lack of verbal expressions of love.

Tears blurred her vision and she tripped over a dead tree limb, falling on her face in the mud.

"Bethel!" Gideon shouted in the distance.

Her heart lurched.

But...nein. Nein.

Words did hurt. Brutally. Stabbing deep in the tender flesh of her heart. It was probably gut she hadn't heard the rest of the men's conversation.

She scrambled to her feet and blindly ran on.

There was nein going back. Not home, not to Gideon.

What had she done to deserve such harsh punishment from Gott? To be so despised and rejected?

"He is despised and rejected of men; a man of sorrows, and acquainted with grief: and we hid as it were our faces from him; he was despised, and we esteemed him not."

Bethel choked out a sob as Isaiah 53:3 came to her mind. Gideon had preached from that very passage last church Sunday. She always had to recite to Daed the passages the preachers had referred to, just to prove she'd listened to their sermons. And she'd continued the habit here, albeit to herself.

But something inside her replayed the words as she ran.

Despised and rejected.

How strange it was to realize that der Herr Himself experienced the same emotions she felt. And how dare she assume she was better than der Herr and didn't deserve it? He was perfect, just, the Son of God; she was a sinful daughter of Eve. Human. She deserved to be despised and rejected. But Gott knew how much it hurt... and still found a way to love all of humanity. To forgive them, even knowing they were bound to make mistakes.

And, like her, Gideon, though a preacher, was still a sinner. He would fail her from time to time, but at least he would take care of her, even if he would never love her.

Knowing that, maybe she could surrender yet again and return home. Well, return to Gideon. He might despise and reject her, their relationship might be destroyed, but he would take care of her. And Reba said she loved her. Actually, she'd said "we." Elam certainly loved her. He always squealed and reached for her when he saw her. Might as well go back for Reba and Elam.

She may not be loved by the one she loved, but he needed her. And he would take care of her.

Bethel stopped running and took a moment to catch her breath. She lifted her muddy hands and tried to find a clean place on her apron to wipe them. Then she used the back of her hand to dab away the tears streaming down her cheeks. Despite her efforts not to, she'd probably smeared mud on her face. She would shower when she got home. Hopefully, she would manage to sneak inside without anyone seeing her disastrously disheveled appearance.

She turned around. Listened for a call. She would answer this time. Then she turned again. Turned a third time. The woods looked the same in every direction. And nobody called for her. Which way was home?

~~~

Gideon yelled himself hoarse, silently cursing himself for his careless words with his every step into the woods. Isaac was his friend. A very gut friend. And he was Bethel's friend. Of course, he would've had Bethel's safety foremost in his mind and he wouldn't have recommended Gideon as an ehemann unless he was confident that Gideon would take care of her. Yet, Gideon had failed again.

Der Herr had brought him and Bethel together, giving Gideon his dream frau, after all. He had acted through Gideon's friend and the bishop to help Gideon move past grief to a more hopeful future. Gideon recalled with despair the look on Isaac's face when Gideon had lashed out at him. Isaac must think Gideon cared only for himself instead of Bethel and her safety. Kish was looking for her, despite risking reinjury to himself, yet Gideon had carelessly voiced feelings he'd honestly moved past, thereby putting Bethel in danger. She'd brought life and laughter back into his heart and by hurting her, he'd only hurt himself. If only he had the bishop's wisdom.

Gott, I am nothing without You. I can't even control my tongue. I hurt my friend, I hurt my frau, I hurt myself.

"Bethel!" he shouted again. Then he stood silently, listening.

Another man shouted in the distance. Kish, probably. It didn't sound like Isaac.

But Kish shouldn't be tramping around in the woods, risking reinjury to the torn muscle that had benched him for the duration of spring training. He was supposed to be in Grand Rapids, participating in therapy sessions with sports therapists, but he'd taken a leave of absence to help his family with their move. And when Gideon had headed for the woods to hunt for Bethel, Kish hadn't hesitated to join in the search.

"Bethel!" Gideon yelled once more.

And still nein answer from her. Of course, as badly as he must've hurt her, she could be cowering in the undergrowth within five feet of him, not daring to breathe.

"I'm sorry," he shouted, in case she was nearby. "I would've chosen you. Ich liebe dich."

He listened again, praying for some sound to let him know where she was.

Instead, nothing. Just the distant shout of her name by another man.

Lord Gott, forgive me for my harsh words. Help me to find her. Please.

<hr>

Bethel stumbled through a muddy ditch full of dirty, semi-melted snow onto a dirt road. She was beyond pride now. She was cold, wet, and hungry. If found, she would hug her rescuer. Or she'd be tempted to. In reality, whoever found her would probably take one look at her wet and filthy clothes and merely point her in the right direction. She would still be grateful.

She stood motionless for a moment on the edge of the road and looked around. If only she could discern the way to Gideon's haus. She took a deep breath and started walking again, needing the exertion to warm herself. If she was going to run away, she would've grabbed her coat.

After walking for what seemed like several miles, she came upon a lopsided buggy stationed alongside the road. A wheel had snapped and a woman knelt beside the vehicle, removing the broken pieces of wood. Not that the effort would do much gut. Most Amish didn't carry a spare wheel and the horse was gone.

Bethel stopped about six or seven feet away. "Can you point me to Preacher Gideon's haus?"

The woman pushed back the black bonnet over her prayer kapp. Bethel almost cried with relief as she recognized the red hair before the woman turned to face her. Naomi.

"What happened to you?" Naomi shot to her feet, dropped the forked tool she'd been holding, and came toward her. "You're filthy."

"I got lost in the woods and fell in the mud." Bethel choked back a sob. The Kaisers might not kum looking for her, but they would definitely search for Naomi. *Danki, Lord.*

Soon she would be warm and fed. Then she would move her suitcase into Elam's room, even though it used to be Lizzie's. Alternately, she could move up to the attic or down to the cellar and that pile of quilts...which she ought to be packing right now.

"I sent the horse on home." Naomi brushed her hands on her apron. "Someone will be along to investigate why the horse returned without the buggy. All we have to do is wait."

"Do you mind if I wait with you?" Bethel's stomach rumbled loudly.

Naomi giggled. "Of course not. If you're hungry, I have some leftover glazed doughnuts in the buggy. I was bringing them home for the frolic. How did you end up in the woods anyway?" Her eyes narrowed as she studied Bethel's face, likely seeing tear tracks in the smeared mud. She arched a brow, then reached inside the buggy and retrieved a bakery box.

"Danki," Bethel nearly gasped.

Naomi handed her the box. "About the woods?"

Bethel didn't want to admit the horrible truth—that Gideon resented her and had yelled at Isaac for his part in forcing them to marry. Though it was nice to know Daed had contacted Isaac first and had taken Isaac's recommendation of Gideon. That meant Daed *had* believed her when she insisted she wasn't pregnant and he was just trying to protect her from Rodney. Although why he needed to do that remained a mystery.

But Gideon…. A fresh ache filled her. She tried to find a way of explaining what had happened to Naomi without painting him in a bad light, but she couldn't.

Instead, more tears escaped.

27

Gideon searched the woods, calling Bethel's name and speaking in a calm, soothing tone, just in case Bethel was hiding and could hear him. But after what seemed like hours of looking, he hadn't kum across any signs of her. Maybe one of the other men had found her or she'd returned to the haus on her own. Telling himself to hope for the best, he headed toward home.

The clearing beside the barn was filled with parked buggies and wagons; the sounds of women conversing drifted out the open windows. Rachel Troyer's voice rose above the rest as she directed someone to put something in a waiting wagon.

Gideon found Kish in front of the barn, grabbing a horse by its harness.

Kish looked at him, his eyebrows rising. "It just ran into the driveway."

Gideon frowned. "It's Naomi's." More drama? Really? He didn't have time to rescue Naomi when he needed to find Bethel.

"Maybe I'll drive out in a buggy and search some more." Kish kicked at something in the driveway.

"She hasn't returned then?" Gideon's heart folded in on itself. He should have known better than to hope she would kum back on her own. She had left him. Unless he could find her and somehow convince her of the authenticity of his love.

Kish's expression was hard. "Did you expect she would?"

"Nein, but I was hopeful."

Kish adjusted his hat on his head. "I'd go rescue Naomi, but I think she would rather stay stranded than have me play the hero. If you don't want to go, I'll tell my daed or yours."

Gideon glanced toward the woods. *Lord Gott, I know I need to keep looking for Bethel, but Naomi needs finding, too. Help us to find them both. Guide us. And show me how to set things right with Bethel. Not only that, but help me to dig up the root that my bitterness sprang from.*

"Well?" Kish took a step nearer to the barn.

Gideon nodded. "I'll go with you to find Naomi. Maybe we'll kum across Bethel on the road toward town. If we don't, I'll return through the woods and call for her some more." Gideon sighed heavily. If only he could take back his horrible words. He should've told Isaac how much he loved Bethel. Then she would've heard the truth rather than the unfiltered overflow of frustration Gideon had held in for so long about having been blackmailed into marriage.

Lord Gott, help me to do a better job of guarding my tongue.

Preacher John and Daed were in the barn, packing tools and equipment for the move. Gideon handed off the reins of Naomi's horse to his daed. "We're going to take a buggy and see if we can find Bethel on the road while we look for the place Naomi got into trouble. Where's Isaac?"

Daed lifted his shoulders in a shrug, but Gideon read condemnation in his gaze. "Still in the woods. He's not going to give up until she's found."

Ouch. Gideon cringed. "I'm not giving up either. Just redirecting the search."

"You really messed up, Sohn. You just undid six months' worth of courtship."

"I haven't courted Bethel for six months." He hadn't been married to her for six weeks even.

Daed just shook his head.

Message received. Gideon had his work cut out for him, provided he found her. "I'm *not* giving up either, Daed. And I'll win her back, if it's the last thing I do. I would die for her."

"Then tell her that. A woman needs to know how much she's loved."

Preacher John nodded his agreement.

"I will." Gideon went to join Kish, who was readying the buggy. *Lord, help us. Please.*

~

A car sped down the dirt road toward them, splattering mud on both sides. Bethel stepped into the grassy area next to the broken-down buggy to wave for help while Naomi gathered the remains of their doughnut picnic.

The car skidded to a stop. An Amish man got out of the passenger seat.

Bethel gasped. A chill ran down her spine. Rodney? How had he found her?

The breeze stirred the hairs of his beard. "Bethel Eicher. I was looking for you."

Bethel backed away, around the rear of the buggy. Naomi went around to the front.

Ach, Naomi. Bethel caught her breath, then let it out in a whoosh.

Naomi glanced over her shoulder at Bethel with a puzzled look, then turned to Rodney. "Can you give us a ride home?"

"Of course." Rodney opened the back door wide.

Naomi smiled politely. "Danki." She looked at Bethel again. "Kum on, Bethel."

"Jah, indeed. Kum on, Bethel." Rodney smirked at her, a sinister gleam in his eyes.

"Nein. We'll wait for her brother." Bethel firmed her shoulders. "Naomi, wait here with me. Please." Hopefully, Naomi heard the desperation in her voice and would stay out of the car.

But, nein. She scrambled into the backseat.

"Kum on. Be wise like your friend." Rodney approached Bethel with slow, deliberate steps, the same way he'd stalked her in the barn. He extended his hand as if expecting her to grab hold of it.

She wanted to hide. If only a pothole would swallow her.

The horse should've showed up at the haus by now. Someone should be coming to help. Where were they?

Lord, we're in danger. Deliver us from evil. Please send Gideon, or Ben, or someone else to rescue us.

A still small voice whispered inside her head: *You trust Gideon to take care of you after he hurt you, but you don't trust Me?*

Bethel winced. But honestly, it was easier to trust a seen Gideon than an unseen Gott.

Leaving the car running, the driver got out. Bethel felt her throat tighten in fear as he leveled a gun at her over the top of the car. "Get in. Now."

Bethel only stared at the gun as she struggled to understand what was happening. A gun? Really? Why? Why was Rodney hanging out with a gun-wielding Englisher? Why did they want her? *Please, Naomi, get out of the car and away from them....*

Rodney came even closer. "Let's go, Bethel. Nothing bad will happen if you cooperate. Get into the car."

Naomi leaned out of the vehicle. "What's going on?"

"Your friend doesn't seem to want a ride home," the driver said. He didn't look away from Bethel, his gun still trained on her.

"Well, I wouldn't want a ride, either, if you were aiming a gun at me." Naomi climbed out of the car and glanced between Bethel and the man with the gun. "Bethel, what's going on?"

"Naomi, this is *Rodney* from my hometown," Bethel said.

Naomi's eyes widened.

"Get back in the car." The gunman waved the weapon at Naomi.

Naomi paled. Wavered.

Bethel glanced from Naomi to the woods. Would one of them be able to run and disappear into the forest without getting shot?

Rodney turned around and gave Naomi a hard shove.

Naomi fell to the ground beside the car. Maybe she could roll under the vehicle and get out of danger that way?

Far in the distance, a buggy turned onto the road and started in their direction. Too far away to be of any help.

"Get up!" Rodney barked.

Bethel swallowed the lump in her throat. "Leave her alone! Take me. I'll go with you." What they wanted her for, she didn't know. But she would surrender for Naomi's sake.

"Oh, I don't think so," Rodney sneered. "She'll fetch a good price, too." Then he kicked at Naomi. "Get up or he'll shoot your friend!"

Price? As if she was for sale! Who would buy a woman—and for what? Nein gut for sure. Bethel's stomach lurched as the images of women from her hometown who'd vanished now paraded through her mind. Bethel's knees shook. She'd lost her sister. Gideon had already lost his Lizzie. Bethel wouldn't let him lose his sister, too. She had to do something and trust der Herr to save her.

Help me trust You, Gott.

She started moving toward the car.

A ways up the road, the buggy stopped. With their backs facing that direction, neither Rodney nor the driver saw it. After a moment, two men got out of the buggy and ran into the woods on opposite sides of the road. Were they coming to help? Bethel could only hope.

Meanwhile, the gun was leveled at Bethel again. She inhaled a shaky breath and stepped slowly toward the car as Naomi struggled to her feet. How could Bethel distract the men long enough for Naomi to escape? And would Naomi be smart and run or would she foolishly try to stay and save Bethel? Bethel was expendable. Gideon could find a third frau easily enough. Or simply hire a mamm's helper.

But Naomi....

Rodney pulled a knife and held it to Naomi's neck. "Get in the car."

"Move it!" the gunman bellowed. The gun shook. His finger shifted.

Okay, Gott. I'm trusting You.

Bethel moved quickly, closing the distance. But she didn't intend to get into the car.

⌒

Gideon's heart pounded as he came on the scene from the right. Kish had gone left. Isaac was in the woods several yards behind Gideon, talking on the phone. Gideon assumed he'd called nine-one-one.

Naomi was crying as she got in the car, moving away from the knife—which was now directed at Bethel. That and the gun.

Bethel marched toward the men, her mouth set. The Amish man with the knife grabbed her, holding the blade against her neck.

"Get in the car. Now." The man with the gun shifted with Bethel's every movement, keeping his sight set on her.

Across the road, Kish picked up something and tossed it in the air a few times. Then he swung his arm. Something flew through the air with a blur and then the gun flew out of the Englischer's hand, landing several feet away. Another blur and the Englisch man fell like Goliath.

The Amish man tightened his grip on Bethel, still holding the knife against her throat. "Don't come any closer or she dies!" He stared across the top of the car in Kish's direction.

Gideon was behind him. And he wasn't going to let Bethel die. He charged the Amish man, though what he would do next, he didn't know. But he wasn't about to stand by and watch as his sister and his frau were kidnapped. Maybe he could subdue the Amish man somehow, at least until the authorities arrived. If Isaac had called the police, they ought to be on their way.

He intended to grab the man by the waist, but the man started to turn, apparently sensing that someone was behind him. His movement brought the knife farther away from Bethel and Gideon grabbed the man and jerked him backward, freeing Bethel completely.

Gideon saw a flash, then felt something pierce his abdomen. A sharp, searing pain. He fell, clutching his belly.

Someone screamed. The ground vibrated with the pounding of footsteps.

"Gideon!" Bethel fell to the ground beside him.

"I wouldn't hurt you deliberately, but you're standing where I'm about to swing," Kish told someone.

There was an angry roar. Gideon wasn't sure whose. Then a thud.

The world dimmed. He fought the darkness and tried to focus on Bethel's face, still beautiful despite being smeared with dirt and mud. Tears streamed down her cheeks. "Ich liebe dich," he strained to say.

"Don't die, okay?" Her voice broke. She yanked her apron off and pressed it against his abdomen.

"I would die for you." She had to know that. "Ich liebe dich."

Gravel scattered. Lights flashed.

"Police! Get your hands up!"

Gideon tried to comply, but something ripped. He tried to bite back a scream.

And his world went dark.

28

Bethel stayed by Gideon's side, crying, as she held the apron in place.

Naomi kept looking at Kish and biting her lip between emotional rants at the men who'd tried to kidnap them.

When the first ambulance arrived, the EMTs shooed Bethel away before loading Gideon on a stretcher.

"I'm going with him," Bethel insisted as she tried to climb into the back of the ambulance.

"He might bleed out, ma'am. We need the space to work." The driver firmly shut the door and then climbed into his seat up front. The vehicle sped away, its siren screaming.

Bethel glanced at Naomi. She paced now, taking frequent glances at Kish.

Then Bethel looked at their first hero, Kish, who stood off to the side, his head bowed, his shoulders slumped, as if he bore the weight of the world. He held his right shoulder with his left hand, rubbing it occasionally. That looked uncomfortable. Gideon had said he was taking time off from the baseball team due to an injury. Had he hurt himself even more severely? It must've required a lot of effort to hurl those rocks and then to swing that bat-sized tree branch at Rodney, hitting him in the knees and knocking him to the ground.

Bethel shuddered as her gaze moved to Rodney, who lay in the road, still yelling, groaning, and cussing, even after the police had swarmed in and put him in handcuffs.

Her gaze moved to Isaac, who held his smartphone out for several police officers to see. He was the only one with the presence of mind to talk to the police and he'd apparently captured everything in a series of photos and videos.

She didn't want to see any of the footage. She looked back at Kish, who massaged his shoulder and gazed at Naomi with longing in his eyes.

Naomi was now huddled on the ground, crying.

Go to her, Kish, Bethel silently urged him. *Or better yet, run to him, Naomi.*

Neither of them moved toward the other.

Bethel sighed. She wanted to do something, to go to Gideon. Instead, she stood there uselessly, praying silently while Isaac talked to the police. She was numb, her thoughts were disjointed and confused, and she felt disoriented. She realized she was probably in shock.

Would Gideon's family even allow her to go to the hospital? Or would they expect her to stay at their haus with Reba and Elam? And what if, Gott forbid, Gideon didn't make it? Would they send her home to Daed? Or would they keep her?

Ach, Gott, please let Gideon live!

He'd said he loved her. Finally. She would forgive him even if he didn't ask her to because Bishop Miah said that forgiveness was more for her benefit. And Gideon was willing to die for her. Tears coursed down her cheeks. Jesus *did* die for her. Maybe she *could* cast all her cares upon Him.

Gott, help me to trust You with everything. Help my unbelief.

Isaac gave her a look, his eyes narrowing, and he stepped nearer, as if preparing to support her with some verbal encouragement or a hug. But then he pulled out his phone again. "I'm calling a driver. You need to be with Gideon at the hospital."

She agreed. It was where she should be as his frau. But was she really a frau or simply a caregiver? Which duty came first? "What about Reba? And Elam? He only married me to have someone to take care of them."

Isaac's expression was one of patience and compassion. He eyed her clothes, muddy from her run through the woods, and then looked upward at her dirty face, her tears. He studied her silently until he held her attention.

"I heard it all." He nodded at the bloody spot in the road where Gideon had confessed his love. "Trust me, you belong by his side. The women of the community are already at the haus with Reba. Let them help."

Naomi came to stand beside Bethel and clasped her hand. "I can go home, too. Someone needs to tell Daed. Your place is with Gid."

A second ambulance arrived and the EMTs checked the gunman's pulse. "It's steady. He's alive."

Kish's expression brightened with obvious relief. According to the Ordnung, an Amish man who killed someone was condemned to hell.

The officer motioned toward Rodney as yet another ambulance pulled up. "Take the screamer away."

The EMTs loaded Rodney into the vehicle and left.

The ensuing quiet was a blessing.

Kish approached Naomi, carrying his hat in his hands like an old-time suitor. "Do you want me to take you home?"

Naomi released Bethel's hand and considered him for a long moment. Then she gulped, swiped at her face, and shook her head. "Nein. I'll walk."

His mouth worked a bit. Then he merely nodded and put his hat back on. "Suit yourself." He turned. "Isaac?"

Isaac hesitated, glancing at the police. "I might be here awhile. I'll walk back to the haus when I'm free to go. Or if I'm allowed to leave when the driver gets here, I'll have him drop Naomi off before he takes Bethel to the hospital. If that's the case, Agnes and I will go with Bethel. She'll need a shower and some clean clothes for herself and Gideon."

Bethel held up her hand. "I'll go with you, Kish, if you don't mind." She turned to Isaac. "You'll have the driver pick me up at the haus?"

"Of course, little sis." He turned back to the officers.

Kish nodded and turned toward the buggy. Then he abruptly pivoted, grasped Naomi by the shoulders, and kissed her on the lips.

Bethel blinked the moisture away from her eyes and stared. His reaction to being rejected by Naomi broke her heart. She knew the feeling of unrequited love. He'd thrown those rocks despite the potential consequences to his body because he loved Naomi. Love. That's what love did. It was willing to face eternal damnation…or death, in Gideon's case…on behalf of the beloved.

She need to get to her ehemann's side!

Kish released Naomi. Took a deep breath. "Have a nice life. Kum on, Bethel." Then he spun around and shuffled off toward the buggy.

Naomi gulped again. Blinked. And burst into tears.

Why couldn't Naomi see how great a sacrifice Kish had made to rescue the woman he loved? Broken hearts could mess up your emotions so badly that you ran away from the very one you love. Naomi needed time to reconcile the man who'd as gut as publicly broken up with her via postcard with the man who'd put his eternal future on the line to save her. Bethel just hoped Naomi would kum to her senses before it was too late.

And as Bethel and Kish rode away, she hoped she would get to the hospital in time to tell Gideon that she loved him, too…before it was too late.

～

An obnoxious beeping sound penetrated the fogginess. Gideon opened his eyes a slit. Before he could register where he was, fatigue overtook him and he closed them again.

More beeps. And then a whirring sound that coincided with something around his upper arm tightening with an uncomfortable grip. He opened his eyes again. Whatever it was that had clutched him now released its hold.

He relaxed again, wanting more sleep.

But now there was a terrible moaning sound. He turned his head, keeping his eyes shut, and tried to block out the noise.

The moaning continued. It wasn't him. Another patient. Then there was a scratching sound.

He gave up and opened his eyes. Registered a gray pleated curtain hanging from a metal rail in the ceiling. He blinked. Where was he? The hospital? What had happened?

He tried to remember. He was stabbed while trying to save Bethel. He moved his hand to try to find the area where he'd been injured.

"Leave it alone." A woman's voice.

He turned his head. A nurse in scrubs stood beside him, keying something into a tablet computer.

"I'll let the doctor know you're awake. We'll monitor you for a bit more to make sure no other bleeding starts, but you'll likely be free to go home later today."

"Am I here alone?" He would need to call a driver. He felt for his wallet, but encountered bare skin. He glanced down. He was dressed in an immodest gown like the one Mamm had worn. His face heated and he tugged the thin blanket higher on his body. "Where are my clothes?"

"Your wife said to toss them since they were torn and stained with blood. Your wallet is in a bag in the safe until you're discharged." The nurse checked the IV bag beside him. "She brought some extra clothes."

"My wife—may I see her?" He *had* to see her. He needed to see for himself that she was alright. Needed to start apologizing and resume courting.

"I'll send someone to summon her as soon as we get you moved."

Moved? To where? But the nurse took her tablet and walked off, leaving him alone in the gray-curtained cubicle next to the moaning man.

Gideon fidgeted. A dull, throbbing pain began in his midsection and radiated everywhere. The room seemed to spin, the dizziness almost making him sick. He needed to see his frau. Why weren't they moving him yet? What would he say to Bethel, when he had so much on his heart? If someone didn't kum soon, he would wrap this blanket around his immodest attire and go looking for her himself!

Just as he was reaching the end of his patience, a male nurse finally showed up and wheeled his bed to another room. This one had the same gray-curtained cubicle but, thankfully, nein moaners.

The nurse took a blanket out of a warmer and spread it over Gideon. "I'll bring your wife back now." He gave Gideon a smile, wrote a quick note on a piece of paper on a tray near the foot of the bed, and left.

A short time later, Bethel was ushered in. She clutched the orange New Testament/Psalms in her hand. Gideon had left the book in their bedroom. She must've grabbed it when she'd packed clean clothes for him. And when she'd changed hers, since she was nein longer wet and muddy.

He reached for her with his left hand, the one that didn't have a needle taped into it. "Bethel. Ach, Bethel."

She laid the Bible beside him on the bed and took his hand in both of hers. "Are you okay? I was so scared." Her eyes held an indefinable emotion. Was it worry? Fear? Hesitation? Or perhaps an inexplicable peace?

He blinked at the sting in his own eyes. "Me, too. I thought I'd lost you. That you'd left me." He swallowed hard. His throat hurt. "Ich liebe dich. I didn't mean what I said to the men in the barn. I would've chosen you. I *had* chosen you. Isaac is your friend—and mine. It's an honor to know he thought highly enough of me to recommend me to your daed. I'm so sorry I let you down."

Bethel leaned over and kissed him lightly. "I forgive you, Gideon. And ich liebe dich."

A flood of relief washed through him at her words. The truth of them was reflected in her eyes. He just wanted to kiss her again… and more. "When I'm released from the hospital, can we go someplace alone? I need to hold you."

"Like that cabin of Gabe's that still has our bed in it?" She gave him a flirty grin.

He smiled. "Ach, yeah."

"I'll see what I can do." She winked

He knew she would make it work, although he would likely be sore and need to take it easy for a few days. Holding her might be the most he could do.

He reached for Bethel's hand and held on tight. She took such gut care of him. But was anyone taking care of her? He remembered the warning he'd received from the disappearing stranger during his last time in the hospital. He wanted to care for her in return. A mental-health break was definitely in order. "Are you here alone?"

Bethel smiled. "Nein. Agnes and Isaac came with me to the hospital. And Bishop Miah showed up with one of his sohns just a few minutes before they brought me in here. Do you know what he said?"

Gideon couldn't venture a guess. He shook his head.

"He said, 'Our love has limits. Gott's love is limitless.' He believes that Gott, in His infinite love, orchestrated the entire situation that brought you and me together and even though I believed Gott was ignoring me, He was actually working behind the scenes. Bishop Miah admitted that he wanted to warn you about Rodney—in typical Bishop Miah fashion, he'd tracked down Daed and asked him point-blank what was going on. But he didn't want to say anything in front of Agnes at her shop the day of his heart attack. Meanwhile, Agnes already knew because Isaac had told her after Daed called him." Bethel's brow furrowed. Her eyes shimmered with tears. "Daed was trying to protect me the best way he could even if that meant lying and blackmailing a stranger after Isaac turned him down."

So, her daed didn't normally blackmail people, but he was desperate enough to do what he felt was necessary to protect his dochter. Admittedly, if the man had merely asked Gideon to marry Bethel in order to save her from a bad guy, he wouldn't have agreed. And he would have missed out on the greatest treasure.

"We can leave the results of our lives in Gott's hands." Gideon gently squeezed Bethel's fingers. "A message I'm still trying to learn."

"Me, too." She swallowed. "But I'm sorry I was forced on you. I know you weren't in any frame of mind to even consider a new frau."

Tears stung his eyes. "I will regret those thoughtless words for the rest of my life. Bethel Magdalene Eicher Kaiser, you are a treasured gift straight from the hand of Gott, who, in His great wisdom and mercy, arranged things so that I fell in love with you first."

When the doctor said he was keeping Gideon at the hospital a couple of nights for observation after some issues with blood loss and infection, Bethel refused to leave her ehemann's side.

On Monday, Gideon called the driver to take them home, where they would pause long enough to pack a bag and tell Naomi where they were going. By now, Reba and Elam were at the new haus, being helped by some of the local women. The entire yard was abuzz with activity as men hauled farm equipment, furniture, and packed boxes to waiting wagons for transport to the new house. Bethel helped Gideon out of the car and wrapped her arm around him; he leaned heavily on her as they slowly climbed the porch steps.

He clutched at the doorpost as they entered the haus. "I need to sit down."

Inside, there was a similar flurry as women helped Naomi finish packing. Bethel frowned. She should've been helping, but she hadn't been able to tear herself away from Gideon.

Naomi came over and gave her a one-armed hug, then did the same to Gideon. He swayed.

"He needs to sit," Bethel explained. Thankfully, the kitchen furniture hadn't been taken out yet. Bethel led him over to the table and he dropped into a chair, gasping. His face was white. Hopefully, the pain medication would kick in soon.

"We found this in Lizzie's sewing room." Naomi pointed to a big box on the table with an envelope taped to the outside.

Bethel slid the box closer to Gideon, then peeled off the envelope and handed it to him. His name was written on it, after all.

He unsealed the envelope and pulled out a sheet of paper.

"I'll go get our bag," Bethel said, wanting to give him some private time to read the note Lizzie had left him.

"Nein, stay," Gideon insisted. "What's mine is yours. You can read it, too."

Bethel stood behind him, her hands on his shoulders, and took a deep breath before reading the letter.

Dear Gideon,

Ich liebe dich. And I always will. But I have a sense that I'm going to be leaving you soon. I don't know why—and I don't want to go. I want to watch our sohn grow up. But I feel strange inside. I'm not afraid though. I know that Gott is in control and when He calls me home, I'll kum gladly.

I asked your daed about your Beth. Turns out he'd gotten some details about her when you stated your interest all those years ago, just in case you ever wanted to reach out to her. Her name is Bethel Eicher. She lives in Mio with her daed and mamm and sister. My pen pal in that area tells me she never married.

If something should happen to me, I hope that you will find her, Gid, with my blessing. You deserve a second chance at love.

This is my gift to you.

Choose love, Gideon.

Always,
Your Lizzie

Bethel didn't know what to say. Lizzie had a premonition she was dying and directed Gideon to find her? That was shocking—just too incredible for words.

Gideon took a moment of silence, running his fingers over Lizzie's writing. Her name. He handed the letter to Naomi, who had been hovering nearby.

Naomi read it quickly and shook her head. "Wow. I never imagined Lizzie could sense something like that." She paused. "I wish..." Her voice trailed off.

Bethel thought she knew just what Naomi was thinking. If only she and Lizzie hadn't jangled so much.

Naomi put her hand on Bethel's arm. "Why don't you open the box?"

Bethel slowly removed the lid and pulled aside some tissue paper to reveal...a quilt.

"Ach, it's beautiful." Bethel reached down and gently touched an edge of the off-white quilt with borders of a lavender-blue and four flowers that resembled violets in the corners. It was unbelievably soft. "I didn't realize Lizzie was an expert quilter. Some quilts like this, in the Victorian Treasure design, sell for thousands of dollars at auction."

Gideon twisted with a groan as he reached for Bethel's hand.

Naomi smiled. "It's lovely. A wedding gift for you and Bethel."

Gideon pulled Bethel's hand up to his lips and kissed her palm. "I can't believe it," he finally said. "'Choose love. Not loss.' And that vision in the hospital...it's as if Lizzie was smiling down on me and Bethel."

"Huh? What vision?" Naomi sounded as confused as Bethel felt.

"You can explain later," Bethel decided. For now, she didn't demand answers. Instead, she returned the quilt to the box, set the letter in on top of it, and replaced the box lid. "It'll look beautiful in our new bedroom," she said quietly. "Or you can give it to Elam someday." She returned her hand to Gideon's shoulder.

"Whatever you want to do is fine by me." Gideon patted her hand. "Put it with the things to be moved. I want a date with my frau."

Bethel decided they *would* save the quilt for Elam. It'd be the perfect wedding gift for him someday, a present from his mamm.

Naomi patted her brother's arm. "We've got this move under control. Just go. Recuperate and get your strength back." She glanced at Bethel. "Enjoy each other." She seemed subdued as she lifted the box from the table.

"I need to pack some things." Bethel headed upstairs.

Naomi followed her. "I made some raisin bread for Gid. I'll send it along."

"Danki." Bethel grabbed a few things and stuffed them into her suitcase. Then she looked at her sister-in-law, who stood in the doorway. "What's wrong, Naomi?" Bethel asked quietly.

"Kish." Naomi shook her head. "His daed said he reinjured himself and had to head back to Grand Rapids to see the team doctor. I doubt he'll kum back. We're finished, this time by my doing. He didn't even say gut-bye."

Unless she counted his "Have a nice life" comment.

Bethel gave her a hug. "I'm sorry." Should Naomi really be surprised? The way she acted after Kish risked his career for her? And his life?

Downstairs again, Gideon took Bethel's hand and she helped him out of the chair. "Danki for taking care of Mamm and Elam for a few days, Naomi," he said. "We'll see you at the new haus."

Bethel picked up their suitcase and supported Gideon as they went back out to the waiting car.

The cabin was as quiet and welcoming as their first visit, but this time, Bridget had stocked the kitchenette cupboards with groceries, including the ingredients for shrimp alfredo and chicken spaghetti. Bethel had spoken with Bridget when she and Gabe visited Gideon in the hospital, so she knew just what they needed.

After he paid the driver, Bethel helped Gideon hobble into the cabin and over to the couch. He sat down, reached up, and pulled her into his arms. She melted against him.

He winced a little from the pain but gave her a big smile. "Bethel Kaiser, ich liebe dich. Today, tomorrow, and for all eternity. Ich liebe dich."

"Ich liebe dich." She kissed him tenderly. "I am so blessed." And she meant it this time.

"And so am I." He ran his fingers over her lips. "As Bishop Miah said, Gott's love is limitless. Choosing love is the best way to live. I'm so glad we're nein longer strangers."

And he kissed her again.

About the Author

A member of the American Christian Fiction Writers, Laura V. Hilton has authored more than two dozen books. She is also a professional book reviewer for the Christian market, with more than a thousand reviews published on the Internet.

Married to a Stranger is Laura's third book in the Amish of Mackinac County series; the previous two were *Firestorm* and *The Amish Candymaker*. Her last series, The Amish of Jamesport, included *The Snow Globe*, *The Postcard*, and *The Birdhouse*. Although not part of that series, her novels *Love by the Numbers*, *The Amish Wanderer*, *The Christmas Admirer*, and *The Amish Firefighter* also take place in Jamesport.

Laura's first series with Whitaker House, The Amish of Seymour County, consists of *Patchwork Dreams*, *A Harvest of Hearts*, and *Promised to Another*. In 2012, *A Harvest of Hearts* received a Laurel Award, placing first in the Amish Genre Clash. Her second series, The Amish of Webster County, includes *Healing Love*, *Surrendered Love*, *Awakened Love*, and *A White Christmas in Webster County*.

Laura and her pastor-husband, Steve, have five children and make their home in Arkansas. To learn more about Laura, read her reviews, and find out about her upcoming releases, readers may visit:

lighthouse-academy.blogspot.com

booksbylaura.blogspot.com

www.familyfiction.com/authors/laura-v-hilton

www.amazon.com/Laura-V.-Hilton/e/B004IRSM5Q